SQUIRE

A MASCOT'S TALE

JOHN M. CUNNINGHAM, JR.

Ashland Park Books
Montgomery, Alabama

ISBN: 978-1-7322488-1-6
Copyright 2019 by Ashland Park Books and John M. Cunningham, Jr.

Cover Design by Teddi Black
Interior Format by Megan McCullough

To my grandparents, Mr. and Mrs. Perry S. Owens and
Mr. and Mrs. Neander D. Cunningham
I miss all of you.

Acknowledgements

Thank you to the following people who helped make this book possible by providing valuable advice during its writing:

Norma Jean Lutz
Joan Deneve
Robyn Hook
Tisha Martin
Jessica Stefani
Cathryn Swalia
Anne Andre
Jean Lutz
Mary Ann Grigsby
Dr. Robert Hopkins
C. Molin

Thank you also to my late dog Jebba, a great canine who inspired this story, and to my Lord and Savior Jesus Christ who called me into this wonderful work called writing.

Recollect that the Almighty, who gave the dog to be companion of our pleasures and our toils, hath invested him with a nature noble and incapable of deceit.

Sir Walter Scott, *The Talisman*

Contents

———◆———

May 1863, Port Hudson, Louisiana

June 1863, Port Hudson, Louisiana

June 1866, Coughlin, Alabama

Preface

———— ◆ ————

Although I am a Southerner, I'm also a historian and former history teacher. My specialty is America's Civil War, a subject I've studied since my early teenage years. Because I'm a historian, I don't take sides in this conflict. Instead, I seek to understand it through writing stories.

I try to place myself inside the heads of all my characters, from the North and South, to understand our ancestors' motives for fighting this bloody war. To understand them more fully, I look at them and their decisions within their historical context according to nineteenth century values—*not* twenty-first century. If we take historical events or quotes out of their proper historical context, our understanding of history suffers.

I love this quote by Cicero, and I always try to apply his principles in my historical study:

"The first law for the historian is that he shall never dare utter an untruth. The second is that he shall suppress nothing that is true. Moreover, there shall be no suspicion of partiality in his writing, or of malice" (Marcus Tullius Cicero, 106-43 B.C.).

I may be contacted at ashlandparkbooks@gmail.com.
Visit my website at www.theauthorscove.com

May-June 1861
Coughlin, Alabama

One

———◆———

Well, I'd sure as sand say he is going with us." Jesse Webb sauntered down the wooden steps of his father-in-law's brick furniture store.

His wife folded her arms, her emerald green hoopskirt spanning its slatted walkway. "Oh no, he's not. Besides, how could you take the most popular dog in Coughlin? He might get killed."

Like a man just ambling through the day's hours, Jesse faced her. Amused, his lips curled up in no great hurry. Then he spoke. "Seems I'd say you're more worried about Squire than me, dear Rachel."

She grasped his sack coat's sleeve. Thin black brows lowered, she leaned into his face so close her fragrant perfume skipped his heart a beat. "Would you please get that nonsense out of your head, Jesse Webb?"

"That is most reassuring, my dear." He gave her lips a quick kiss before he went to his wagon.

In the wagon bed was Squire, a dog whose shaggy golden-colored coat draped his back. His triangular ears, bent forward like flaps, sat atop his wedge-shaped head. His curved tail, upraised with fur hanging from it like feathers, swished back and forth, resembling a plume. He propped his sizable forepaws atop the wagon bed's upper edge. His molasses eyes twinkled, as though he understood he was the topic of their dispute.

The wagon creaked as Jesse climbed up onto its bench.

"He's not going with you." Rachel hastened inside the store and slammed its door behind her so hard its windows rattled.

"You're right, my dear." Jesse popped his whip. "Squire's going with my whole regiment." The two horses pulling his wagon turned southward, down Main Street, which was white with oyster shells clear down to the Mobile & Ohio railroad's red brick depot on the edge of town. They'd been brought up via rail car from nearby Mobile a few years ago.

Just beyond the town its militia, the Coughlin Rifles, assembled on a grassy field while other militia units from nearby towns arrived. The Rifles elected Jesse their captain.

Squire panted behind him. His breath warmed Jesse's head; his tongue slobbered his neck; his fur held the odor of dirt.

"You're it, boy. Everyone in my regiment has elected you our mascot. You're the most popular dog in Coughlin. That, my boy, is a genuine fact for sure."

Squire barked, as though he understood. Then he bounded out of the wagon and lit out after a squirrel.

Hands cupped round his mouth, Jesse yelled for him to come back.

Squire gained on the zigzagging rodent. He was the fastest dog in the county. If he was a betting man, which he wasn't, Jesse would bet he'd even give greyhounds a respectable race.

A flurry of gray wings swooped down. White patches on the wings and tail—a mockingbird's attack. When Squire whirled and sprang at her, his jaws clamped air. The bird flew into a pine tree.

Jesse loathed mockingbirds. She must have a nest somewhere. "Come on, boy," he shouted. "Let's get on to drill now."

Squire sat. Not a muscle did he move, nor a whisker did he twitch. Like a statue, very still, his large eyes fixed toward a treetop.

Lieutenant Mitchell Hayes jogged up to him. "Hurry, Jesse. I mean captain, sir. You'll be late for drill."

"Calm down, Mitch." Jesse eyed Squire. He looked back at Mitch.

Mitchell yanked off his cap and waved it back and forth as though shooing flies. "Colonel Stonebridge sent me to fetch you. Let's go. Fast, before he gets his dander up."

"First find out what our boy's staring at so hard, that he finds so interesting, would you?"

Mitchell ran to the tree, stooped, and looked up. "All I see are a bunch of branches and pine needles."

"Well, he's found something he thinks is important."

Sighing, Mitchell hurried closer and stooped lower. Humor suffused his broad face. "He's trapped a squirrel. Poor little critter's clinging to a branch and shaking his tail at him."

"Probably the same one he was chasing. Would have caught him, I'd say for a fact, if it hadn't been for that dumb bird. Climb on aboard. I'll take you back to camp. We'll let my boy have his fun."

Mitchell scrambled onto the wagon bed. "Right. I hate it when the colonel yells at people for being late. Makes me nervous, it does."

Something always roused Mitchell's excitable nature. Jesse wished his friend didn't take everything so seriously all the time. The war was starting; it was going to be fun. He couldn't wait to get in on the action.

Jesse sailed his straw hat onto the kitchen counter. Here above the store he and Rachel lived with Rachel's widower father, Robert Montgomery. Jesse gave Rachel a peck on her cheek.

The aroma of baking ham pervaded the room. If Rachel ever loved anything approaching wifely duties, it was cooking, her culinary talents famous far and wide throughout the region. At social functions she shone as their queen, on condition she could bring her meals and everyone enjoyed themselves. Her biggest compliments came when folks helped themselves to third helpings of her food. The surest way to insult her was to not eat anything even if your stomach lacked space for more of her tasty delights.

"Where's Squire?" Rachel looked past his shoulder at the open door behind him.

"Just lazing about under a tree, snoring." Jesse chuckled. "He ran after a squirrel and cornered it up in its branches then forgot about him. Little fellow's probably still up it."

Rachel erupted into giggles. "That's my boy."

"You mean my boy, dear. He's my boy, not yours."

"Humph! I think not."

"Your father's gone over to fetch him. Is my uniform finished?"

"What? Oh. Only the frock coat's left. You can try on the shirt and trousers after supper."

"An excellent seamstress you are, dear. I am positive everything will fit fine and dandy."

"Humph."

Jesse sauntered down the central hallway. Upon turning into the parlor overlooking Main Street, he plopped down in an oak chair. He, his older brother Elliott, and younger sister Emma grew up in this town.

*Elliott...Marsden...*Jesse leapt from his chair when his late brother's image flashed in his brain. His fists telegraphed pain to his knuckles as his fingers dug into his palm. "Hampton Lafayette Marsden," he muttered, "we'd better not ever see each other again. If we do...Rachel, I'll..." Jesse shook his head. No, he couldn't do it to Marsden. He wanted to, after what that man did to Elliott, but...He shook his head again. Unfortunately, Emma wouldn't approve, either. She was down in Mobile, married to a bank cashier who aspired to become a bank president.

But his mother and father...what would they have thought if he'd done it? "You let Mister Montgomery down, Father. You were supposed to be his business partner." *Till you took to heavy drinking after Mother died, staggering around town. You became the local drunk everyone avoided.* "Folks gossiped about you, Father. And how they gossiped! Ha. Why should I even care about what you'd think?"

He undid his bow tie and sailed it across the carpeted floor. He'd graduated the university in Tuscaloosa with high marks, sold his family's home, and obtained a bank loan to buy a share in his father-in-law's business. He'd be a good business partner, the best business partner Mister Montgomery ever had. He'd not become like his father.

"I'll restore our family's reputation, Father, the good reputation you lost. And I'll never touch a drop of liquor for any reason. I'll not discredit the Webb family's name."

He arose from his chair, went to a double-hung window, and opened it.

Outside, across the narrow street, Joses, barber Miller's only slave, swept the raised walkway in front of Miller's barbershop.

"Joses!" Jesse shouted. "How are you?"

Joses paused his sweeping and looked up at him. "Doing fine, Mistah Webb! Doing quite fine!" He resumed sweeping.

Charging Joses's broom, Squire raced within Jesse's view. Snapping at its straw bristles, he pounced around it as Joses moved from one platform section to the next. Laughing, Joses held the broom high and aimed its wide bristly end at Squire. Squire sprang for it; his jaws clamped it for a few seconds before he dropped back on all fours.

Miller barreled out of his shop. "Quit playing with that dog, Joses."

"Sir, I was—"

"Sweep. Sweep. It's time to close up."

"Squire," Mister Montgomery yelled. He, too, approached within Jesse's view. "Here, boy. Come here right now."

Squire trotted to Mister Montgomery's side.

Jesse closed the window. Slavery. He loathed it. It was America's worst sin, no two ways about it. Mister Miller was wrong to stop Joses and Squire from having a little fun. Yet withholding his objections to the institution often nagged Jesse like mosquitoes around a campfire. Some days, his heart almost ripped apart like broken stitches sundering a seam. When Alabama withdrew from the Union and Lincoln declared his blockade of Southern ports after fellow Southerners captured Fort Sumter, Jesse and his conscience brawled a "knock-down, drag out" for weeks. Should he fight for his state's independence, or stay out of the war because he hated slavery? Lincoln's blockade threatened the South's economy. He'd sent out a call for volunteers to invade his beloved Dixieland.

Finally, lured by the promise of wartime adventure and unable to let down his friends and his state he, with Mitchell's help, raised a company they called the Rifles. It joined a regiment commanded by Colonel Edward Stonebridge—West Point educated, veteran of the war against Mexico, and a large slave-owning planter not many miles across the county line.

The clap of the kitchen door followed by two sharp barks and booming laughter brought him back into the kitchen.

Squire's tail high and batting air, he threw his forepaws into Rachel's hoopskirt. She grasped them. They did a little dance. "Well, hello, Sir Squire." She spoke in high-pitched, baby talk. "Look, I have something for you." She led him to a fat ceramic jar on the counter. From this, she produced a cracker.

Squire snatched it from her hand. Within seconds the cracker became crumbs. He licked its remnants off the floor. His begging eyes gazed up at her. She winked at him before tossing another one at his forepaws. He made short work of it, then padded over to Jesse. Standing almost knee-high to him, Squire sat and lifted his left paw.

Jesse gave it a gentle shake. "Howdy there, Squire."

Squire lowered it and offered his right paw.

Jesse also shook it. "Howdy there again, pardner."

Mister Montgomery hung his tweed cap on a wall peg. "The way you two carry on about that dog, you'd think he was your child."

"He is my child," Rachel said. "I'm the one who found him hiding under that sofa downstairs."

"He has a real mother somewhere," Mister Montgomery said. "A pity we could never find who he belonged to when he was a puppy."

"Well, at least we tried finding his owner." Jesse joined Rachel's father at the dining table. "I'd say we tried pretty hard. I did have fun training him in those days."

After licking up the crumbs of his second cracker, Squire went to his water bowl in a corner. Like always, he was a messy drinker, sloshing water into his mouth while splattering numerous droplets on the floor. One would've thought he'd wandered a desert for a year, the way he drank it.

Her skirt rustling, Rachel glided to Jesse, glanced at Squire, and then tweaked Jesse's cheek. "You really trained him well, didn't you?"

"I can't help it if he thinks like a cat sometimes. Besides, the war won't last but a few months or so. Squire and I will be back before Christmas."

"Humph."

Jesse sighed. She sure was an amenable gal, wasn't she? Well, she wouldn't change his decision about his dog, not by a long rifle shot.

Rachel gathered up some thick rags and returned to the oven.

Mister Montgomery spread his linen napkin in his lap. "If you two will please shut up and listen, I have an idea how we'll resolve this matter."

"It's already been resolved." Rachel set the ham before them. "Squire's not going."

"Suppose Squire wants to go?"

"He's a dog, Father. He can't decide such things for himself."

"I beg to differ." Jesse twirled his fork between his fingers. "Squire's got more than air between those funny ears of his. Mister Montgomery, sir. What is your idea?"

"We'll discuss it after supper." Mister Montgomery picked up his fork. "Peaceably. Like adults."

Squire padded over to Jesse, rested his muzzle on his lap, and rolled his pleading eyes up toward him.

Jesse chuckled. Typical dog, his boy. Always begging for food.

While cumulus clouds scudded across June's morning sky, Jesse and Squire sauntered along Holly Street's clay path, their daily constitutional near an end. Flapping wings whistling, three mourning doves flew out of their way. Two servants whom he knew belonged to Mrs. Moore hurried past them on an errand.

He scratched his left arm. Servants. Slavery. His insides squirmed like angry worms. "You understand, don't you, boy? About this slavery business?" He talked as though Squire understood his every word. "I mean, I'd be doing my friends a disservice if I don't fight with them. I'd feel like I betrayed them. They did elect me their captain, after all, mainly because it was my idea raising a company, anyway, I'd say. To help defend our state and stop the Yankees from trying to push us around. I hate slavery and all that, the good Lord knows I do, but still, they have no right trying to tell us how to manage our own affairs. It's a matter of states' rights, boy. Well, what I'm saying is, what I'm honestly trying to say is, I had to do it. I was honor-bound to do it. And if I hadn't done it, Rachel and Mister Montgomery might suffer because of it. He might lose all his customers. Honor's the point, boy. Honor is all that matters in this whole entire world."

Tail high, Squire trotted ahead.

When Jesse turned onto Main Street, his feet crunched oyster shells. His mind raged like a hurricane devastating a coastal town.

Honor *was* all that mattered, wasn't it? Was he honorable? Was he really just fighting for Alabama's rights, or was he also defending slavery? No man had the right to own another man. It was immoral. It was a sin in the eyes of Almighty God. His fists clenched; his fingernails dug into his palms. Up ahead was a Methodist church with a towering steeple. "Do you know something, my boy? There are times like this when I question my honor and my courage. I worry too much about people's opinions of me. Why, I can't even find it in me to voice my true feelings on this slavery issue. Why…uh… Look at who's back."

A boulder of a man dressed in a blue militia uniform peeked in the furniture store's window. He must've come in on the train. Jesse had heard it pull into the depot several minutes ago. Drawing closer, he gritted his teeth. Hampton Lafayette Marsden, Elliott's killer. Jesse's rage boiled. His pistol… in his bedroom. If he could just… "Why'd you come back here?"

Marsden spun on his heel and faced him, his powerful shoulders thrust back. He wore a neat brown beard, trimmed close, and a walrus mustache. His thick brows arched high as he looked beyond Jesse instead of in his eye, a peculiar bit of unspoken language meant to make Jesse feel inferior.

But Jesse, wise to this game, wouldn't play it. No way would Marsden's attempts at belittling him succeed.

"Well, well. Look what the swine dragged in." Marsden tweaked Jesse's shirt collar.

"I'd say you can't read, Marsden. Didn't you notice the sign on the window? The store doesn't open till ten."

Marsden's falcon eyes, framing his aquiline nose, peered down at Squire. "Whose mongrel is that?"

"He happens to be my dog." Jesse reared back to slug him, till he remembered his promise to Rachel that he wouldn't avenge his brother's death.

Growling, Squire crouched.

"Easy there, boy." Jesse patted Squire's head. "Marsden, if you have any sense about you, you'll get back on that train before it starts moving again."

"I'm a colonel now, Webb. What are you? A private? A corporal? Don't go ordering me around else I'll have your hide. Where's Rachel?"

"None of your business."

"Who's down there?" Mister Montgomery shouted from an upstairs window.

Jesse stepped out from the tin overhang and shouted up at the second floor. "Marsden has returned, sir. It seems he desires entry into our fine establishment."

"It's closed."

"I told him that, sir. He hasn't learned to read signs yet."

The window slammed shut. A minute later, Mister Montgomery barged out the store. "My daughter never wants to see you again, H.L., not after what you did to her. Turn your body around and get your body back on that train before it departs this town."

"You and she made the mistake, my dear sir, when you did not hearken to my words. I would have made her a prominent and affluent lady in Mobile."

"She married an honorable man. That's all I care about. You're going back to the depot. You won't leave my sight till you're riding that train."

The train's whistle cut the air.

"Too late, Mister Montgomery," Marsden said. "Think I'll stay. Train heading for Mobile isn't due here till tomorrow."

"Then you'll hire a horse at the stables and ride back to Mobile. The stable owner's a close friend."

"Do you think you could use some help, Mister Montgomery?" Jesse said.

"As in Squire?"

"Yes, sir."

"Indeed. Don't try running away, H.L. Squire here's the fastest dog in this county. Maybe two counties. Maybe even the state."

Squire growled again—low, guttural, menacing.

Marsden shot him a concerned look. "I won't be running."

"I figured as much. To the stables for a horse. Move it."

Never before had Squire seen so many people gathered at the depot. Tail thumping and tongue lolling, he searched for his master among the ranks of men standing at attention. They all wore the same clothes. No sign of him, but he knew his master was among them. Why else were they here? He moved forward; a leash jerked him back. He whimpered. He hated leashes. He hated not being with his master.

"No, boy."

Upon his mistress's firm command, Squire stayed put. A man astride his horse in the soldiers' front ranks, Squire recognized. On the depot's platform stood a lady he also recognized. She and the man had visited the furniture store many times together. Squire liked the man on the horse. Every time he visited he brought Squire a treat.

"...and let every one of you, brave and gallant lads of our two counties, be assured that we are sending forth our prayers for you every day," the lady on the platform said. "We ladies, your mothers and your sisters and your daughters and your cousins and your aunts and your nieces, and every one of us here today, say to you now—go forth and smite the foe. Drive them back. Back to their homes, we all say..."

Her speechifying dragged on. For how long, Squire didn't know. He listened to his mistress and her friends talk but had no notion what they were saying.

"Well, now, ain't that woman a sure 'nough purty speaker," James Henley, a free man of color employed by Mister Montgomery, said. James was one of several employees.

"She's a windbag," Rachel said.

"She's got more air in herself than a balloon," James said.

"She needs to let Reverend Adamson speak."

"Well, it's about time." Matilda Rutherford clapped silently when the elderly minister tapped Mrs. Stonebridge's shoulder.

Hands clasped as though in prayer, Colonel Stonebridge's wife ended her speech, bowed her head, and stepped down the depot steps where she joined her husband.

A long drawn out prayer followed Reverend Adamson's brief sermon. Once he finished, Colonel Stonebridge ordered the soldiers to "fall out."

Jesse strode to Rachel and embraced her.

Squire barked for attention to no avail. Why didn't his master speak to him? What did he do wrong? His leash loosened, slackened, dropped from his mistress's hand. He almost jumped up on his master, till it tightened again when Mister Montgomery grabbed it.

"Back before Christmas, my darling gal. I'll be back before Christmas." Jesse's and Rachel's lips pressed together in the longest kiss Squire ever saw. His master broke from his mistress, shook Mister Montgomery's hand farewell. Touching his kepi's visor, he bid Matilda and James goodbye.

Shouted orders sent the men to the rail coaches.

Squire searched for his master. Where did he go? He barked and barked and barked. Where was he? Why didn't he speak to him?

The train hissed, gathered steam. The last men approached the last coach.

"Now, Father?" Rachel looked at him.

"Now," Mister Montgomery said.

Squire's leash went limp. Turning, he threw his forepaws up into her hoopskirt.

Her countenance gentle, she winked at him. "Guess you decided to keep us company, huh?"

Squire licked her knuckles and then lit out after the train, leaping into the last coach just before its door shut. He jumped onto a laughing soldier's lap and peered out a window. His mistress crushed something beneath her nose. A rag of some sort. What was it? Was she sad? Why?

March 1863

Port Hudson, Louisiana

Two

———— ◆ ————

Captain Jesse Webb forced his eyes open and rubbed the sleep from them. Outside his cabin, starlight shimmered and seeped through cracks separating its upper willow logs. Days after their arrival in October he, Lieutenants Mitchell Hayes and Richard Utley of his company, along with another company's officers, threw it up within two days to ward off winter's chill.

He moaned, his body aching from his makeshift bed—a flimsy hay mattress atop an old door affixed to the cabin wall.

Something prodded his chin, his shoulder next.

"Well, hello to you again, boy," he whispered, so as not to awaken his snoring friends. He reached over and scratched Squire behind his ears. "Now what are you doing wanting to play this hour of the night, huh?"

Squire's tongue drooped inches from his nose. Rough, moist licks smothered Jesse's face and hands.

As Jesse rolled off his bed, Squire's tongue caught him behind his right ear. Not much maneuvering space in this cabin, but it did have standing room. He got to his feet. Two chimneys flanked the roof, their fires dead. Fortunately, no longer was the weather unbearably cold, just tolerably cool. If Utley was awake, he'd have kept their fires burning. Of all this cabin's occupants, Utley hated the cold worse than any of them.

Once Squire nudged him outside, he leaned against Jesse's legs.

Jesse looked down at him. "Some short war we're in, huh, boy?"

Squire rolled over, his belly exposed and his legs kicking like a newborn pup. Kneeling, Jesse threaded his fingers through his dog's thick fur. When Jesse scratched his belly, Squire shut his eyes and stopped kicking, his legs almost totally outstretched and his mouth closed.

"I'd say you like being spoiled." Jesse stood, his hands on his hips. "Glad you've survived all we've been through together so far… Pensacola, Island Number Ten upriver after we surrendered to the Yanks. We might've been split up permanent if I hadn't spied a boat on that creek. You and me, boy, we sure sneaked away from 'em, didn't we? You and me crossing that lake on that boat together like we were going fishing like we used to do back home. What an adventure that was, getting away from those Yanks, eh?"

Squire rolled over on his legs, leapt to all fours, threw his forepaws forward, and thrust up his tail. He sat on his hindquarters. His long muzzle parted in what resembled a smile.

"You enjoyed our time in Vicksburg after we made our way there, didn't you? Then Colonel Stonebridge got his release in a prisoner swap. The rest of our men, too, all swapped in a prisoner exchange. Glad we have our regiment back together. Aren't you?"

Squire yipped, as though he agreed with Jesse's words.

Jesse's thoughts wandered back to his escape…and to Rachel. He touched his pocket. No, Rachel's tintype was no longer there. He remembered rowing the boat across the huge lake in deep darkness, Squire in its bows. He'd bent over to pick up a rope he'd been dragging behind him. It must've happened then. That must've been when Rachel's tintype fell out of his pocket and splashed silently into the water. It'd been over a year since he'd last kissed her, during a thirty-day furlough from his Pensacola post. She'd once again begged him to let Squire stay with her, but again, he left the decision up to his dog. His dog, once again, chose to accompany him.

He scoffed at himself. How could he have been so naive as to believe this would be a glorious little war, a grand adventure, a diversion from his day-to-day routine? How could he have believed he'd be home before Christmas? All it took was one battle to kill that notion—blood, death, scattered and shattered arms and legs…and… Jesse shuddered…*and decapitated heads.*

Now he existed on a Louisiana bluff, isolated by the Mississippi River, ravines, swamps, canebrakes, and to his immediate north by the town he defended. More hamlet than town, Port Hudson, a mere twenty-eight streets crisscrossed its acreage. Isolated, too, from his beloved Rachel. He patted his trouser pocket, safe haven for her most recent letter.

From the sentinel post on the eastern bank downriver a signal rocket, death's grim herald, streaked the darkness with brilliant bursts of light. A rapid succession of musketry erupted from the river batteries farther south. Jesse ducked inside his cabin and buckled on his waist belt.

Mitchell bolted upright in his bed above him. "The Yanks. It's about time."

"Is it the whole fleet?" Utley, now on his feet, spoke in a nasal monotone.

The cabin's other occupants bounded off their beds, threw on their shirts, buckled on their sabers, and grabbed their revolvers. As they dashed outside, incoming mortar shells seized their attention. Unlike their bombardment earlier in the day, the mortar boats at Prophet's Island downriver finally found their range. Their iron balls screeched through the star-spangled sky in great arcs, smashing earth, scattering women who'd been visiting the garrison's camps. Scooping up children, numerous ladies raced past Jesse and into the woods, the swamp, and onto the steamboat wharf. Older children and men who'd also been visiting Port Hudson followed them.

His revolver drawn, Jesse hurried to some soldiers who'd tossed aside their card game at the first signal rocket. "Fall in, men. Come on, now. Let's go. Fall in."

Drummers beat the long roll. Mortar fire and broadsides intensified. Distant shells crashed. From every direction, officers darted through their camps repeating Jesse's words to their men.

His tail high, Squire beat a retreat away from the battle.

Within minutes bonfires blazed along the river's western bank. Mesmerized, Jesse watched them. All around him soldiers made battle preparations, yet he stayed put, transfixed by the dancing flames shooting skyward, wavering back and forth like fiends, illuminating the mighty Mississippi, devouring the pine knots heaped together for this attack. For Jesse…a lump swelled his throat…and time… everything…stood…still.

Roars from the garrison's lowest river battery jerked Jesse out of his daze. Through the bonfires' dense smoke, swirling around and obscuring the vessels, came flashes from the approaching ships' guns. Of little use because of their smoke, the bonfires died as quickly as they'd sprung to life.

Jesse jogged to the precipitous bluff near Battery Number One, the northernmost cannon in the gauntlet of nineteen guns. Here the Mississippi made a sharp turn. Ever since the Yankees' ineffective bombardment earlier in the afternoon its cannoneers, standing behind their sodded earthworks, eagerly awaited this Yankee attempt to pass them.

While the ships steamed closer, Jesse half-cocked his revolver's hammer. With a flask, he poured gunpowder down one of its cylinder's chambers. His men rammed balls down their musket barrels or aimed at the river far below. Let his boys get off some decent shots, those poor Yankee tars would be swimming in blood.

"I figured on them getting on up here today or tomorrow." Jesse dropped a pistol ball in its chamber.

"My conclusion likewise, sir." Utley grabbed the rammer attached beneath his revolver's barrel and pulled it down.

"It'd sure be nice if our fine government sent us some better guns. Ten more rifled cannon, a thousand Enfields, and a hundred ironclads, too, would be a dandy addition to our defenses here."

"If you say so, sir."

"I do say so, Zero."

"Zero?"

"Never mind, Utley." Jesse chuckled to himself. Utley's personality reminded him of a number—zero—as in zero personality. He continued loading the remaining chambers in his pistol's cylinder.

From their river post they spotted two steam transports docked at the wharf, the vessels illuminated by their lights. The boats' crews quit unloading their cargo when screaming women and children ran up the gangplanks onto the vessels. Officers shouted unintelligible orders; sailors cast off from the wharf. The steamboats hastened upriver.

Hooves pounded the earth behind Jesse. Turning at the sound, he spied the garrison's commander, Franklin Gardner, galloping toward the cannoneers. "Why don't you fire on those boats?" Gardner aimed his sword at the fleeing transports.

Before Jesse could respond, Private Hearn spun on him. "They are our transports, you infernal thief."

The general rode off.

Jesse grinned, likewise Colonel Stonebridge, who'd arrived in time to hear the incident. Most likely, Hearn didn't recognize the general. Not in this darkness. A West Point educated officer, born in New York and reared in Iowa, Gardner had married into a prominent Louisiana family. Everyone loved and respected him.

Jesse's attention returned to the approaching ships. Onward they steamed, the van of more Union ships bent on their destruction. Their flashing muzzles thundered. The air pulsed. Shells exploded. His ears rang while the earth shuddered as though blasting it from its orbit. Into a swirling bank of smoke, the vessels plunged. Battery Number One boomed with ear-splitting fury. Jesse fired his revolver at the two large vessels lashed together, creeping past.

Chewing the end of an unlit cigar, his air nonchalant, Colonel Hampton Lafayette Marsden watched shrieking mortar shells burst over the treetops like a fiery meteor shower. Several crashed near his position; several fell short without detonating; others buried themselves in the earth and exploded from the ground seconds later, spraying dirt and shrapnel everywhere. Where was the enemy? Why wasn't he coming?

Marsden's comrades also observed the show. This wasn't their first engagement; they'd all seen this "elephant" before. Those who'd not "seen the elephant" yet, who'd not experienced their first battle— many of them wide-eyed—cowered in ditches behind an earthen parapet. For Marsden and his men, however, this current river battle offered a measure of entertainment. Though the mortar shells and naval guns pounded the bluff, shattered the air and cut down trees, they couldn't inflict much damage on Marsden's position. The enemy's troops, that's who he longed to lock bayonets with.

Officially designated as unattached, his regiment currently served in General S.B. Maxey's brigade, posted in William Slaughter's cornfield smack dab in the center of the garrison's landward defenses designated the Center Wing. Unlike the rugged terrain dominating Port Hudson's landscape, this center wing, situated some two miles east of the hamlet, spread out flat as a flapjack just beyond a mile.

Work on their defenses was as yet unfinished. They'd first started building their defensive perimeter one and a half miles below Port Hudson, on the Mississippi River. From there the earthen parapet made a crooked path northward. Because the slaves they'd impressed from nearby parishes to do the work poked around, as did the soldiers who helped, progress on the fortifications limped along. Eventually, according to the plan, the parapets would form an irregular arc linking the Mississippi River north of the town to its southern starting point. Though outnumbered by the enemy, Port Hudson's jagged terrain gave them an advantage if their armies ever clashed.

The river battle's rumble intensified.

Marsden imagined cannoneers sweating at their artillery, sponging the hot bores, ramming the shells home. He shifted his feet. He needed to be out there, amidst the action. He reached for his saber inside the scabbard dangling off his sword belt buckled round his waist. Drawing the blade, he sliced air then sheathed it again. He was a great commander, a very great commander.

At Fort Donelson, he'd fought like a wildcat. One day, the Confederacy would recognize his military genius. His dear father may be Mobile's great big nabob cotton factor, but he could do something his father could never do. He could fight. No way could his dear, precious father criticize his fighting skills.

Sergeant Major Esau Winder stepped away from the breastworks.

"The enemy isn't coming," Marsden said, the word *enemy* his preferred term for his Union opponents.

"I ain't so sure, Colonel." Winder's voice was gruff.

"Bah! I'm never wrong." Marsden broke from his men, their gazes transfixed on the exploding sky. He swaggered to a ravine off the south side of a narrow lane, which ran through a sally port past William

Slaughter's residence. Numerous white outbuildings surrounded that planter's big house.

A ragtag lot, most of his men were, dressed in variegated shirts and trousers. Though it wasn't their fault, he wished they wore proper uniforms. When he first organized his regiment back in '61, their uniforms were made of the finest blue and gray cloth. But the war exacted a toll, not only on their clothes but also on them. They ought to look like soldiers, not a bunch of coon hunters. As their commander, he deserved to lead a grand-looking regiment into battle, brass buttons gleaming and uniforms spotless.

The battle's gunfire slackened. Flashes decreased in frequency. Marsden muttered. It couldn't stop now, not before he got into the fracas. He returned to the breastworks. "Sergeant Major, tell Bailey to bring me my horse."

"Where you heading off to, sir?" Winder cracked his knuckles.

"General Gardner's headquarters."

Winder blinked at him quizzically.

Marsden stared straight into Winder's face instead of past it. Battling his mounting temper, he said, "Listen, old man. My reasons are my reasons. Got that?"

"Begging the colonel's pardon, but forty-four ain't that old."

His eyes suddenly shifted away from his sergeant major. "You are fully cognizant of the fact that General Rust's brigade has been out there, way beyond our fortifications, endeavoring to make General Banks's enemy boys attack us."

Winder nodded.

"Well, his objective was to lure them here so we could counterattack. He's failed." Marsden's fist smacked his palm. "I'm going to talk some sense into our illustrious garrison commander, Sergeant Major. I'm telling Gardner to give me Rust's command. I will make them attack us. I am the man who should have Rust's authority."

"My, my. Look at who's coming." Winder cracked his knuckles again.

Marsden spotted them before Winder did. Outside the breastworks, off in the distance, four men approached the sally port. They came in a rank, rather than a file. The two men on the flanks rode horses, the two in the middle plodded, and ahead of them trotted a shaggy dog.

"Ain't that Webb's dumb doggie?" Winder said.

"Appears so."

"The thieving cur stole my socks."

"Filthy mongrel." Marsden drew a penknife from his trouser pocket, set its blade along his cigar's cap, and snipped it off. He struck a match and lit up. He scowled at Squire. How he'd love to rip apart that dog.

A few weeks ago, while chasing a rat through his camp, Squire knocked over a washerwoman as she hung Marsden's trousers to dry. The trousers flew out of her hands and landed in the dirt yards from her near-empty clothes basket. The rat scurried over them. Squire caught the rodent in a matter of seconds. Triumphantly, he stood atop Marsden's clothes, dirty paws and all, and held the pest high between his jaws, its limp tail almost trailing the ground.

Squire's audience cheered.

Dirty clothes were not something Marsden considered funny. He puffed his cigar.

The four men and Squire finally halted in front of him. The two soldiers on horseback saluted. The men in the middle, wearing dusty blue uniforms, didn't. Squire sat, his long muzzle tight.

"We found 'em hidin' in the woods, sir." The Rebel corporal indicated the men withholding salutes.

"Squire flushed them out of hiding, sir," the second Southern soldier said.

"Jumped out of hidin', them men did." The amused corporal's narrow shoulders sort of bounced while he talked. "Like a pair of scaredy rabbits, them was. Squire put the snarl on 'em. We're takin' 'em to the provost marshal. They claim they're desertin'"

"You men get on back to your regiment. I'll handle it from here."

"Sir, we were ordered to—"

"I told you I'd handle it."

After a moment's hesitation, the Confederate troopers trotted their horses back down Slaughter's road in the direction from which they came.

Marsden sat on a log and puffed his cigar. He studied the no-count enemy who'd deserted their flag. Squire sniffed their trousers.

"Where you from?" Marsden puffed out a smoke ring.

"Massachusetts." The first deserter, tall and skinny as a telegraph pole, displayed a gap separating his two front teeth when he spoke. "The name's George Eakin."

"I spent some time at your Fort Warren. Terrible hotel. Its food stank, its service stank, my room stank. Glad when I got freed in a prisoner swap." Marsden's cool gaze wandered to the second soldier, whose jutting jaw was firm and whose expression suggested a person who'd just swallowed a bitter lemon. "What about you?"

The soldier's calloused eyes shifted from Marsden to Squire.

"Your name, man." Marsden's forefinger tapped his cigar's burning end. Ashes hit the soldier's square-toed shoe. "Give me your name."

"Smythe."

"Your forename."

"Huh?"

"Your forename. I asked for your forename. That means your first name, you ignoramus."

"Just Smythe."

"Your first name is Just?"

Smythe gazed at the breastworks.

"Look at me when I'm talking to you."

"Don't take it personal, Colonel," Eakin said. "Nobody knows his first name. We were thinking on the way here that we'd like to join you."

"You would, huh?" He ought to be glad to have these new men join his ranks, even if they were only two, but he wasn't. For all he knew, they were saying this to avoid a prison camp. Salisbury Prison, in North Carolina? Perhaps. Even if sincere, how could he trust such cowards who'd deserted their flag? They might also desert their new flag. "Why?"

Distant shells crashed.

"General Banks has slaves in his army now," Eakin said.

"Slaves?"

"Former slaves. Call themselves the Native Guards. Smythe and me'll be plucked roosters before we fight alongside them."

"I'll be more'n plucked." Smythe looked Marsden in the eye.

Winder studied Smythe's shoes.

"Do you fancy those, Sergeant Major?" Marsden said.

"Not the shoes, sir," Winder said. "I'm having a pair of 'em made at Lieutenant Bransom's shoe shop. It's the socks I need to go with 'em, sir. The cur stole my old socks and ripped 'em to shreds."

"Remove your shoes, Smythe. And take off your socks."

"We came here in good faith, trying to join your Rebel army," Smythe said. "You've no cause to make me lose my—"

"Take them off."

Smythe spit in the dirt.

Winder slid his bowie knife from its leather sheath and aimed it at Smythe's stomach. "The colonel said take them off."

Smythe grunted, plopped down on the ground, and worked off his right shoe, which he hurled at a stump.

Quick as a flea, Squire sprang on it and dragged it across the dirt. Then he faced them. His upraised tail brushed the air with broad strokes. The gleam in his molasses eyes said, "Chase me."

"I'll get him." Winder charged Squire.

Squire bolted down the road, faster than Winder could catch him.

Three

———◆———

Squire trotted toward the corral at the north end of town where he'd buried his coveted prize, Smythe's shoe, which he'd stolen a few days ago. An urge to dig it up drove him there. He wanted to chew it, to gnaw it, this desire mounting with his every step. After a soldier left, he flattened himself on his belly and crawled along the hard earth, its rank odors assaulting his nostrils. As he wriggled into the corral beneath its lowest rail, a horse's tail swished near his face.

In the corral's farthest corner, Squire started digging. Rapidly his forepaws worked, spraying chunks of warm dirt beneath his belly. He stopped. He sniffed the hole. Leather! Leather! Faster he dug…and harder. His heart drummed his chest till his nails scraped the shoe.

Clattering distracted him. His muzzle lifted in the breeze; his nose quivered. He sampled a banquet of smells. Then one special scent roused his interest—salt pork, his favorite food. Crawling out from the corral, he next turned the corner behind the canvas-covered wagons choking a dusty street. Their four-mule teams clopped at an even pace. When his keen nose led him to the pork wagon, he darted behind it and noticed a lid missing from one of its upright barrels.

He sprang toward the wagon's end gate.

"No, Squire." The sharp command sounded from a soldier inside.

Squire ran closer and jumped higher, still not quite clearing the gate.

The soldier inside the wagon poked his head past a barrel. "We got these off the Yanks, Squire. They've all gone back to Baton Rouge and left their supply wagons behind. This is our food, not yours. Get."

Squire didn't "get." He barked and leaped and barked and leaped and cavorted around the wagons all the way to a small frame house when, fur bristling, his antics ceased. An unfamiliar odor he smelled. He pricked his ears…and strange steps he heard, the squish of grass beneath merciless paws. He scurried to the house's small porch and maneuvered behind a rocking chair. Peering between two of its spindles he awaited the intruder. A bulldog.

No ordinary bulldog. Scars marred his broad forehead and forelegs. Hate brimmed his eyes. Squire sensed trouble. Should he flee? Should he attack? Something inside him blared like a bugle: *Watch out!*

The bulldog spotted him. And charged.

Squire toppled the chair in flight. He swerved past a wagon and crashed into a stranger's legs the precise moment the stranger turned from the wagon's end gate. This mishap caused a delay of seconds, enough time for Squire's foe to catch up. Squire sprinted around the man.

His vicious eyes glaring, the bulldog gave chase.

Jesse shoved his revolver down his holster and snatched his scabbard from off his bed. "Stupid doggone drills," he muttered. "Should've gone back to Coughlin months ago."

"Then get shot for desertion." Utley rose up from his stool, on which he'd been sitting.

"Maybe not such a good idea that, either." Jesse wondered how the furniture store fared. Did it have a lot of business? Considering the South's hard times these days, he doubted it. At least Rachel and James were helping Mister Montgomery, that is, on the condition his father-in-law could still afford to pay James. He moved toward his cabin's door. "Our wonderful dress parade in a half hour. Ain't our drills grand?"

"Well, a very restful Sunday lies just around the bend." Utley buttoned his frock coat, grabbed his kepi from off another stool, and plopped it on his balding head. "I am glad we at least will have to do nothing then."

"And at least I'll have more time to give our boy the attention he deserves. I can't help but feel guilty when I can't play with him. I know if I were a dog, I wouldn't like being ignored."

"Well, if I were born into the feline species, I would not care. I would just as soon be left alone."

Jesse smiled at Utley's feeble attempt at humor.

They stepped out into the afternoon's crisp air and sauntered toward the batteries frowning down at the river from the forbidding bluff. Shaped like pentagons, the works' flame-belching cannons promised destruction to any foe who dared venture past. Rather than engineers, who usually built such fortifications, artillerymen erected them, packed earth overlaid by green sod. They did such a fine job they made General Gardner, an engineer himself, proud of their work.

"Glad only that first pair of ships got past us the other night." Jesse gestured downriver, at a distant island.

"Admiral Farragut's flagship and her consort were the pair that got through." Utley looked upriver. "So the rumor goes. It came from one of our prisoners we captured from the ship that grounded on a shoal."

"We sure blasted her to kingdom come." Jesse pivoted from the river. "Just glad none of our boys got killed."

"Those ships we repulsed are still down at that island. They will make another attempt at it in the future."

"I reckon their mortar boats'll keep on pounding us when they get the notion. I'd say it was a pity Colonel Marsden's men weren't attacked."

Utley cleared his throat. "You would like to see that man dead, would you not?"

"He killed my brother. He should've been arrested for their duel. I should have been arrested also, being how I was Elliott's second. I have no inkling how we got away with it." Jesse's face burned; every muscle in his body tensed. "I don't give a cat's meow if I get arrested, not after he killed Elliott. It's only because I gave Rachel my word that I wouldn't fight him that I haven't done it."

"Your Rachel is wise."

Shouts quickened their pace.

"Cap'n Webb! Cap'n Webb!" A corporal astride a gray horse galloped up to him. He swung off his saddle and thrust the reins in Jesse's hand. "Squire's skirmishing for his life. Too dangerous to break it up, and none of us in town are toting our guns. The horse, compliments of Colonel Stonebridge. Hurry, sir. Bring your pistol."

Jesse sprang into the horse's saddle. His heels bumped the animal's barrel. The horse galloped toward town. Utley and the corporal followed at a run.

Down the middle of a Port Hudson street, Jesse rode smack into a raucous mob. Soldiers and civilians screamed, waved arms, flung down hats. Rising in his saddle, he peered across their heads. His jaw went slack.

Brindle bulldog and golden mix-breed flashed within this circle of humanity. Dirt and dust swirled round the battling beasts. Squire's teeth lashed at the bulldog. The bulldog sprang for Squire's head. Squire danced aside; the bulldog smashed his left shoulder; Squire tumbled over. The bulldog pounced.

Squire rolled clear, regained all fours quicker than the bulldog's jaws could clutch him.

Leaping off his horse, Jesse tethered it at a watering trough. He'd work his way through the crowd and shoot Squire's foe. "Let me through." He nudged two men aside. "Let me through. Let me through, I say."

The deafening roar drowned his screams. Jostling men backed up, making a path for the dogs. Jesse forced himself between them.

Though not stocky and muscular like the bulldog, Squire held two aces in his paws—speed and nimbleness. No way could he defeat an experienced fighter like the bulldog, though. All the bulldog needed to do was grab Squire's nose or neck and lock them in his tenacious grip and shake Squire hard enough to rip apart his muscles. He almost grabbed him once, but so far, Squire's agility had saved him. Question was, how long could his boy last?

Squire darted under a wagon behind one of its rear wheels. The crowd's noise tapered off.

Growling and glaring at Squire, the bulldog lowered his head.

His ears flattened against his head, Squire drew back his lips and snarled. Terror dilated his eyes. His hackles rose. The air pulsed.

Pistol in hand, Jesse drew a bead on a patch of skin between the bulldog's ears. He squeezed the trigger. *Click.* Jesse swore.

"Quit teasing him, Nero," a heavyset old man wearing a battered top hat shouted, mopping his brow with his sweat-soaked handkerchief. Though his wide girth hindered his swiftness, he managed to move within sight of his dog fairly fast.

Jesse jammed his pistol down in its holster. He knew what the old man was doing. By running to where Nero could observe him, he was making his dog fight harder to please him. He'd heard this was one of the tactics owners of fighting dogs used. He sprinted to the man. "Call him off, mister."

"Why?" The man didn't bother looking at him—too busy urging on his dog.

"My dog's under that wagon."

"Ain't much of one, is he?"

"Mister…" Jesse clenched his fists.

The old man lifted his hat.

As though on cue, Nero charged beneath the wagon.

Squire bolted back out, onto the street, and sprinted toward some stores, dodging around hitching posts and barrels and crates, his enemy on his tail.

The old man followed him. Jesse raced way ahead of the crowd.

Squire wove around watering troughs.

Nero gained on him.

Jesse and the old man shouted at the top of their lungs. To Jesse's fearful astonishment, Nero almost equaled Squire's speed.

"Kill! Kill!" the old man screamed.

"Run, Squire! Run!" Jesse and the spectators yelled.

Mitchell hurried to Jesse. "Squire's starting to get tuckered out."

Jesse's attention didn't waver from the dogfight. "I'll have that old man's head if his crazy dog kills Squire."

Nero reversed course and lunged for Squire's nose.

Squire dodged him by a whisker and darted through a store's open doorway, its owner one of those who'd fled in a transport when the Yankee navy tried passing them.

Nero pursued.

A crash sounded.

Jesse bounded inside and over a fallen shelf right behind Nero. Shattered glass crunched underfoot. The fallen shelf delayed Nero by seconds, long enough for Squire to scramble atop a high counter. Squire glared down at Nero, and Nero glared up at him.

How did his boy jump that high? Jesse fast found the answer—a small overturned table. He'd probably hopped atop it then sprang from it onto the counter.

Spectators packing the store cheered Squire, though at a distance lest the bulldog turn on one of them.

"Hold it right there, mister." Revolver drawn and cocked, Jesse closed on Nero's owner as the man started turning the table upright. Though his gun was unloaded, Jesse figured the old man didn't know that.

The man dropped the table upended. He hastened behind the counter to a chair, upright and nearer Squire. Patting it, he shouted Nero's name. "Use this, boy. Kill him. Kill him."

Nero made for the end of the counter to go around it to the chair. His attention diverted from Squire, Squire jumped him, seized his neck between his teeth, and squeezed his struggling enemy harder and harder. Nero fell over on his back …his legs flailing…weakening…slowly…slowly…dead. Cheers erupted throughout the store.

Whimpering, Squire hobbled to Jesse. His left hind paw trailed blood.

Jesse dropped to one knee. His fingers probed the mangled fur and bloody withers. Ragged gashes lacerated Squire's skin. Thankfully, his fur's thick padding, a double coat of it, saved him.

The old man stormed up to him. "Your dog killed my champion. I paid lots of money for Nero. He won me plenty, too. Made a good living fighting him." The man's glare, black as iron, blazed from his coarse face.

"If you didn't let your dog out of his cage and let Squire bump into you, he'd have been long gone from your sick animal." Colonel Stonebridge strode to them. "I saw it happen, Captain Webb. I wasn't but a block away when the incident started."

"Squire ain't no real fighter," another soldier said.

"But he sure is smarter and quicker," Mitchell said. "He's got lots of wits about him. All your dog ever got was brawn."

The spectators exploded into guffaws.

"Either him or your dog, mister," Jesse said. "It looks like it was going to be your dog. A mercy to Nero Squire killed him. At least he doesn't have to suffer your barbarity anymore. No dog deserves to be treated the way men the likes of you treat them. Making a living gambling with a dog's life is a disgrace."

"Look at his hind leg." Colonel Stonebridge pointed. "Seems our boy injured his foot."

"I reckon on that store's shattered glass, sir. Bottles or something when the shelf fell." Jesse inspected Squire's bloody left hind foot. "With your permission, Colonel, I'll take him to Doctor Carter. I may be late for dress parade."

"Permission granted."

Carefully, Jesse slid his arms beneath Squire and picked him up.

"I'll kill him." The old man waved his fist. "As sure as my name's Aaron Blevin, I'm gonna kill your dog."

While day slowly surrendered to night, Marsden jogged toward the sally port on the lane rolling through his breastworks. "Mister Blevin. Stop a minute."

The old man halted the two mules drawing his wagon. On the wagon bench beside him, his daughter Giselle slipped her snuffbox inside her faded blue reticule.

Marsden remembered them from a few months earlier when they passed through Port Hudson to catch a flatboat across the river. He'd probably returned to Port Hudson the same way, or by one of their transport steamers.

"Where's your dog?" Marsden aimed his cigar at the empty cage.

Blevin spat a stream of tobacco before he removed his top hat from off his hairless head. With a broad sweep of his forearm, he swiped perspiration off his creviced brow. "Dumped him in the river. I should of never let him outta his cage. I wanted him to go after some tramp of a cur and get hisself some fighting practice. The tramp of a cur killed him."

"A cur with gold-colored fur?"

"Lots of fur. Not real big and not real small. Taller than Nero was, though, but not by much. Some idiot officer owned him." He turned his head away from Marsden and spat.

"Was that officer perchance clean-shaven? Wavy brown hair sort of combed straight back? And the dog's name. Was it perchance Squire?"

"That's him."

"The fool's name is Jesse Webb. I don't much care for him or his mangy dog. It's a pity Nero didn't kill him."

"Tsk, tsk." Giselle tied her reticule's drawstrings.

Marsden tipped his forage cap at her. "I trust none of Webb's men harmed you, miss."

"I was at the hotel."

"General Gardner's headquarters?"

"Uh-huh."

Not what he'd call a screamer, Giselle. But neither was she homely, thanks to her owning a most beautiful pair of emerald eyes, shimmering like jewels above the smidgen of freckles gathered near her oval face's flat cheeks. A black snood kept her dusky red chignon in place. She looked to be no older than eighteen. Her thin lips curled, as though amused at something behind him.

Marsden followed her gaze. Several soldiers, also Smythe and Eakin, gawked at her from a distance, apparently buying into her coquettish games. "The men around here seem to like you, Miss Blevin."

"Ain't never met 'em, me and Papa travelin' and all. Most folks livin' in this town knew me, 'cept most of 'em cleared out after y'all moved in."

"What've the Bluebellies been doing in these parts lately?" Blevin said. "I heard tell their cavalry was operating on the river's western side, but I didn't see hide nor hair of them."

"Well, sir, General Maxey's brigade, most of it, is out skirmishing with them. We got left behind to guard the works. About three days ago, we fought their ships when they tried running our batteries. Then their army started pulling back, pillaging every home and farm they could lay their hands on. Some of our boys managed to steal a large number of their commissary wagons."

"Those must of been the wagons I saw in town." Blevin swatted at mosquitoes buzzing around his large ears.

"Where are you heading now?"

"Home, if the Yanks ain't torched it. And they better not have harmed my other fighting dogs."

"That would be a shame, sir."

"You'd better believe this, Colonel. And I don't mind telling you since you seem to hate that tramp of a cur same as me. First chance I get, I'm bringing back every fighter I own to hunt him down and kill him."

"Where did you say you lived?"

"Not far. A small farm off the Clinton and Port Hudson Railroad. My nephew Zack manages it for me so I can fight my dogs. Make more money fighting dogs than I do raising cotton."

Marsden tugged and twisted his mustache. "Bringing all those killer dogs through our picket line will most likely prove problematic."

"You saying I shouldn't get back at Webb and his dog?"

"Not at all. I'm merely suggesting that you bide your time and await the appropriate opportunity, till I can dispatch my sergeant major to get you. You can trust him, Mister Blevin. He hates Squire as much as I do. He'll sneak you in."

Blevin replaced his battered top hat on his head and produced a business card from his coat pocket. He handed it to Marsden. "My address." After they shook hands, Blevin drove the mules pulling his wagon through the sally port.

As Marsden returned to his regiment, he caught Eakin and Smythe glaring at him. The garrison's provost marshal made a mistake when he released them. Those two, he'd best keep a sharp eye on. Especially Smythe, since he now owned no socks and, thanks to Webb's dog, he'd also lost a shoe.

Four

———◆———

High-pitched barks hastened Jesse and Mitchell down a field hospital's narrow path. "No mistaking what those barks mean." Jesse passed the hospital's yellow flag drooping from a pole.

"Poor Squire's miserable," Mitchell said.

"That, my friend, is a fact."

Inside his crate, atop a long table, Squire greeted them with two happy barks. His tail batted the crate's sides and a white cotton bandage, knotted behind his ears, swathed his chest and withers. Another bandage wrapped his injured hind paw. The crate's slats, spaced about two inches apart, allowed him plenty of breathing room.

"There's our boy." Jesse hurried to his dog. "I haven't forgotten you. Why, there's nothing in this whole entire world that can make me forget you." He offered Squire his knuckles.

Squire poked his tongue between the crate's slats and licked them, fast and rough, as though licking a bowl of ice cream.

Jesse extended his fingers farther in and patted Squire's head. "You won't be in here too long, boy. That's a guarantee."

"You're one lucky critter." Big hands on his knees, Mitchell bent forward. He stuck his hand between the slats.

Squire's teeth grasped it, but they didn't break Mitchell's skin.

"Good thing crazy Nero didn't get a proper hold on you. You'd have sure nuff been a-goner." Mitchell pulled his hand from Squire's mouth. "I love it when he grabs my hand like that, Jesse. It feels good."

Jesse reached between the slats a second time and patted Squire's whiskered muzzle. "You know something, boy? You're the best dog in this whole entire world, and I hate the fact I have to lock you up like this. Doctor Carter promised me it'd only be a couple of weeks. You'll be all right, boy. My solemn promise."

Jesse cringed. Squire's butchered fur, Squire's bandages...Jesse rammed his fist in his palm. He should've listened to Rachel. He should've never suggested Squire be their regimental mascot, nor should he have let him come with them.

Jesse stroked Squire's paw. "I'm sorry this happened, boy. So very, very sorry. It's my fault. Next chance I get, soon as things around here settle down, I'll request a furlough home so I can take you back to sweet Rachel. I should've left you with her during my furlough last year, when I had the chance, but I figured on us staying in Pensacola more permanently. Stupid, I was."

An evening breeze rushed into Marsden's wall tent on the eastern edge of town. As he sat at his small pine desk, he grabbed a sheet of stationery out of its drawer and slapped it down beside a flickering lantern. A soldier in a nearby camp played "Aura Lee" on his harmonica; a washerwoman hummed its tune.

Saturating his tent space was the smell of tobacco, a reminder that he needed another cigar. First, though, he'd scribble a letter to Blevin. He seized up his steel-tipped pen, dipped it in his inkwell, and began writing.

Port Hudson, Louisiana March 28, 1863

Mister Aaron Blevin—

> *My dear sir, because of my pressing duties, I have been unable to write you until now. You may have heard about the action we've been having here. Until a few days ago, enemy ships have been bombarding us from long range. They have driven off all the*

transports here and forced General Gardner to move the landing farther north to Thompson's Creek. Our boys have been working night and day unloading transports there. Not much damage done to us, however.

The enemy burned the sugar mill across the river from us, but our batteries drove them off. Some of their cavalry attacked one of our steamers. It carried a load of molasses.

Were you cognizant of the fact that some of the enemy have come up the railroad from New Orleans? They forced our boys out of Pontchatoula. It is my understanding that General Pemberton, Vicksburg's commander, has dispatched reinforcements. Our General Gardner has dispatched some as well, but again he has left me out of the fun.

Generally, routine has returned to our garrison—drilling, fatigue duty, details. Boring.

I have conceived a most brilliant idea. If you and your lovely daughter will rendezvous with me at Peterson's sugar cane field, on the Sugarhouse Road at seven o'clock on the evening of the 31st instant, I can neglect my military obligations long enough for us to discuss it. Upon your agreement to my plan, and on condition that it finds success, of which I have no doubt, I will deliver the tramp of a cur to your doorstep. We must be careful that no one discovers our meeting.

Colonel Hampton Lafayette Marsden

He'd hand this letter to Winder and dispatch him to deliver it to Blevin. He swaggered out of his tent and moved down the road toward the river. "Sweet revenge, Webb, for stealing Rachel from me."

Five

—◆—

His saddle creaking, Marsden rode his stallion past cane fields sprouting their crop. A star-lit sky guided his path. *Revenge.* The word pounded his rib cage, pulsed his brain, and snatched his sleep. Revenge. Since he'd met the Blevins, he'd forged an alliance, the intent of which was to exact Webb's demise. He'd done nothing wrong. No, it was Rachel who'd dealt him an injustice. And it was Webb who dealt him an injustice, all high and mighty Jesse Webb. Soon, he'd expose Webb's "honor" business as a fraud.

Rachel would rue the day she married Webb. Childhood friend or not, she'd discover she didn't know her husband as well as she thought she did.

Up ahead, a large silhouette sharpened into focus. A buggy, and the flickering of its lanterns lured him closer. Within minutes, he reined in his horse alongside it.

"You're late." Blevin spoke from the buggy seat.

Marsden swung down from his saddle, moved around the other side of Blevin's vehicle, and assisted Giselle down.

Blevin set aside his buggy horses' reins and climbed out.

"Some unexpected army business to attend to, Mister Blevin. Usually, I'm the most punctual soldier in the garrison." Marsden pulled off his gauntlets, held them in his left hand, and scanned Giselle from feet to face.

Her homespun dress hung about her slender figure to midway past her calves. Cold craftiness hardened her round face; her alluring emerald eyes glowed in the moonlight. A pretty pair of orbs they were. So green, so nice.

Unsure of how she'd receive his comment, Marsden cleared his throat and shifted his attention to her father, though he was addressing her. "For my plan to succeed, Miss Blevin, you will need to conceal your flesh more. And, uh, you'll have to quit dipping snuff… at least while you're in town."

"Ain't goin' to stop doin' nothin' till I hear the plan." Giselle waved her snuff box at him.

"It's a good one. We'll meander down this road a distance and discuss it. Let me tell you a little about my background first. I'm from Mobile. My father's a cotton factor. I was in that same business till the war started. My father was one of the city's leaders."

"Figger you're rich, then." Giselle's tone wielded a twinge of envy.

Marsden ignored her words. He recounted his and Rachel's first meeting in her father's store on one breezy March day back in '57, while Webb was away attending the university. He needed some furniture for the new room that laborers had added to his house. Unable to find something suitable in Mobile, he considered ordering pieces from up north because even with shipping it'd be cheaper than what he'd have to pay furniture builders in Mobile. He was on the verge of doing this when a friend mentioned Mister Montgomery's store and his "screamer of a girl" Rachel. His curiosity about her led him to follow his friend's advice. On the day he visited the store he met Webb's older brother, Elliott. And when he laid eyes on Rachel for the first time, and Rachel him, some mysterious force neither could identify drew them toward each other. His friend had been right. She was a screamer, so beautiful, in fact, that he ordered more furniture than he needed.

He slapped his gauntlets against his thigh. "Her father liked me at first. She and I entered into a courtship. He even approved of our getting married, especially after she assured me she and Webb grew up together and were always no more than friends. Some six months after our courtship began, Webb graduated from the university and moved back to Coughlin. Rachel got all sweet on him. Their relationship turned serious. Elliott told him about our courting, our…" Marsden stalked away from the wagon several steps, turned about, and continued. "That no good…" He bit his lip. "Elliott had gone to Mobile, seeking me out at my father's office. Someone told him I'd gone to Pensacola on business and mentioned the Bobcat Saloon, which most people in the office, including my father, knew I frequented."

Giselle's lashes blinked quizzically as he approached his story's climax.

Hundreds of times, he'd mentally rehearsed the horrible incident. Dark shadows filled the saloon's four corners. Two candlelit chandeliers shimmered over men clustered around tables, hunched over cards and drinking beer. The congenial society of gamblers held no attraction for him this night. "I'd always gone to this saloon for one purpose, and one purpose only."

"Yes?" Giselle fluttered her eyelashes.

"To visit a lady who worked there. Stella Rogers. When I arrived, she was decked out in a scarlet dress and ostrich feathers, standing at the bar beside the stairs. We couldn't be seen together, so I first pretended not to notice her. After I looked around to be sure I didn't spot any familiar faces, I followed her up the stairs."

Blevin grinned.

Marsden suspected what Blevin might be thinking about Stella and him, and he almost…*No! Won't say it.* He swallowed his anger. "While Stella and I were upstairs…in the corridor, Mister Blevin… Elliott entered the establishment. Once he saw us coming back down the stairs, he followed me outside when I left. He waited till I'd gotten down the street a piece before he followed me. Once he caught up, he accused Stella and me of some horrible things, things that were not true. He threatened to tell his brother."

"Why was he hunting you down?" Blevin said.

"His intention was to stop Rachel and me from courting. He claimed he suspected something wasn't right about me. He was determined to discover what it was. Then he planned on telling his brother and Rachel about it."

"I reckon he found out." Giselle opened her snuff box, reached for some snuff, but closed it as though having second thoughts about dipping it.

"I tried explaining," Marsden continued. "Told him his accusations were falsehoods and misunderstandings. Did the man listen? No! He turned deaf ears on me. When I defended Stella's honor, he defied me and ridiculed her more. I hated his leering face, and it was imperative I shut him up. He allowed me no choice but to challenge him to a duel. One week later, after making the necessary arrangements, we fought our duel. Webb served as his brother's second, of course. I shot Elliott clean through the heart. That was a mistake, and something I'll have to explain to Rachel one day at the right opportunity. That's why I won't fight Webb in another duel. I must use other means."

"Who is this Stella girl?" Thrusting his hands in his pockets, Blevin rocked back on his heels.

"A lady, sir." Marsden pumped his fists hard. Stella's identity was nobody's business but his own. True, Webb and Rachel did know about her, thanks to the duel, but they didn't know anything beyond her first name. "She was a very nice lady. I said we were in the corridor together...on the second floor. Nothing more." He raised his palm. "I swear it."

"Rachel ain't pledged herself to you no more after you killed Elliott." Giselle's cold face yielded to its gentler features.

So, his gamble paid off. Giselle was the correct person, all right. Those bright green orbs of hers might just achieve his objective.

"What kind of feller is Webb?" Giselle slipped her snuff box inside her reticule.

"Struts around like some cock of the walk, bragging about how honorable and upright he is. His sense of honor is his biggest vulnerability. His father was a partner in the furniture business, same as Webb is now. After Webb's mother died, his father took to heavy drinking and became the town drunk. He lost his family's honor, and Webb's trying hard to recover it."

"Is that Webb feller a drinking man, too? Or is he a religious sort?"

"He's not a Bible-thumper, Miss Blevin, if that's what you mean. But he's always been a teetotaler, far as I know. He's afraid he'll end up like his father. Some men in this world just can't handle their liquor, I suppose, and Webb thinks he's one of them. It is my opinion you can destroy his honor for good."

"And if I succeed, she will up and fall back into your arms."

"You understand me correctly, miss."

"What makes you think she'll do that?" Blevin said.

"She will. I know she will. Say she doesn't, though. I've at least gotten my revenge on her for rejecting me. Once your beautiful daughter destroys Webb's honor, I will write Rachel and perchance persuade others to do the same. We will tell her what a rat her husband has become."

"Papa, can I help this feller? It sounds like fun."

"I'll help any man who'll help us get the cur." Blevin and Marsden shook hands. "Colonel, I place my lovely daughter into your service."

"Dispatch Giselle to Port Hudson at the end of the week. We mustn't let on we know each other, at least not at first. If Webb gets wind I'm behind his demise, well, I have my reasons for avoiding him at present."

"Some of your men saw you and us jawing the other day," Blevin said.

Giselle's eyes turned to ice. "I can handle them fellers."

"Good girl." Marsden proceeded to outline his plan for destroying Webb's honor and thus, his and Rachel's marriage.

April 1863
Port Hudson, Louisiana

Six

---◆---

ail wagging and tongue lolling, Squire trotted along Port Hudson's dusty streets, happy to be released from his crate and recovered from his wounds.

"Pree-sent, arms!"

"Order, arms!"

"Ground, arms!"

These shouted orders and other commands echoed all around him. This meant his master would be ignoring him for a spell. Since he'd heard his master say the word *drill*, he figured that must be the reason for the shouts. He'd heard them almost every day, and a long time ago he'd learned not to seek attention during drill. No amount of barking or capering brought the reward of his master's voice. So, he explored. This day, such roaming and exploring brought him to the town's common where tents were pitched in neat rows. He sat on a church's front steps and briefly watched some soldiers go through the manual of arms.

From here Squire wandered onto a road leading to the town's depot. He arrived the same time a train, its couplers clanking, screeched to a halt on its tracks. Its bulbous stack billowed pungent pine smoke. His nostrils quivered.

Not much to the train—one locomotive pulling seven cars. Of these cars, only one carried passengers. The others were either flat or box cars. Women and girls piled out of the passenger car. Hoopskirts bouncing, they hastened past Squire.

Squire sniffed the earth. In no great hurry, he stretched out on a covered porch attached to a building opposite the depot. He rolled on his side, shut his eyes. The pleasant breeze rolling past him stirred the tips of his coat. Lost in limitless time, he napped.

"Gotcha, you furry little bandit."

Startled awake, Squire recognized the speaker. Sour-faced Smythe, bearing down on him, his thick fingers splayed wide ready to grasp his throat. This was no game. The man was after him. He bounded off toward the depot, across the tracks, and ducked beneath a pup tent pitched near the hotel.

"I see you in there, you little thief." Smythe slowed to a walk. He bent low, his arms extended to grasp Squire and…

Squire wriggled backward out of the tent's rear flaps and then sprinted toward the hotel.

The man screamed, gave chase, stumbled over a stump, smacked the ground.

Bolting past the hotel, Squire darted beneath a hoopskirt that flew up like a giant clam's shell. It dropped back over him. Crouched low, he listened to the pleasant voices outside.

"What's your hurry, soldier?" Squire's rescuer said.

"I seen a big dog running this way," Smythe said, puffing hard. "Golden-colored fur, shaggy coat. You seen where he went?"

"He turned tail down yonder, heading for the landing."

"Thanks."

A pause.

"Haven't I seen you before?" The man asked the question.

"Maybe. I think I seen you at the breastworks that time my papa and Colonel Marsden were having themselves a chitchat a while back."

"Oh, I do recollect seeing you now. I'm Smythe. Just Smythe, as in just call me Smythe. Maybe we'll see each other again sometime."

"You don't talk like us, Mister Smythe. You sound like one of them Yankee fellers."

"Not anymore. Bye."

To Squire, it seemed an age before Giselle spoke again. "He's gone."

A sliver of light widened beneath her slowly lifting skirt. Squire scurried out. Crisp air and pleasant smells poured through his nostrils. Freedom. He launched into wild leaps and barks.

"Enjoy it now, you worthless, stupid dog." Her opened parasol held over her head with one hand, her other hand adjusted her bonnet's big bow. "I saved you for Papa. You're going to be his next bait dog." She walked toward the tracks, Squire alongside her.

"There's my good boy."

At the sound of his master's voice, Squire bounded high, his barks gleeful.

Jesse's lips spread into a wide grin. "Calm down, boy. I haven't been gone that long."

After further capering Squire sat erect, his head lifted high, his eyes fixed on his master. His warm heart pounded steady. His master. Squire adored him.

"Our drill's over," Jesse told him. "C'mon. Let's go."

"He's a smart animal," Giselle said. "Is he your dog?"

"Yes, miss. He's my regiment's mascot. His name's Squire."

"What a precious name! Some Yankee feller was chasing him. I let him hide beneath my skirt."

"Smythe chasing him, probably. I'm much obliged to you, miss." He tipped his kepi goodbye then snapped his fingers twice.

Squire obeyed Jesse's signal and followed him. But he did look back once.

Giselle thinned her lips.

Something was wrong. Squire sensed it.

Jesse matched Colonel Stonebridge's stride through the regiment's camp.

"I'm sorry, Jesse," the colonel said. "General Beall denied your request for a furlough."

Campfires sparked to life as they skirted past several fly tents, some willow log cabins, and a gaping hole their Alabama boys dug for an oven. Sniffing the ground, Squire accompanied them before he padded to a soldier pulling a spoon from his haversack.

"Have you asked General Gardner, sir?" Jesse said.

"Same story. It can't be done yet."

They halted near the bluff's edge. Beyond the winding Mississippi, the sunset painted the sky a purplish-crimson hue. Jesse's mind tumbled. Rachel, Mister Montgomery…how were they faring? If Squire got killed…would Rachel be able to forgive him if Squire died? Would she forgive his selfishness wanting to bring Squire to war? "I won't desert, sir. On my honor, I won't. Please, sir. I must get Squire on back to my Rachel before he gets killed."

"I cannot disobey my superiors' orders. You are aware of that."

"Then I'd say my word's not good enough for any of you. That's it. Everyone knows how much I hate this lousy war." He frowned at the coal-black clouds. An angry scream clutched his throat. "And its killing. And…and they're all scared I'll desert. But I won't, sir. On my word of honor, I won't."

Up went Stonebridge's hand, palm out. "Hold it right there, Captain Webb. I know you well enough to know you always keep your word. You're not the only one who hates killing. All us sensible people do. But we're locked into it now. We all have to see it through to the end. It's another matter of honor, Jesse. Besides, the Federals still threaten our garrison."

"Well, I'd say Banks achieved his objective last month when he distracted us long enough for Farragut to try and run past our batteries. Doesn't Banks have but one division left in Baton Rouge? Isn't he campaigning up the Red River?"

"Not just one division. All his cavalry and siege artillery remain in Baton Rouge also. General Rust's division moved out today for Jackson. General Buford's division will be pulling out of here soon. As for Grant, he's still trying to take Vicksburg."

"Well, sir, I'd say we're rid of Banks for a spell, else General Gardner wouldn't be ordering them elsewhere."

"How long will Banks leave us alone, Jesse? Your guess is as good as any man's. Next time, his maneuvers against us might be of a more serious nature and intent." Stonebridge's arm swept toward the river. "Some two or three hundred miles of the great Mississippi separates us from Vicksburg. If we surrender, the Yanks will control the entire river and seriously cripple our country. We need every man here till it's over."

They watched Squire, snarling and pawing and jumping back and forth between two chortling soldiers lying on their backs, a friendly tussling contest.

"Look at him," Stonebridge said. "Our boy's a morale builder. He's one of us."

"I can sort of see things that way, sir, I reckon. With your permission?"

"Granted."

Jesse saluted and trudged off. This whole entire war was one big ole serious mistake.

Seven

————◆————

Marsden stepped out from his tent into the boiling noonday sun. "Eakin!"

Whistling and swinging his arms, the gap-toothed deserter loped past him.

"Get over here, you blockhead. On the double-quick."

Eakin quieted. His pea-sized eyeballs slid Marsden's direction. "You talking to me, Colonel?"

"Confound it. I gave you an order."

Eakin stuck his hands in his pockets, kicked a rock against a tree, then shuffled to him.

Marsden's hand latched onto the deserter's forearm and yanked him inside. "What does 'clean' mean?"

Eakin snapped to attention. "Clean, sir. It is the absence of dirt, stains, or any other real or imagined blemishes on one's person or property."

"Cut the smart talk, unless you enjoy digging ditches for a month."

His demeanor apathetic, Eakin's erect posture slouched.

Marsden slid his fingers along the edge of his desk before he thrust his dirty fingertips into Eakin's face. "Do you understand how to clean things properly, or is it too complicated an assignment for your pitiful little mouse brain to comprehend?"

"I dusted it this morning, sir, before company drill as you ordered."

Marsden poked Eakin's chest to emphasize his point. "Explain this dust on my desk. And on my chair."

"It must have floated in…sir."

"Not this much dust. Moreover, my tent door's flaps were closed most of the morning." Marsden spotted a slave carrying an oak bucket. "Perchance I can locate a black man who will teach you."

Eakin flushed redder than an apple. "Cleaning's a slave's chore anyway, sir. Slaves crawling all over this stinking hole. Go find you one. Make him do it instead of me."

Marsden wondered why this idiot, this treasonous turncoat, should be under his command. He never trusted traitors. "Either obey my orders and get this place looking decent, else I'll clap you in irons so fast your big elephant ears'll fall off."

Blood drained from Eakin's face.

"Till you prove I can trust you, Eakin, I'll always dangle that threat over your head." Marsden jerked up his fist. "By a thread. Like Damocles's sword."

"Do you, er, want me cleaning your quarters again tomorrow morning?"

"I want you cleaning it again today, with a slave teaching you how to do it."

"Sir! I…I…" Eakin stammered out a few unintelligible words.

"Didn't the bugler play dinner call a few minutes ago? Go feed your ugly face and report back within the hour. Dismissed."

Eakin turned to leave.

"Eakin."

Eakin did an abrupt about-face, snapped to attention, and saluted Marsden.

When Marsden withheld his salute, Eakin stormed out.

Marsden snatched a square of Corporal Bailey's cornbread from his plate. He bit into it. *Ugh. Too gritty.* He dropped it and went to his writing desk. Bailey possessed none of Rachel's culinary endowments. But then, who did? Hopefully, Giselle met Webb today.

Marsden picked up his leather cigar case and slid off its cover. He slid it shut. He'd smoke later. Fortunately, he didn't have to break his teeth on Bailey's cornbread this time. He'd been invited to General

Maxey's quarters for finer fare, compliments of the ladies from nearby Clinton.

He stowed Stella's most recent letter in a small walnut box. Though she still lived in Pensacola, she'd found employment at a different saloon a few miles outside of that town.

Had his aide-de-camp, Lieutenant Felix Ransom, located Smythe yet? They'd reported him absent at company drill. Well, he'd best get moving. He was famished, and he needed to partake before General Maxey and his aides devoured all the food. An hour remained before skirmish drill. He plopped his forage cap on his head when a grumble snatched his attention.

Winder and Ransom shoved stumbling Smythe through Marsden's tent door.

"Sir, he was caught heading for Ross's Landing, sir," Ransom said.

"Trying to run the guard again, Smythe?" Marsden looked past him, at soldiers walking toward their camps. "Plan on swimming the river to the enemy ships at that island?"

"I was hunting that dog," Smythe said.

"The mongrel?" A wave of his hand dismissed his blond aide-de-camp. He turned back to Smythe. "Don't you realize how many weeks you've wasted trying to catch him? What would you have done if you'd caught him?"

"Choked him to death."

"Shooting him would be easier."

"More painful choking him."

"You'll never catch a dog, you dolt. And you'll certainly never catch Squire."

"Almost cornered him yesterday under a tent."

"Sure you did." Smythe's chasing the mongrel wouldn't do. If, by some good fortune, the fool did catch him and kill him, it'd derail his own plan. Marsden stroked his beard while studying Smythe's blistered bare feet. "What would you say if we found your stolen shoe? Would you cease pursuing the mongrel and attend all the drills?"

"Provided I get it back, Colonel. I still got my other shoe."

"You will do it, idiot, else you'll be court-martialed, whether I do or whether I don't give you back your shoe."

Marsden swaggered to his cot at the rear of his tent, bent beneath it, and returned seconds later, Smythe's shoe in hand. Twelve days ago, a cavalryman found it in the corral. Fortunately, Winder, in town on regimental business, was passing the stables when the soldier picked it up. When he recognized the shoe, he recovered it. Figuring it might be useful one day in managing Smythe, Marsden decided to lie about how long it'd been in his possession. He tossed Smythe his shoe.

Smythe caught it.

"Sergeant Major Winder found it yesterday evening over near the swamp. The mongrel buried it there."

"What was the sergeant major doing in the swamp, sir?"

Winder cracked his knuckles. "Gator hunting."

Smythe grunted and touched his forehead in a lazy salute.

"Dismissed," Marsden said.

After Smythe and Winder left, Marsden made haste for General Maxey's quarters.

Jesse swallowed a morsel of bland beef, slammed down his fork so hard the mess table wobbled, and shoved the plate at Utley, who sat opposite him. Jesse pulled a face.

His expression grave, Utley nudged it over to Mitchell.

Mitchell shoved it back to Jesse.

Jesse shoved it to the table's center. Blue beef, bland beef, he'd eaten enough of that fodder for today. From his shirt pocket, he withdrew a letter he'd received an hour earlier. Only now did he have time to read it. Written on an envelope, it was sealed inside another, wider envelope. Proper stationery was a rare commodity these days.

Panting, Squire sat on the ground beside Jesse. His big eyes appeared eager and hungry. His tongue drooped out the side of his mouth; saliva dripped from it in long strands. He barked twice, asking for a share of the food, Jesse assumed.

For the moment, though, everyone ignored him.

"From Rachel?" Utley said.

"Or Emma?" Mitchell said.

Jesse held it at an angle. "It's scrawl. Definitely from dear Rachel. Sister Emma's penmanship is practically perfect." He thumped the signature. "Ha! I am sure enough right. Written four months ago, judging by the date, and I'm just now getting it. Our postal service is getting downright efficient these days."

Whimpering, Squire padded over to Mitchell and nuzzled his calf.

"Now you look here, boy." Mitchell scratched him behind his ears. "We'll feed you in a few dang minutes."

Squire withdrew from Mitch and returned to Jesse. Up on his hind legs he rose, his forelegs propped across Jesse's lap, saliva building a warm puddle on his trousers. His sad-eyed pleas stirred Jesse's heart.

"I see you, good boy. Just you be patient a minute." Jesse squinted while he read her short letter. He tossed a scrap of beef behind Squire.

Squire leapt on it and wolfed it down. His black nose to the ground, he sniffed the earth hoping to find more.

"Yes, siree." Jesse leaned back on his stool. "She has become a nurse. Would all you imagine that, would you?"

Squire barked.

"Well, well. Let us have a look at this." Jesse opened the envelope on which she'd written and pulled out a red bandana accompanied by a small card. On it, Rachel had printed the words more legibly: "To Squire."

"My boy." Jesse waved the bandana at him.

Squire quit sniffing and looked up, ears perked and friendly eyes alert.

"My, what a dandy looking bandana." Mitchell set down his cup of coffee.

"Rachel sure was thoughtful making you this, boy. Sewing's not exactly her forte, not like her cooking, I'd say."

Squire rested his muzzle on Jesse's lap. He secured the bandana around his neck, its knot tight but the bandana loose enough so as not to choke him.

Rachel was too good of a lady for him, Jesse told himself. His sister, Emma, participated in a military aide society in Mobile, and Rachel left Coughlin to work in one of that city's hospitals, along with her closest friend, Matilda Rutherford. They were staying with Emma and Emma's husband.

Why she became a nurse, he didn't know. He did know certain people might gossip—that she'd become disrespectable—because she roamed hospitals in close proximity to strange men. Not disrespectable in his eyes, though. Under ordinary circumstances he would've forbade it, but these were not ordinary times. Lots of ladies were doing it. Many proved themselves better at it than men. He loved her for it, and he could tell by Utley's and Mitchell's reactions that they also respected her decision.

A leaflet suddenly landed on his table.

"Colonel Cox." Jesse got to his feet, as did his messmates.

With his deep brown, waist-length beard Lieutenant Colonel Cox, Colonel Stonebridge's second-in-command, resembled an Old Testament prophet. An Old Testament prophet? Weren't they sort of fiery?

"I'm hoping that in your spare time, you gentlemen will read it," Cox said. "Its message is urgent for all of our souls."

Jesse picked it up and scanned its title: *Religion Is Not Enough.* "Sir?"

"Religion cannot save us, Captain."

"Er, yes, sir." If ever a Christian walked the whole entire earth, it was Colonel Cox. His lifestyle stood out among everyone else's, and Jesse respected him. Everyone in the garrison did, as far as he knew.

The lieutenant colonel moved on toward another camp farther down the bluff.

Giggling behind him roused Jesse's interest—Squire's rescuer, twirling a familiar pink parasol opened wide against the noon sun. She basked in the attention of a half-dozen officers, her mouth wide with merriment. Skirt swishing, she moved straight to him.

"You remember me, Cap'n?" She peered at him beneath her dark lashes.

Mitchell and Utley stood.

"I remember. You rescued my dog," Jesse said.

"I declare! You is so right." She offered him a hand clad in faded kid gloves. "Folks in these here parts call me Giselle."

"Your last name, might I ask?"

"Uh…uh…it's uh…" Her voice squeaked. "B-Blevin."

Scowling, Jesse recoiled.

"I ain't my papa, and I…I hated that Yankee feller gone off chasin' your dog. Your dog's got hisself some very sweet looks."

"He's the best dog I've ever owned," Jesse said.

Squire started toward her, but Jesse snapped his fingers twice, calling him back.

"She won't hurt him," Mitchell said.

"Why not, Mitch?" Jesse said. "Her daddy's dog almost killed him."

"Did you see her at the fight?"

Jesse glared at Giselle as though driving a spike through her heart. "People who fight dogs ought to be imprisoned. For life. Or better than that, hanged."

Giselle's demeanor cooled. "Despite what my papa does, Cap'n, I like dogs. I've been tryin' for years to make him quit fightin''em."

"I believe men live on the moon, too." Jesse snapped his fingers twice again. Squire followed him back inside his cabin.

He sat on his bunk. His palms pressured his eyes. Giselle was up to something. *She's after Squire.*

But if that were true, why didn't she take him that day she nabbed him beneath her skirt? Something odd about her. He couldn't quite put his finger on it, but he did not like her. Not one bit. Jesse plucked his watch from his vest pocket.

Squire brushed against his legs.

Jesse stroked his back. "Almost time for skirmish drill, my boy."

Squire stretched out beside him, his eyes closed. Content, his dog seemed to be. Surely, his boy knew how much everyone in the garrison loved him.

Jesse slapped his knees. "General Gardner sure has a knack for keeping us busy around here. Not much time for us to play, is it?"

Squire rolled over on his side; he snored.

A cool breeze rippling his fur, Squire tagged after his master. Myriad stars glittered across the coal-painted sky. Outside a tent, a girl dropped back behind her female companions to speak to a familiar-looking man outside its door. Seconds later, the girl rejoined her friends. The man re-entered his tent.

"So-o-o," Jesse said to Squire, "looks like Giselle and Marsden are acquainted. Come on, boy."

Jesse's long strides, swiftly swinging arms, and cold eyes told Squire he was angry. When he barged into the man's tent and started shouting, Squire sensed, no, he smelled his master's hatred of the man.

Fists planted on his desk, Marsden glared at them from behind it. "Out."

"I saw you talking to Blevin's daughter," Jesse said. "You two conspiring against me? You hire her to do something to Squire?"

Marsden sniffed. "Get out. Now."

"Not till you tell me what you two are up to...sir!"

"We're up to nothing. Leave."

Shouting. Oh, how Squire hated it! He scooted to Marsden's cot. His nose quivered. He sniffed around it. Linen, tobacco, wool, and myriad other odors swirled. Maybe he'd find something interesting, perhaps a snack.

"You two talked at the sally port the day of Squire's fight," Jesse said. "I got that from some of your men."

"I have no cause to deny it, but say I was plotting against you and your filthy mongrel, I'm not stupid enough to do it in front of people. As for what you just witnessed, I was merely inquiring as to whether the Yankees ransacked their house like they did so many others during their recent withdrawal."

"Well, I'd say she's up to something. What is it?"

"Ask her."

"What do you have against Squire?"

Marsden snickered. "I wouldn't mourn if your mongrel bites the dust. He's ill-mannered and a thief."

"Thieving's his only vice. Besides, he doesn't mean anything by it. To him, it's a game."

"Time you start teaching him manners."

"You keep avoiding me, Marsden. Just you keep on doing it. One day, I'm getting you for killing Elliott."

"Out. I'm busy. You will cease lecturing me else I'll have you clapped in irons."

"For what?"

"Out!"

Squire sniffed a linen shirt sleeve draping the cot's edge. He snatched its cuff between his teeth, dragged its shirt onto the floor, and shook it so fiercely it slapped air. Something fell out of it, landing at his forepaws. His nose nudged the thing—metallic, like something his master used to carry—Rachel's tintype.

Quietness settled inside the tent. No more shouting between his master and the man behind the desk. Caught up in their anger, both men had forgotten him.

Squire seized the cold metal between his teeth, held it high and proudly, like a trophy, then trotted out.

His every muscle practically played out, Marsden trudged toward his tent pitched beside a flickering street lamp on the town's outskirts. Like a landlocked lighthouse, it guided him in. Earlier in the evening, he'd visited his regiment's camps and discussed military matters with his officers and sergeants. Fist to his mouth, he let go a yawn. Tonight, hopefully, would be tranquil.

And tomorrow...tomorrow...tomorrow Giselle better make more progress with Webb than she did today.

A pity Webb didn't imbibe. He could really get him in trouble. Spike Webb's canteen with rum and get him so spiffed he'd become the same buffoon his father was. Ah, but if he made him drunk and his superiors discovered the deed, he'd be the one facing a court-martial instead.

"Mistah colonel." Smythe, swinging a jug, staggered toward him. "Mistah colonel. Mistah colonel."

Marsden halted. "Where'd you acquire that rum?"

"From my jug, shuh." Reeling and red-eyed, Smythe leaned into his face.

Cursing, Marsden shoved him back. "A polecat smells better than you."

Smythe turned the jug upside down. "Hee, hee. Gone. All gone." He leaned sideways, back into Marsden's face. "You make me shick, mistah colonel. Shick. Shick." The jug dropped from his hand, shattered at Marsden's feet. From his belt, he drew a knife. It flashed in the evening light.

Marsden's eyes caught two provost guards bearing down on them.

Smythe slashed at Marsden. In his drunken fury, the blade missed him.

Marsden shoved him aside. "You'll answer for this, you cowardly blockhead."

The guards reached them at a run.

"Sober him up and lock him up." Marsden kicked the jug's shards. "I'll teach him not to assault me."

"My pleasure, Colonel." A guard jerked Smythe to his feet.

Long shadows of pines and magnolia trees deepened into darkness. Though starlight filtered through the foliage, Squire's surroundings dimmed. He followed a wagon path leading up a much-gouged hill. Heaviness burdened his legs, as though loaded with sand. He still hadn't grown used to this rugged terrain, this rising and dropping of numerous ridges, the gorges pocking the ground everywhere. He set down Rachel's tintype and stretched out alongside it. The hard ground cooled his belly. Cicadas raised a ruckus. His tongue drooped. He panted. When he finally fell asleep, he dreamed about chasing squirrels.

Sometime later, Squire awoke. He didn't know how long he'd slept. He only knew that stars dotted the dark expanse and a pleasant breeze ruffled his fur. He seized Rachel's tintype between his teeth, trotted to some bushes near a building and buried it, his trophy

Thirst traveled the length of his tongue. Water. He'd not tasted it in a while. He lifted his muzzle, sniffed the air. Yes. He knew where the water was. He smelled it. He'd drunk from its creek before. His eyes detected the smell's source. He trotted toward the liquid ribbon wending over the earth.

Like a puppy chasing a ball, he scurried to it. Twigs broke and leaves crackled beneath his paws. Tail up, his muzzle touched the murky water. His tongue sloshed it into his mouth.

On the stream's opposite bank, something aroused his curiosity. He raised his head, his ears at attention. His nose twitched. Slowly, the noise approached. It stopped. On the stream's fringe, the bushes rustled. He watched them; he sniffed; he waited. The thing stepped into view.

It was a dog, a female dog. Where did she come from?

Her short tail tucked between her hindquarters, she worked her way down the bank's steep slope as though she'd not seen Squire. Her long ears hugged her head. After slinking a good distance past Squire, she stopped. Like a perfect lady, she lowered her muzzle till it touched the water, but she did not drink sloppily like Squire.

Squire squared his body. He stood more erect, curled back his lips, and held his tail high, waving it. He next paddled across the creek and climbed the bank as agilely as a cat. Back on firmer land, he shook the water off his fur.

She continued lapping, paying him as much heed as an old stump.

He stared down at her from the creekbank.

She lifted her muzzle. Her nose twitched. Then she looked up at him. A wide-eyed friendliness beckoned him forward.

For a fleeting second, they faced each other. Then they both looked away. She wanted peace, and so did he.

Determined to learn who this strange dog was, Squire approached her. She, too, made her approach. Their muzzles touched. They circled each other as they tried to pick up each other's scent.

The strange dog licked Squire's mouth, tucked her tail between her legs, and then dropped to the ground and rolled over on her back, her belly exposed.

The wind blew a stick off a tree. It struck her between the eyes. Startled, she jumped to her feet and took off running. Beyond the creek, up another slope, through trees and brush she kicked up dust between herself and Squire.

Squire's long legs pumped hard in pursuit, till she got so far ahead he stopped to catch his wind. She ran faster than him, the first dog who'd ever outrun him. He dropped back for a spell. Sitting on the northern edge of the woods, he panted. She wouldn't outrun him again. He sniffed earth then lifted his muzzle to search the air for her scent. Wherever it led, he'd follow.

It led to another ridge, which he descended in no great hurry. Before him rose a forested canopy. Mighty trees spread their foliage over the earth. He picked up his pace. He stepped into a clearing. He surveyed a mass of brush and logs. Somewhere down there was his lady, amid the forest. He continued down the well-worn path. Briars clutched at his fur. There she was, way down near the creek's edge, curled beside a dead tree, her muzzle tucked into her belly.

Every vein in Squire's body turned to ice. Two huge eyes skimmed the creek's surface, heading toward his lady. An alligator. Didn't she hear it coming? What was wrong? Squire jumped wildly and raised a string of warning barks.

The gator didn't see him. The lady saw neither Squire nor the gator.

Eight

---◆---

Squire crouched and crept through the tall grass toward the giant reptile. A fierce determination to rescue his lady mounted within him. But how…how could he stop so huge, so massive, so powerful a beast?

The gator lumbered up a wagon path and onto land, his powerful tail trailing behind him. Fatal intent accompanied his every step. As certain as lightning in a thunderstorm, he was sneaking up on Squire's lady.

The lady lifted her nose. Perhaps she smelled the alligator. No, she'd fastened her attention on Squire. Squire rose to all fours and, pumping his legs like pistons driving a locomotive full steam, he sprinted to her and pounced before the gator closed in.

Spotting the gator, the lady hurtled up the ridge, Squire on her tail.

The gator's legs worked hard to gain on them, but only briefly. His short burst of speed exhausted, he turned and headed back for the swamp.

Squire caught up with his lady; their pace slackened to a trot. Side-by-side, they hurried back to Squire's master's camp.

Giselle peered over other ladies' shoulders, covered by either muslin or lace mantelets. Just beyond them, soldiers stood at attention in two ranks, their musket butts grounded at their sides.

The afternoon's heat pounded hard; sweat glistened on the men's dirty cheeks. Though proud in bearing, their uniforms lacked a uniform appearance. Many men did wear gray. Others wore varied combinations of colors or clothes brought over from their civilian lives—flannel shirts, checkered shirts, striped trousers and white linen shirts. Nothing was uniform about the Confederacy's army.

Twirling her parasol, Giselle searched for Jesse among these men. His uniform was iron gray—trousers, vest, frock coat. Faded, but it was, at least, gray.

"You got stars in your eyes?" a girl said.

Giselle shifted her attention to the speaker, Henrietta Phipps. "I ain't interested in generals and colonels."

"Every girl's got a interest in generals and colonels."

"Not me." *Stupid girl.*

Henrietta quieted and admired the soldiers. The same age as Giselle, she lived a few miles from her father's farm. Her hair was dusty brown, her nose and ears large. Her homespun calico dress hung close about her limbs. Poor girls such as her couldn't afford crinoline. A dull yellow, prints of small blue flowers dotted its fabric and red bows smothered its shoulders. It was a dress as plain-looking and tasteless as Henrietta herself.

In addition to cotton growing, Henrietta's father dabbled in horses, raised guard geese, and owned quite a pack of dogs. Not that he was any great dog lover, either. For him, breeding them was a business, a means of earning extra money by selling them to whoever wanted one regardless of how the buyer treated the animal. Some dogs he sold to Giselle's father, who used them as bait dogs.

The only crinoline cage Giselle owned, the one that had hidden Squire from Smythe, came from her father's winnings and what money he'd earned growing cotton.

"Who's the lucky feller you plannin' on catchin'?" Giselle finally spoke again.

Henrietta's lower lip trembled.

"Now don't go off frettin'. I ain't gettin' 'tween you two, whoever he is."

Henrietta turned her back on Giselle.

"You can tell me. I ain't goin' to do nothin'."

Henrietta sighed. "Colonel…Colonel Cox."

"Colonel Stonebridge's regiment? The lieutenant colonel? Who commands one of his battalions? Cap'n Webb's?"

"Y-Yes."

"Why, ain't that just sweet as candy." Giselle looked where her friend looked—Squire and a gaunt-looking black dog trotting together.

Henrietta clapped.

Startled, Squire jumped. The black dog kept her course.

"It can't be," Henrietta said. "The deaf dog that dug herself outta Pa's pen last week. I was sure she was a-goner when she done that."

"Reckon she's a survivor." Giselle latched onto an idea, a way to keep her promise to Marsden. She grasped Henrietta's hand. "Let's go."

"Why?"

Giselle dragged Henrietta toward Webb's cabin. Some minutes later they found the dogs stretched out on the ground, Squire on his side, his legs extended, and the lady curled, her muzzle tucked into her stomach. Their eyes half-opened, they seemed to be enjoying the warm day and each other's company.

Henrietta pointed at Squire. "Seen that dog around here a lot. Never cared to ask who owns him."

"He's what them soldiers call a mascot." Slowly, lest the dog flee, Giselle stepped up to Squire's lady. Her fingers wiggled at her in a non-threatening manner.

Squire cocked his curious face at her; his lady got to her feet, then made her cautious approach.

"Whatcha doing?" Henrietta said.

"What does it look like I'm doin'?"

"You and that dog being friends?"

"We ain't friends."

"I'm surprised she don't remember that time you kept whacking her bottom with my broom. Too stupid to remember, I reckon."

"She should've never tried gettin' hold of my hoop. I ain't got but the one I'm wearin'."

"That's what dogs do, Giselle. Of all people, you ought to know that."

Giselle stretched forth her knuckles for the dog to sniff them. Ever so slowly, her other hand shifted beneath the dog's chin and briefly scratched it. "Ain't no dog got manners. Always gnawin' and chewin' up things and stinkin' up a room. World would be a better place without 'em, far as I'm concerned."

"What about your pa's gambling? Suppose there weren't no more dogs on this here earth. How would he make hisself some money? His farm's not making him much of a living."

"For now, I want to be her friend."

Henrietta eyed her skeptically.

"I mean it, Henrietta. I want that dog."

"Why?"

"Oh, darlin', I reckon I'd better 'fess up. I need her to help me catch Cap'n Webb."

"He ain't wearing stars."

"Well, my dear, if you don't help me, I will catch me a man who does wear them stars."

"You wouldn't dare."

"I wouldn't? Do you for sure believe that?"

"Well, you promise you ain't gonna get 'tween me and the lieutenant colonel?"

Giselle, reaching inside her reticule for her snuff box, put on an icy smile, the kind of smile that when those who knew her saw it, knew she meant business.

Nine

————◆————

Two nights later Jesse posted himself on the fork of two distillery roads. Beneath him yawned a deep ravine, its rustling trees silhouettes against the moonlight. Here, outside Port Hudson's defensive perimeter, the woods thickened. Squire, his lady, and Sergeant Hickam stood beside him. Tonight, they'd help the provost guards find the stills.

This time of year, all the planters' sugar did was stay in hogsheads, useless to anyone. In their minds, their only choice was to make rum, or else go penniless, thanks to the war denying them the opportunity to sell their sugar. Soldiers purchased it at a dollar an ounce. Jesse knew many officers who drank rum punch at night. Intoxicated officers, though, risked getting arrested.

More than an hour had elapsed since he'd dispatched Mitchell and Utley. Though he'd heard no shots fired, he worried. Had they encountered any difficulties at the stills? Ordinarily, he'd have accompanied them, but this time he waited here to catch any rum smugglers who might try to slip past them. Five men patrolled the immediate vicinity.

"You'll find the smugglers if they try anything, won't you, boy?" He patted Squire's head. To Squire's lady, he winked and added: "You'll help too, gal."

Squire's lady jogged to the ravine's edge, where Squire joined her. They stared at the opposite ridge. Lady sat; her left hind foot battled fleas.

Poor gal. What must it be like, being a dog and missing out on all life's wonderful sounds? What heartless wretch abandoned such a fine animal to nature's whims? Blevin? No. Maybe not. Squire's lady was no fighting dog. She was deaf. What use would he have for a deaf dog, except perhaps to train his fighters as a bait dog, and if he wanted to use her for that, he wouldn't have abandoned her this way. His own dogs would have killed her. Blevin's cruelty…the man ought to be put before a firing squad and shot.

Sergeant Hickam's long legs carried him quickly toward the dogs. He pointed at Squire. "Just thinking about dogs courting, Cap'n. Whoever heard of courting dogs?"

"A funny notion, I reckon. I may just write Rachel and tell her Squire's found himself a lady friend. It'll put a giggle in her."

"Wonder how she manages, being deaf and all."

"Well, at least her nose is in good working order. I'm sure that helps her get on along."

Squire snapped to attention and aimed his muzzle down the ravine. His ears perked. Sharp teeth bared, he growled low.

"What is it, Squire? Something out there?"

"I see him, Cap'n." Hickam indicated a brief clearing among the trees. "He's heading up the other side yonder."

"Go fetch him, boy."

Squire shot down the steep slope, his lady behind him, weaving through trees and brush and jumping logs. Jesse and Hickam struggled behind them, navigating the difficult terrain with more care as they worked their way into the ravine. Shrubs lashed at Jesse; limbs broke against his face. He stumbled once, looked up, and saw the man scrambling over some undergrowth.

The man glanced back once, twice at the dogs gaining on him.

"Back! Back dogs! Back!" He swung toward them.

Squire slammed into his chest and knocked him onto his back. His lady seized the man's trouser leg between her teeth.

The man screamed, moaned, and kicked his free foot. His New England accent was unmistakable.

"It's Eakin," Jesse told Hickam.

Squire straddled Eakin. Growling, fiercely shaking his head, his teeth butchered Eakin's shirt and locked onto his shoulder. Her legs splayed, the lady tugged and ripped his trousers. Cursing, Eakin yelled at the dogs to get off him.

"Good boy." Jesse snapped his fingers once.

Squire returned to his side, as did Squire's lady.

"On your feet," Jesse said.

Eakin stood, spit dirt, and massaged his bitten shoulder between winces. "Your dog almost killed me."

"If he was out for blood, you'd have been dead by now."

"My shoulder hurts."

"Let's see, now. Are you trying to desert again?"

"No, Captain."

"Are you lost?"

"Running from a still. Got away while Lieutenant Utley's boys smashed it up."

"So-o-o, you're a smuggler, are you? I'd say you were smuggling rum to our men."

"You arresting me and court-martialing me the way your friend Marsden is doing to Smythe?"

Jesse bristled. "We're not friends."

"Arrest me, sir, that'll make you two of a kind." Eakin tilted his head at the lady. "Who does blackie belong to?"

"Me. Squire found her and brought her to me."

"Sir, are you sure she's a stray?"

"I'm sure."

"She's not. I know who she belongs to."

"Impossible."

Hickam jerked Eakin into his face. "How'd you know this?"

"Some other girl. Henrietta Phipps, I think she called herself. As plain looking as a whitewashed fence." Eakin smirked. "She's been flirting with Colonel Cox. Not very good at it."

"The brown-haired gal hanging around our camp recently," Jesse said.

"She's the one. This afternoon, she asked me about her friend's black dog. Said it'd run away from home. Gave me her name and Miss Blevin's in case I found it."

"Did you happen to see Miss Blevin?"

"No, sir."

When the five men on patrol worked their way down the gorge, Jesse put Eakin in their custody. "Lock him in the guardhouse after Doctor Carter tends his shoulder."

"Do you think the girl's lying about the deaf dog?" Hickam said once they took Eakin away.

"I'll ask Colonel Cox about it tomorrow."

Ten

---◆---

Next morning, a Sunday, Catholic Confederates attended divine services. The Protestants among them had no chaplain; therefore, many rode the train to nearby Clinton to attend church. Jesse, Mitch, and Utley attended an Episcopal church. Lieutenant Colonel Cox visited a Baptist church in the region.

No opportunity presented itself for Jesse to speak to Cox in Clinton or on the train. Back at their camp, he found the colonel sitting outside his tent reading his worn Bible, his brow as creviced as Port Hudson's terrain evidencing his total concentration. He penciled notes on the page's margin.

Wiping his sweaty palms on his trousers, Jesse cleared his throat. "Uh, sir, I'm mighty sorry to disturb your devotions."

Face grave, Cox looked up at him.

"May I, uh, would you mind if we chatted a short minute?"

"Continue."

"Are you, uh, are you seeing someone named Henrietta Phipps?"

Cox closed his Bible. "Seeing her?"

"Yes, sir."

"If you mean am I visiting her, the answer is no." Cox set his Bible aside. "She does visit me. We are not courting, you understand. She is not a woman of faith and her education is in…shall we say…to put it politely…her education has not progressed much."

"Yes, sir. Has she mentioned anything to you about a dog?"

"Her father raises them and sells them. Capital job you and your men did catching those smugglers, by the way."

Jesse's erect posture relaxed. He risked a grateful smile at Cox's compliment. "Thank you, sir." When Cox returned his smile, it put Jesse even more at ease. "Sir, what about a black dog? A female dog, sir? One that's deaf?"

"I do believe I recollect her giving such a dog a mention, something about it belonging to one of her friends, that it was lost or something of that order."

Jesse pointed at his Bible. "What book of the Bible are you reading?"

"My favorite. Galatians. The parson preached a sermon on it this morning. It's all about the grace of God."

"I'll have to read it sometime."

Cox's deep blue eyes turned briefly sad. "'Tis a pity we Protestants have no chaplain. The gospel of Jesus Christ is the most important message in the world."

Jesse saluted and turned to leave.

"Captain."

He looked back at Cox, whose grave expression pierced him so deeply he squirmed.

"Have you read the leaflet I gave you a few weeks ago?"

Jesse's brain scrambled to remember. *Leaflet. Leaflet.* If he didn't remember it, he'd have to lie and possibly disappoint the colonel, but if he lied, he might then be questioned about its contents, questions he could not answer, which would then lay bare his untruth.

"*Religion is Not Enough.*"

"Sir?"

"The title of the leaflet. It appears you did not read it, then."

"Sir…" Jesse shifted uneasily. "I intend to."

"Yes, Captain Webb. I'm quite sure you intend to."

"I'm not opposed to religion. I attended church today same as you."

When Cox opened his mouth to speak again, Jesse excused himself. As much as he admired the colonel, he wasn't in the mood to discuss religion. He called Squire away from his playtime with Private Perkins.

Squire bounded away from the soldier, getting to his feet after their friendly wrestling match. He threw his forepaws on Jesse's chest.

Jesse grabbed them. Gently, he set them back down. "Squire, let's you and me go for a walk to the depot. Since this is Sunday, we have time for some fun."

Tail high and wagging, Squire barked.

"See you later, Perkins." Jesse waved at him.

"All righty, Captain." Perkins waved back. "So long, Mister Squire!"

Squire barked again.

"Well, I found the confirmation I needed, boy. The dunderhead Eakin did tell me the truth about Henrietta."

Squire barked twice more.

Eleven

———— ◆ ————

Giselle reined in the mules drawing her wagon, halting it on a practically deserted street at a vacant hardware store. A four-seat vehicle, leather-covered hickory slats made its top. A smattering of civilians milled about the area. Distant shouts echoed—officers drilling their men.

"Now where do you reckon that dog is?" Henrietta climbed down from the vehicle's creaking bench. She stuck her hand inside her pink skirt's pocket and pulled out a thin rope, a large loop tied by a slipknot at the end.

"Go on, now." Giselle fluttered her fingers at her. "Hurry up and get movin'. Get on over to your colonel's camp. If them dogs ain't huntin' trouble, they're likely there."

"Can't you come with me, Giselle? Please?"

"Listen, darlin'. I'm s'posed to be frettin' 'bout Webb's opinion of me, ain't I? Besides, he might not let me have the dog if it's me who gets her. It's all part of our plan, remember?"

"Suppose the dogs ain't where you say?"

"I reckon you'll just have to come on back and tell me, then. I'll think of somethin'. And remember what I told you to tell Cap'n Webb if you see him. Now don't keep standin' there like a bump on a log. Get movin'."

Henrietta hurried down a dusty street and disappeared around a corner several blocks away.

Giselle reached inside her reticule for her snuff box. Cox, Webb, they weren't no different than Cody Ragland, who did her a sinful deed. Three years ago, eager and excited, she'd waited at the justice of the peace's office to say her "I do's" to that louse. Seconds dragged into minutes. He left her waiting at that office for an hour. Embarrassed, humiliated, and all in front of her small group of friends, Cousin Zack, and her father. Not to mention Cody's sinful betrayal. He never arrived, and she never set her peepers on him again. She was sixteen at the time. Last she heard, he got himself killed somewhere in Virginia. Malvern Hill, she thought the place was called.

Except for her papa and cousin Zachary, who supported her in everything she did, she'd vowed a one-woman war against men. Like an older brother to her, Zack was. She recalled a day a year ago, in early May, when a messenger brought her word of his wound at Shiloh. No hint of its seriousness in the message. He was hospitalized at a hotel in Corinth, Mississippi. This was all that messenger told her.

Out of the war for good, Zachary returned to Clinton and their farm after his wound mended. The doctor fitted him with a wooden leg below his knee, but he still needed a crutch. She didn't think the war's wound would ever be fully healed, at least not in his mind, despite his surprising progress.

Every time she'd come into town he'd wanted to accompany her, but she always refused his offer. "I ain't some rich lily needin' an escort," she told him, on more than one occasion. This day, before she left home, she hinted he might be useful coming into town later.

Her father agreed.

What to do now, she wondered. *No sign of that disgustin' Marsden. Probably off marchin' his soldiers somewhere.* At least this beat staying home doing womanly chores. She might as well sit here and wait for Henrietta to bring back that dog, her father's new bait dog. In the meantime, she dipped snuff.

Jesse sauntered to Squire and his lady playing outside his cabin. Squire charged her and jumped back, charged her and jumped back, nipping at her exposed belly and feet. She rolled over, leaped onto her legs, and went after Squire like she meant business. Their playful barks echoed across the camp. Ever since Squire befriended his lady, they spent almost as much time at camp as they did roaming.

"All right, boys and gals. Dee-licious blue beef time again. Cornbread hour's here. Yum. Yum." Jesse chuckled. "Come and get it!"

Mitchell and Utley pulled stools out of their cabin and set them around their table. Three other cabin messmates joined them.

"Not as tasty-deelicious as Rachel's cooking," Mitchell said.

"There is not a single person walking this whole entire earth who can cook better than my darling," Jesse said. "And I sure do wish she was here. She'd do us right, I'd say, and she'd enjoy doing it."

"Don't mean this personally," Mitchell said, "but not even a cook possessing Rachel's culinary talents can do much with our victuals here, what with our corn spoiled and all our cattle the unhealthiest lot of beef I've ever set my poor eyes upon. Those boys back east get the better end of things, I'll bet."

Utley sipped his beer and screwed up his face. "Blah! Vinegar."

"Vinegar is the beverage you prefer most, is it not, Utley?" Smiling, Jesse winked at his messmates.

Utley slammed his mug down next to his plate. "I am tired of drinking this home brew. It tastes like it."

Jesse and everyone around their table laughed.

"It's about the only thing potable enough for us to drink around here," Mitchell said. "Give our Tennessee brethren who brew it credit for trying, though."

"Molasses, corn, and water's the recipe," one of their other messmates said. "I watched them making it a while back."

"Well, I'd just as soon not drink it." Jesse reached for his mug of so-called coffee, a home brew made from parched rye and wheat, something both he and fellow teetotaler Colonel Cox drank at meals. "Come on, Squire. Come on, Lady. Let's eat."

"Her name's Daisy."

Jesse started at the voice. A young girl wearing calico approached from behind their cabin. "Daisy?" He got up from his stool.

Mitchell jumped to his feet. "Now you wait a dad-burn minute. That dog's ours."

"Our boy found her." Utley tossed his beer's remnants on the ground. "And what's his is ours."

"Supposing she belongs to someone else?" Henrietta stuck her hands inside her skirt pockets.

Jesse slapped his arms across his chest. "Like who?"

"My friend."

"And what might her name be?"

"Giselle Blevin, and I am Henrietta Phipps. Daisy wandered off from Giselle's home the other day. Pa gave her Daisy on condition her pa didn't make her fight."

This was the gal Eakin mentioned a few nights ago? The one who'd been visiting Colonel Cox? "I heard she belonged to Miss Blevin. So how come I never heard her mention this dog?"

"Well...well...well she kept figuring Daisy would come back." Henrietta tilted her head at Squire. "Don't your dog wander off at times?"

Henrietta's point was valid. Jesse couldn't deny it. "How come you're here to claim her instead of Miss Blevin?"

"Because she's scared if she did—"

"Giselle ought to be here claiming her, not you."

"Not if some feller might think she's fibbing and would try stopping her from fetching Daisy home. It hurts my friend plumb awful when folks think she's a fibber on account of her pa. She loves dogs."

"Uh-huh. Well, I am Captain Webb, the man who didn't believe her."

"I figured you was." Thin rope in hand, Henrietta passed its loop over Daisy's head and neck, keeping the loop loose. "Goodbye, Captain. Thank you for taking such good care of my friend's dog." She led Daisy away.

Squire barked after her and started following.

Through cupped hands, Jesse shouted for Squire to come back. Squire kept following a minute or two longer before he returned, probably torn between Lady and his master. At least, that's what Jesse figured. Who knew what all went on inside a dog's head.

Perhaps he ought to test Giselle's sincerity. He'd give her the benefit of a doubt, or at least let her tell her side of the story. Just because her father hated dogs didn't mean she did. Did it? After all, his father had been a drinker whereas he'd never touched a drop. Maybe he'd been unfair.

Twelve

—◆—

Marsden pulled an envelope from his desk drawer, the only stationery during these difficult days. He grasped his pencil beside his empty inkwell and began his Sunday missive.

April 11, 1863

My dearest Stella,

Finally, I have exterminated one pesky mouse, that dunderhead Smythe, the poltroon about whom I wrote you earlier. A provost dispatched him with one shot when he broke out of the guardhouse and reached for the provost's revolver.

Unfortunately, that ninny Eakin still hangs around. Webb threw him in the guardhouse for a few days. I think he enjoys watching Eakin annoy me. But me? Well, I shall relish my revenge once it is complete. And it will be completed, dearest Stella, before one of us gets transferred. It will be Webb's high-blown honor that will be his demise; he will become a disgrace like his father. I needn't kill him. The humiliation I plan for him shall accomplish that.

My greatest desire at this present time, next to destroying Webb, is for the enemy to attack us. War suits me well, I think. I shall become a general before it all ends. Then we'll see what Father thinks of me. At this point in my life, I really do not care.

He considers himself mankind's greatest gift. A joke, a very grand and very sad joke, he has become to me now. If Father were to die tomorrow, or today, I would celebrate a toast to the event on his grave, and drink champagne, our personal favorite.

It is rumored that the enemy has been operating around Milliken's Bend and New Carthage, south of Vicksburg but on the Mississippi's western bank, I believe. Grant still thinks he can capture that town. Let us say I was in command there instead of General Pemberton, I'd rout him so fast his head would spin off his neck. One day, President Davis will discover my genius. I only hope it is not too late.

Since enemy vessels are now north of us, we're cut off from our supply line on the Red River. Now, our wagons transport supplies from Osyka, Mississippi, while some fool officers leave other supplies on the landing to be washed away by the river.

You say that....

A presence entered Marsden's tent.

Marsden set aside his letter.

The visitor, leaning on a crutch, hobbled toward him. His shoulder-length brown hair was shaggy. His jutting chin, stubbly. His shirt was made of red flannel, and his trousers of brown jean cloth. A faded gray slouch hat shaded his weather-beaten brow. Out of his battered boot, a sheathed knife protruded. Marsden might have pitied the man's misfortune at having lost a limb, but the wickedness kindling the visitor's squinting eyes vanquished all his sympathies.

"Zack Blevin," the man said.

"Miss Blevin's brother?" Marsden said.

"Cousin, Colonel." Zack eyeballed a heavy oak chair, the one Marsden purchased from a Port Hudson store months earlier. "Mind if I sit a spell?"

"Permission granted."

Zack maneuvered himself over to the chair and dropped into it clumsily. Puffing, he laid his crutch across its arms like a bridge and patted his wooden prosthesis. "I lost my leg at Shiloh."

"A bloody affair I heard."

"You heard right."

"Well?" Marsden aimed his pencil at him. "State your purpose for being here."

"Giselle sent me to deliver a message."

"I figured she was up to something when she took the deaf mongrel."

"Word travels like the wind around here, don't it?"

"We are a small garrison. A few thousand men."

Zack's tongue swiped his lips. "Tomorrow, she'll be back here to change your luck. She'll need your sergeant major's help. And you can look for her to bring that ole deaf dawg along."

"What about her friend? The one who stole the deaf cur?"

"She ain't coming."

"Will she be able to convince Webb the dog belongs to her?"

"Colonel, if she's a mind to, she can convince a snake he's a worm."

Thirteen

——◆——

Jesse and Mitchell strolled back to their camp. Squire lagged behind them, his tail low.

"Squire hasn't seemed himself these past few days," Jesse said. "Used to be, he'd charge way ahead of us when we attacked the stills, like it was a game."

"Now our boy's holding back," Mitchell said. "Know what he did last night when we started pouring rum out of those hogsheads? Why, he up and stretched himself out on the ground and closed his eyes. Looked to me like he was as much interested in what we were doing as he was in a rock. Something's bothering him worse'n skeeters."

"I'd say he's been spending more time hanging around our camp most days, like he was waiting for his gal to come on back or something."

Mitchell shook his head. "We'll never see our poor Lady again."

"I can't accept that."

The friends halted.

Mitchell pointed at Winder. "What's he up to?"

Sitting on a stool, his large hands clasped between his knees, Winder watched a cribbage game between Colonel Cox and Major Boudreaux, a Louisiana officer.

Then Giselle approached, accompanied by Daisy who held her stubby tail high while Giselle strained at her taut leash. The dog moved eagerly left and right. Giselle made a face as though having trouble controlling Daisy's excitement.

Scattered soldiers stood and tipped their caps, greeting her arrival. From a nearby river battery, several whistled and made wolf calls. She grunted and jerked the leash, heeling Daisy.

Squire bounded toward his lady, cavorted all around her, his ecstatic barks flying out his mouth. Playfully, he pounced on his friend. Daisy's tail wagged; she joined his barking. Squire's tail brushed the air, its strokes broad and happy.

Giselle's red curls bounced when she burst into laughter.

Jesse and Mitchell strode to the dogs.

"Get that cur out of here," Winder snapped.

Giselle's eyes flashed. "You ain't got no right talkin' to Daisy that a-way!"

"I'll say anything I please, woman." He grasped his holstered pistol. "That dog comes any closer, I'll shoot her."

"Silence." Cox glared at them.

Winder stalked off.

"Dear me." Giselle nervously twisted the indigo bow securing her bonnet on her head. "Do you think the sergeant man means it?"

"I can't say for a fact, but I will say if Winder does try to harm either of our dogs, he'll regret it for the rest of his livelong days." Jesse grasped Giselle's elbow and steered her back in the town's direction. "Let's have a little talk, miss."

"Of course."

Tongue drooping and bent ears flapping, Squire and Daisy trotted ahead, Daisy still on her long leash.

"What does Winder have against your dog?" Jesse said.

"Some silly notion about gnawing up them socks that Yankee feller gave him. She ain't done it, course. That sergeant feller just thinks she done it."

"Seems both our dogs get accused of things."

Giselle stopped walking. Her gaze fell upon him, her beautiful eyes, so sad yet so pretty...Jesse gulped. A pity she didn't share Rachel's education.

Jesse shifted his feet. "I reckon I ought to plead guilty, too."

"Of what?"

"Of accusing you of things."

Giselle lowered her dark lashes. "Don't fret none about it, darlin' Cap'n. I'm used to gettin' accused of things I ain't done."

Their walk resumed...silence. Jesse grappled with his thoughts. This gal seemed so sincere.

Once they entered the town, Giselle spoke. "I reckoned Squire missed my Daisy. That's why I brung her here. You see, I ain't really sech a bad person. I wouldn't dream of hurtin' your dog."

Yes, she was sincere. Jesse's doubts vanished.

Side-by-side in the dirt, Squire and Daisy stretched out, their eyes closed and their muzzles rested on their forepaws.

"Papa ain't always fought dogs. He owns a farm, too."

"How many acres?"

"About half the parish."

Jesse's jaw went slack.

Giselle's curls bounced again when she burst into flirtatious laughter. "Aw! I'm just joshin'. He ain't got that much of a farm."

Jesse chuckled. This gal owned a sense of humor, something he appreciated in the fairer sex. Back when they were children, he and Rachel loved laughing and teasing and often got in trouble when their humor and pranks went a bit too far. Giselle's giggles reminded him of Rachel.

"Only three slaves workin' it now. We used to have five, but two of 'em went with them Yanks when they come here last month. We got us two servants, too, but that ain't much. Cousin Zack does most of the farm managin'. He saw to it we didn't lose no more slaves to them Bluebellies."

Jesse squatted and stroked Squire's back.

Squire turned his head and bathed Jesse's face with fast, rough licks.

"Why did your father start fighting dogs?" Jesse moved his hands to Squire's chest. His fingers vanished through Squire's thick fur.

Giselle patted Daisy's head. "My mama's papa fought cocks. So when her and Papa got hitched, he bought hisself a few birds and tried doin' it. His birds ain't never won him much money, so he worked harder at cotton growin'. But he ain't never much cared for farmin', 'cause he's got a gambler's blood, so he hired Cousin Zack to do the farm managin'. He trusted Zack more'n a stranger doin' it, and all Papa really wanted to do was gamble. A friend suggested he try gamblin' on fightin' dogs. He learned he had a good eye for pickin' out four-legged champions, so after the first dog he bought won him lots of money, he started buyin' more of 'em and fightin' 'em. This was when he started makin' what he called 'real money.'"

"Real money on a dog's death." Jesse's insides roiled. The man was a barbarian.

"I cried and begged and did everything I could to stop Papa from fightin' 'em, but it was like talkin' to an ole post. It's awful, seein' 'em gettin' hurt and dyin'.'' She choked as though stifling a sob. "I...I can't stand it

"I understand."

Giselle squeezed her eyes shut.

"Why did your father let you have Daisy?" Jesse helped her stand.

"He ain't got no choice. My friend Henrietta's papa gave her to me, on condition my papa didn't use her to train his fighters, since she was deaf and all, and her papa sorta likes me, and Papa ain't fond of gettin' on his bad side since he lets Papa buy his other dogs at half-price. Them is his bait dogs, the ones he uses to train his fighters." Giselle's vacant gaze fixed on a small, shuttered house. "He makes me go to them fights. Except for that, he don't much care what I do."

Jesse grunted. Not only was the man a barbarian, he was a lousy father. If he and Rachel ever had a daughter, he'd never let her do anything and everything she wanted. His household would have rules as firm and fixed as the Laws of the Medes and Persians.

Henrietta met them from around a corner. She slapped her hands on her hips. "Now where in tarnation you been, Giselle? We got to get ourselves back home."

Giselle touched Jesse's coat sleeve. "Do forgive me, Cap'n Webb. I came with my friend. It ain't like me to go gallavantin' off alone like this and all."

"It sure ain't," Henrietta said.

Giselle let go Jesse's coat. "But I just had to tell you my story. Private-like. You do understand, don't you?"

"Yes," Jesse said. "I'll accompany you to your wagon."

"Thank you, sir."

Daisy got up, Squire got up. The dogs followed them to the girls' wagon.

While the afternoon slowly died, and long shadows played across her lawn, Giselle joined her father at their paddock. Inside it, one of their slaves walked a copper-colored bulldog, a harness strapped around his muscular shoulders. The animal dragged a canvas sack bulging with rocks and sand. His battered head and nub of a left ear bore battle scars. His eyes glinted fiendishly and, panting hard, his saliva-soaked tongue dangled between flashing teeth. Brutus, her father named him. He liked Roman names. He once told her his dogs were his gladiators and he was their emperor and thus, he gave them such names.

Sweaty beads coursed down the skinny slave's hollow cheeks. "Can't we stop walking, Marse Aaron?"

"You'll stop when I tell you to, Henry," Blevin said.

"But we been walking well nigh all afternoon, suh, and Brutus is getting worn out and I'm plumb tuckered—"

"Stop complaining, else you're gonna get lashes from the rawhide."

"But—"

"You heard me. Soften him up, or any of my dogs, by not making them exercise, I'm locking you in Nero's cage. Bread and water you're gonna get, as well as the rawhide."

"You treat me like you treat them dogs, I'm getting mean as them, too."

"That done it!" Giselle screamed. "Papa, I'll go fetch the rawhide." She headed for their small white house.

"Where's Daisy?" her father asked.

"Locked in my room. Whimperin'."

"See that post?"

Giselle stopped mid-stride and looked where her father pointed. Off to their right and inside a wide pen stood a T-shaped oak post. Five tall, narrow iron cages stood in another pen beside it, all of the cages padlocked except Nero's and Brutus's cages. The other three dogs, chained inside their cages, glowered at them.

"Tomorrow, I'm chaining the deaf dog to it and give my gladiators some practice. Which one do you think needs it most? Brutus, Cato, or Caesar?"

"Not yet, Papa. Webb's breakin', but I don't think he's broke all the way yet."

"He believed your story?"

"He seemed like he did. That Sergeant Winder feller ought to be a actor, he was so good at bein' convincin'. Henrietta done a good job of actin', too."

Blevin guffawed. "Why, ain't you the devil, daughter. You mix truth with lies and mess up a man's mind. A devil in a dress you are."

"Shush, Papa. I just told two little lies, about beggin' you not to fight your dogs and Henrietta's papa givin' me deaf Daisy. Ain't you proud of me?"

Blevin beamed. "I'm the proudest papa alive. You're one girl who knows how to take care of herself. So was your ma."

"Want me to go fetch the rawhide whip now?"

Blevin turned his attention back to Henry, who'd resumed walking Brutus. "Naw. Long as Henry exercises my dogs and does like he's told…"

Muttering, Henry shot them a hateful glance.

"Henry's gettin' too big for his britches, Papa."

"Look out, Henry," Blevin said. "Watch your attitude, else my dogs'll have some fun with you."

Giselle flounced off. Time to start thinking on what would she wear next time she visited Webb's camp.

Not a day passed throughout the following week that Giselle didn't visit Jesse's camp. On these visits, she always accompanied Henrietta so she'd look like one of those self-righteous women who poked their noses up in the air. Modestly clothed to the final button at her throat, her calico and osnaburg dresses helped bait her fish. If Webb was the sort who liked his women loose, she'd have obliged him, but that evening on the Sugarhouse Road Marsden told her otherwise, so she clothed herself as modestly as she could manage.

She only regretted her father couldn't afford the more expensive dresses, made of silk or muslin, like those snobby nabob women wore. A cameo pendant hung beneath her throat, the profile of a lady. Mrs. Webb often wore a cameo pendant bearing the profile of a cat, Marsden told her. Giselle didn't own one of those, but she wasn't fretting about it. If she wore a cameo exactly like Mrs. Webb's, her attempt to remind Webb of his wife would be too obvious.

Of one thing she was fully aware, though, the one major thing working against her and Marsden's plan—her talking. Mrs. Webb owned some book-learning, whereas she didn't, and thus Mrs. Webb spoke more proper English. Though Giselle never cared about talking right, this was one time she regretted her lack of verbal skills. Perhaps her pretended love of dogs would help make up for it, if she could keep convincing Webb about it.

At first, she worried. Would Webb catch on to her trickery? No hint of suspicion crossed his lips, though. He was dumber than she first figured. Her charms and her flatteries thwarted any doubts that might have crept into his mind. Her biggest talent was using her pretty peepers to attract men. Slowly, as each day passed, she giggled and fluttered her eyelashes and manipulated her way into his heart, and all this despite her limited education. When it came to using a man, flattery was a powerful tool, even a big college-educated man like Webb. *Men. Humph! Peas in a pod.* To get her way, all a girl need do was feed their pride and flatter them to the skies.

Her pretended humor, though, finally snared him for good. On the Sugarhouse Road, Marsden told her Webb liked being teased, and this she played up for all it was worth. The way she teased him reminded him of his wife, he told her one Sunday afternoon after Henrietta left them to visit Colonel Cox.

"Me? Remind you of your missus?"

"It's the honest to goodness truth," Jesse said. "I'd say for a fact."

"You miss her, don't you?"

Jesse swallowed hard. Yes, he missed her.

"Do you write her a lot?"

"Every chance I get."

"I ain't doubtin' it. I see love in them purty peepers of yours, Mister Jesse Webb." Her fingertips touched his cheeks.

Jesse grabbed her hand and lowered it. "You're teasing me again."

"Ain't doin' it this time. You do got a pair of purty eyes."

"So do you."

His face beamed, and she knew she'd suckered him in. He wasn't going to be her lover, on account of his fine and fancy book-learning and her lack thereof, but at least she'd made him a friend. For the time being, a friend was good enough. Her gaze wandered toward Daisy, nipping at Squire's feet. Squire barked and leaped back, out of Daisy's reach. *Deaf Daisy, you done your part. Now you ain't got no right to live.*

Fourteen

hen the train eastbound from Vicksburg, Mississippi
screeched to a halt at Newton Station's depot, Rachel
Webb's and Matilda Rutherford's gasps echoed its other
passengers'. They and three other nurses were on their way back to
Jackson with their matron, Mrs. Harris. Their coach, the train's last
car, was the only passenger coach this freight train pulled.

Swarming the brick depot, some hundred whooping Bluecoats
smashed its windows with the butts of their carbines. One skinny
man jiggled its doorknob. Failing to open it, he shouted something
unintelligible. Another man flung it open from inside. Guffawing
soldiers charged into the building like stampeding bulls.

"Yankees." Rachel huffed contemptuously. "Probably looking for
something they can steal."

"Y-Yankees," Matilda, sitting beside her, said.

"They better not touch my nurses." Mrs. Harris's narrowed eyes
followed the Yankees' boisterous activity.

A pang stabbed Rachel's chest. She'd hoped to find someone in
Jackson, an honorable and upstanding gentleman, who could take her
to Port Hudson. The only way she could get there was to persuade
such a person to take her since her husband's garrison didn't have
a connection to one of the main rail lines. From what she'd heard,

its single rail connection stopped at a town not many miles from it. Clinton, she thought the town was called. She so missed her darling Jesse and Squire.

"Rachel. Your earrings." Matilda pointed at them.

Rachel touched the opals dangling off her ears. "My what?"

Matilda leaned past her, opened their window, and tossed hers out.

"Why did you do that?"

"Do you want the dirty Yankees to get 'em off us?"

All around them, passengers tossed valuables out their windows—wallets, reticules, bracelets. "I'm keeping my earrings, Mattie, and my bracelet and my cameo and—"

Rowdiness outside stifled Rachel's words. She peeked out her window again. Now the soldiers were smashing the freight cars' doors.

"Psst! George. Take a look at their guns." The gentleman behind Rachel uttered these words.

"Carbines, eh?" George said. "Likely they're cavalry. This must be a raid."

"Pretty smart observation for you two Rebels." A swaggering lieutenant strode from the coach's rear.

Rachel gave a start. She didn't hear him enter. She shuddered when he passed her. He took up a position at the front of the coach, his arms folded over his broad chest. His blue slouch hat held a black ostrich feather. His blue-steel gaze wandered to her.

Rachel flinched. Did she detect lust in his eyes? She clenched her hands in her lap. Another cold ripple crawled down her spine. *Yes. It's lust.*

"We are your conquerors." He spread his arms grandly. "No one will rescue you Rebs. We've also seized your telegraph station. Before we're done, every rail and crosstie will be torn up. Your supply line will be destroyed."

"You're some high and mighty," George's friend shouted at him. "If our army was here you wouldn't be talking so big."

Another man, sitting across the aisle from Rachel, spat at him.

"Where's your commanding officer?" Mrs. Harris snapped. "I'll give him a piece of my mind."

"Our commanding officer? He's Colonel Benjamin Grierson." The lieutenant locked his lascivious countenance back on Rachel; his lips twisted cruelly. "He'll be along shortly. He was a music teacher before the war. Just think. You all got captured by a mere music teacher. He's putting a good hurt on you traitors, isn't he?" His index finger beckoned Rachel forward.

Fingers digging into her sweaty palms, Rachel shook her head no.

"What's wrong, fine-looking Rebel lady? Scared the big bad Yankee's going to get you?"

"I'm married," Rachel said.

"So am I."

"My husband's in Port Hudson."

He winked at her. "Guess he's not in these parts, is he? He'll never know unless you tell him. Come on now. All I want is a little kiss." His forefinger touched his dusty cheek. "A small little peck. See? Right here."

"Stop it." Mrs. Harris rose from her seat and advanced on him.

Fists doubled, George, whose iron gray hair told Rachel he was probably too old for the army, flanked her on the left.

"You two going to stop me?" The officer chuckled.

George assumed a boxer's stance, his fists raised, ready to punch the officer's face.

The officer planted his hands on his hips. "Go ahead, old man. Hit me."

"Mister Collins used to be a boxer," someone shouted.

"I was the best amateur fighter in this county." George gestured at Rachel and her friends. "You'd best quit insulting our great Southern ladies."

Rachel welcomed the idea that popped into her head. She left her seat. "You said Colonel Grierson taught music before the war?"

"Your ears work properly, fine-looking Rebel lady." The Yankee's attention shifted back to her.

"Tell me, my gallant lieutenant, does he sing alto or soprano?"

Hee-haws from the coach's passengers.

Rachel burst into laughter. "Why, my dog Squire's howl is probably prettier than his voice."

Several people doubled over, tears streaking their cheeks they laughed so hard.

Stiffening, the lieutenant thrust up his square chin. "He happens to play the piano."

"How? Like a monkey?" Rachel's hands banged an imaginary piano, slapping air right and left, doing her best monkey imitation.

The mob's laughter roared.

"Lieutenant Tate!" A major ducked his head inside the coach. "Get your body out here. On the double-quick. Colonel Blackburn's restored order, and we've started inspecting the freight cars. Colonel Grierson'll be here soon."

Rachel breathed a sigh of relief. Now, another task presented itself—finding a decent gentleman citizen who could escort her and Matilda to Port Hudson.

May 1863
Port Hudson, Louisiana

Fifteen

———◆———

Marsden studied Colonel William Miles's sappers and miners moving around several wagons, hefting out the scows they'd brought with their expedition. A wise precaution, he grudgingly admitted, since they'd encountered the swollen Amite River.

Two scows already bobbed on the river's surface. Parallel to the riverbank, they floated alongside each other. Five twenty-foot timbers equipped with iron claws secured the first scow to a wooden abutment. Planks, flushed together like a boardwalk, lay across these timbers, forming the first section of this temporary bridge. Five more long timbers stretched from the second scow to the first one's gunwale. Sappers and miners, holding ropes, knelt in the scows and bent over their sides and looped ropes over the timbers, then lashed the timbers to the scow's cleats.

Another scow dropped alongside the second one. A soldier tossed its anchor into the water.

"Do you think we'll catch the Yanks?" Lieutenant Ransom stepped up alongside him.

"Not if Miles stays in command." Yawning, Marsden drew a cigar from his shirt pocket. "And not if we can't get across this river faster."

The cigar fell from his hand. Exhaustion spread through his arms and legs. Two days of hard marching to overtake a Yankee cavalry outfit raiding southward through Mississippi taxed his strength.

And here it was, the first day of May. Not one Bluecoat seen yet. Throughout Mississippi and Louisiana Pemberton's soldiers, and Gardner's too, sought the elusive Union column. Marsden's muscles craved sleep. His heart screamed for a fight.

"Do you figure General Gardner is right about the Yankees heading for Baton Rouge?" Ransom asked. "There've been so many rumors rampaging through the area."

"We can't be certain about anything now, can we? All I know is, he's been wreaking havoc on our railroad and telegraph wires."

"Do we know who's leading the raid?"

"I don't."

Two to a plank, men heaved lumber from off the ground, which they then hauled to the riverbank.

Heavy breathing behind him turned Marsden around, where he encountered Winder's remorseless face. The sergeant major drew him aside. "Sir, last night, Eakin said he's going to have your head. I reckon that means he plans on killing you, sir."

"Who told you that?"

"Corporal Johnson. He came to me this morning. Said Eakin blamed you for Smythe getting killed."

"Smythe can blame himself for that."

"Want me to arrest him?"

"I'm well able to handle it."

The sergeant major saluted. He strode off toward the river.

Gray-haired Colonel Miles approached Marsden. "It won't be much longer."

"It's been too long. Your Legion should've gotten us across the river an hour ago." Fuming, Marsden showed Miles his back. General Gardner was stupid, putting that second-rate tactician in command of this expedition. He was too old for the army.

"You're the best man for everything, so you believe," Miles said sourly.

"I am."

"You're about as useful an officer as a pair of britches on a snake."

"Sir. You sound like my father, sir. I am insulted."

"I am not your father. I am, at this present time, your commanding officer. Don't you ever forget it." Miles strode off.

Marsden scooped his cigar from off the ground. He'd show General Gardner, he'd show Colonel Miles, he'd show his father, everyone, what an illustrious commander he was. Before this war ended, his name would be heralded throughout the South. It would stand alongside Robert E. Lee's and Bedford Forrest's. Never again would his father belittle him or criticize him, not for anything, not after he became famous.

"If you care asking me, I'd say hunting deer and turkey suits me a whole lot finer than killing snakes." Jesse navigated a path through the timbers. Squire, wading through the gorge's dense foliage, scouted ahead.

"Come on now. Rattlesnakes do taste good." Mitchell panted and puffed behind him. "A Mississippi gentleman I met a few years ago introduced them to me."

"Was it a friendly introduction? Did the snake say howdy-do?"

Mitchell chuckled. "We all called him the Snake Man. He knew more about rattlesnakes than anything I could learn about them in a lifetime."

"Bully for him."

"Honest, Jesse. This hound dog of his used to find 'em, and one time this rattler bit his dog. But did that snake kill him? No, siree. His dog clenched that thing between his teeth and killed it mighty doggone fast. That's what the Snake Man told me happened. His dog did get powerful sick and all that, but his hound, well, he didn't die. No, siree."

"That story's about as believable as me catching a great big ole whale on a trout line. I am sure one happy man we didn't see any today. Not even a cottonmouth, which we were more likely to encounter in that swamp beyond the river's bend." He halted briefly to catch his breath. What a stupid notion, climbing all over these ravines. He resumed his hard march. "I am sure as sand happy about that, too. Know something, Mitch? I'd say those Yanks would be fools to attack us at this point. They'd never get through all these ravines."

"Sometimes men do desperate things in war."

Jesse grasped some large bushes. Their thick limbs scratched his palms. Using them as leverage, he pulled himself higher up the gorge's steep side.

Squire slid backward and stumbled over Jesse's foot, but scrambled to his paws and finished the long climb up the steep, broken ravine to the lip of the ridge where Jesse, on surer footing, heaved himself up onto a more level surface. While Mitchell rambled on about snakes, the Mississippi Snake Man and the Snake Man's dog, Giselle floated into Jesse's thoughts.

He'd not seen her in days. Why hadn't she returned to the camp? She wasn't his type— too underbred—even if she was truthful about loving dogs and loathing dogfights. Unlike Giselle, Rachel was educated. Not one of those female seminaries of higher education, but she at least graduated from a local academy.

However, Jesse found himself liking Giselle since they'd become more acquainted. Not loving. Such a thing could never happen. He was, though, starting to fancy her as a friend.

Squire trotted a path toward a hill. Behind this hill, several wooden buildings housed the garrison's commissary stores, gristmill, and arsenal.

Winded, and his legs aching from his climbs, Jesse leaned against the gristmill's side. With an exhausted gasp, Mitchell halted beside him.

Meandering around trees and brush, Squire's muzzle probed the earth. He sniffed. His big paws struck the dirt. He sniffed again near a bush.

"I'll bet she's in camp waiting for you." Mitchell cocked his head back against the mill, his eyes shut against the sun. "She hasn't been around for the past several days."

"Giselle?"

"I'm certainly not talking about your Rachel."

"We're just friends."

"Suppose Rachel shows up here to do her nursing, huh? Suppose she sees you two going off by your lonesomes and talking like y'all do, huh? Suppose she gets the wrong notion about you two, huh?"

"Stop it, Mitch. She'll never find out. Even if she does, I'll tell her the truth."

"You'll tell her you two are just friends?"

"What else would I tell her?"

Mitchell opened his eyes. "Now you listen to reason. I don't trust that woman."

"Don't I recall you telling me once she wouldn't hurt Squire?"

"I'm not talking about…what I'm saying is…" Mitchell stomped his foot. He wiggled his index finger in Jesse's face. "Listen to me, will you? If Rachel does come here to do her nursing, she won't cotton to Giselle. She may even mistake her for your mistress."

"Not to worry, my worrisome friend. My Rachel will understand, though I doubt I'll see her again till after the war. Say, what's our boy found?" Jesse squatted when Squire trotted to him, something metallic in his mouth.

Wagging his tail, Squire dropped it at his feet, then looked at him, his eyes aglow.

Jesse scooped it up and threw back his head, chuckles welling inside him burst out of his mouth. Smiling at him from this tintype— Rachel. She always smiled in her photos, for the simple reason no one else she knew did it and thus, she wanted to be different in this regard. *Dear Rachel, always trying to stand out from everyone else.* Though she kept her lips closed, they were curled upward between dimples. Mischief shaded her amused expression. Jesse praised Squire and gave him a hearty pat on his head. He and Mitchell resumed their walk back to camp.

"I wonder where Squire got this. Marsden is the only person I can figure." He briefly broke his stride. "Of course." He resumed walking. "That day I caught him with Giselle and went inside his tent and yelled at him. Our boy was with me then. He must have stolen it, brought it here, and buried it."

Mitchell's booming laughter scared off birds. "Of course! Of course!"

Upon their return to camp they spotted Giselle sitting on a stump, shoulders slumped, weeping. Her trembling hands covered her face. Several soldiers clustered around her, trying to console her.

"Something must've happened to Daisy," Jesse whispered to Mitchell as they walked up to her.

"I hope not," Mitchell whispered back.

"What's happened, Miss Blevin? Are you all right?"

"No I ain't!" Giselle screamed, suddenly looking up. "Papa chained Daisy to a post and sicced Brutus on her. She ain't stood no chance." She erupted into another bout of sobs.

"I'm sorry. So terribly, terribly sorry."

"We ought to chain her old man to a post," Utley muttered.

"Teach him what it feels like," a nearby corporal said.

"My opinion exactly," Mitchell said.

Jesse shared their sentiments, but uttered no remark. He couldn't find the right words.

Tail drooping, Squire sniffed around her hoopskirt's battered hem as though searching for his lady.

Jesse grasped Giselle's moist hand. He led her to the road joining the depot, his ears attentive during her babbling about poor Daisy.

Sniffling, she glimpsed Rachel's tintype in his hand. "Is...is that your missus?"

"Yes." Jesse showed it to her, hoping it'd divert her thoughts from her dog's tragedy.

"She's purty."

"I think so." He handed it to her so she'd have a closer look.

When his column halted on a road leading to the Tickfaw River, Marsden squirmed in his saddle. The sun inched lower behind the treetops. The dying day cooled. It'd taken five hours to cross the temporary bridge Miles's men built on the Amite and now, some six miles from the Tickfaw, they'd joined other commands searching for the Yankee raiders.

All around him, soldiers lounged and chattered. Their muskets lay close by, either on the ground, across their laps, or in their hands. Strung out ahead, Miles's Legion likewise rested.

Marsden dismounted his stallion when Ransom strode to him from the column's van. He flicked dust off his coat sleeve before saluting.

"Well? Tell me what you learned, Lieutenant," Marsden said.

"The other commanders we met here, sir, they told Colonel Miles they fought a skirmish at the Tickfaw Bridge. It appears we missed the fun, sir."

Marsden swore. "It's Miles's fault. That wouldn't have happened if I'd commanded this expedition."

"Yes, sir."

Marsden swaggered past Ransom. At the head of the column, he spotted Miles consulting with several other commanders. Miles flashed an annoyed look before he gestured him to join their circle.

"Marsden, we're staying here till my scouts return." Miles thumped the map he was holding.

"The Yankees are camped about four or five miles to our front, Colonel Marsden." This came from a goateed colonel Marsden didn't know.

"I hope our scouts aren't absent for long," Marsden said. "When did the skirmish occur?"

"Close to noon," the goateed colonel said.

"We've transported four wounded prisoners to the rear," Miles said. "We got our information on the skirmish from them." Miles opened his map.

Marsden and the other commanders gathered round him.

"What say you, Marsden?" Miles looked up. "Want to make a wager the Yanks are still four miles to our front?"

"I wager on horses and cards. Nothing else."

"Does your small little brain know how to read a map?" Miles said.

Hot blood shot to Marsden's head. He was about to give this two-bit Napoleon some sound military advice, but not now. No one belittled him!

Marsden spotted Eakin slipping into a thicket. Leaving his fellow colonels, he pursued. Crisp leaves crunched beneath his rapid strides.

Flashes of Eakin's white shirt...between the timbers...the man swiftly gaining ground.

Moving toward the river, is he? Trying to sneak around our regiments? What's that coward up to? Marsden flipped up his holster's flap and drew his revolver. "Come back here, Eakin. Back, or I'll shoot."

Eakin ran faster.

"Stop, else I'll shoot a hole in your dumb head." He cocked the hammer. "Blast. He's out of range."

The Yankee zigzagged deeper into trees and foliage.

His weariness suddenly gone, Marsden took off after him again. Through briars, shrubs, and underbrush, he dared not lose sight of him. He was glad, though, when Eakin's run dropped to a staggering walk. Marsden slowed his pace; his chest heaved as he gulped air. "I see you, Eakin," Marsden shouted at last. "Might as well surrender."

Eakin, head bent low, made for the road.

Thumb on his revolver's hammer, Marsden aimed it at him.

Eakin stumbled to the ground. "Don't kill me!"

Marsden lowered his gun. Eakin's cry didn't sound like it was meant for him.

Marsden crept forward. The smell of fresh leaves filled his nostrils. Birds rustled nearby. By the time he reached Eakin, Eakin dropped back behind some brush. Marsden peered past a tall oak. A Union lieutenant sat propped against a pine tree, his left shoulder swathed in a bandage, his right hand aiming a revolver at Eakin. "You're a deserter."

"I…I'm no deserter."

"Why the blue trousers, then? And the blue kepi and the U.S. buckle on your waist belt?"

Marsden stepped into view. "Drop your weapon, Yank."

Startled, the man scowled at Marsden. "Get outta my face, Reb."

Marsden gestured at Eakin to stay put. To the young officer, he said, "The man threatened my life a few hours ago."

"I did not," Eakin screamed.

"Sergeant Winder said you'd have my head."

"Sir, Colonel, sir. I didn't plan on killing you. I was just angry." Eakin smirked. "Stella's family got mad at her, too, didn't they?"

Marsden slumped as though Eakin's words knocked the wind out of him. "How'd you know about Stella?"

"You make me clean your quarters like a slave, remember?"

Eakin must've gone through that last letter from her, the one he'd carelessly left on his desk a few days ago. Sensing Eakin might divulge Stella's identity to the wrong people, such as Webb or his friends, Marsden directed his attention to the enemy officer. "We're of the same mind regarding chicken-livered fools, but if you kill Eakin, well, you might as well say 'hello' to your grave."

"Worth it if I can kill yellow dogs like him."

"Are you certain it's worth your life?"

The Yankee hesitated, grimaced, and tossed aside his revolver.

"He is a deserter," Marsden said. "Joined our army about two months ago. He's in my regiment. From the look of things, he's trying to desert again. He will be punished, that I assure you." Marsden kicked the hat, sporting a black ostrich feather, which lay at the officer's feet. "What's your name?"

"Tate. Second lieutenant. Seventh Illinois Cavalry."

"Any more of you in these parts?"

"Maybe there are, maybe there aren't."

"Well, then. Tell me this. Do you value your life?"

Tate sighed. "Your scouts found our lieutenant colonel down the road a piece, shot up pretty badly, and three other wounded men. The rest of us went on toward Greensburg after our fight at the bridge. We've destroyed your supply lines to Vicksburg and your trains bringing in supplies. We'll reach Baton Rouge by tomorrow. We've outsmarted you at every turn, Johnny Reb. No way you can catch us."

"Maybe. But I have caught you."

Tate reached for his hat. "I'll give you that, Reb. I was trying to hide here till nightfall before getting out of here, but this traitor tripped over my legs." Screwing up his face, Tate touched his bandaged shoulder. "I'm at your mercy, now."

"Eakin isn't." Marsden cocked his pistol's hammer. Approaching hoofbeats stalled his trigger finger. No, he'd better not do it. Not yet, for through the brush he recognized Ransom galloping their direction.

"Over here, Ransom!" Marsden yelled. "I got us another Yankee prisoner. And Eakin trying to desert again."

Ransom reined in his horse. "Colonel Miles dispatched me to find you when he saw you leave the conference. Congratulations on your captures, sir."

"Easy as pie." Marsden gestured to Tate. "On your feet, Yank. You too, Eakin. Let's move."

The day after their arrival at Osyka, Mississippi, while his men broke camp to head north toward Jackson, Marsden stopped Captain Broussard on the street. "I'll take it."

"Sir, it's for Colonel Miles," Broussard said.

Marsden snatched Broussard's note.

"Sir. I must protest."

"Duly noted."

The captain's cheeks puffed.

Marsden skimmed the note's brief contents before handing it back to Broussard. Looking past him, he said, "Tell Colonel Miles that Generals Pemberton and Gardner have changed our orders. We're returning to Port Hudson."

Indignant, Broussard strode off to find Miles.

"Port Hudson, is it?" Lieutenant Tate, sitting in a nearby wagon with four other wounded prisoners, asked this question. Two shotgun-toting guards flanked them.

"You have a mighty fine set of ears."

"Now then, that is just something."

Marsden swaggered up to him. "What?"

"A few days back, we were raiding Newton Station. I went inside this rail coach that arrived not long after we did and this Rebel lady, when I told her our Colonel Grierson was a music teacher before the war, well, she started making jokes about my colonel's musical talents. She mentioned this dog…called him Squire I believe…said her dog's howl was prettier than his voice. She held her dander up pretty high, because when we tore up the railroad we delayed her trip to Port Hudson. She called herself a nurse, claimed she was going to see her husband."

"Tell me, my esteemed adversary. Did she reveal to you her name?"

"No, but her hair was dark as a raven, and she…yes…she wore a cameo pendant. Its relief was…let me try to remember…Yes! A cat."

Rachel. He was sure of it. "Your information is most appreciated, Tate." Marsden left, his saber jangling.

Sixteen

———◆———

Two days later Marsden dismounted his stallion in front of his tent. General Gardner changed his orders to Colonel Miles. Instead of returning to Port Hudson, he was sent to Olive Branch, Louisiana, whereas Marsden's regiment returned to the garrison. Whistling the jaunty strains of "Bonnie Blue Flag," his forefinger signaled Zack Blevin, who sat on his wagon bench beside a black driver. After the driver assisted him down, Zack hobbled behind Marsden on his crutch.

"What news?" Marsden said.

Zack settled into a chair and removed his battered slouch hat from off his shaggy-haired head. "My cousin's done what you asked her to do. She and Webb are on the friendly side of things now. And I've heard folks around here jawing about them. They think she's his mistress 'cause she visits him a lot, even when Webb swears they ain't."

"Are you certain about this? Absolutely certain?"

"Like you told me once, this is a small garrison, and getting smaller by all I can reckon. Two days ago, General Gregg's brigade left for Vicksburg."

"I heard about Gregg's transfer."

"It's all for the best, I reckon. Fewer mouths to feed. The food supplies are shrinking up."

"Nobody does anything right in this place. If they'd let me take charge of the commissary department—"

"Frank and me came for the dawg. Figured it'd be easier us getting it than you bringing it to our farm like y'all first planned. We've been coming every day this past week, waiting for you to get back."

"Frank?"

"My wagon driver. On the wagon bench. Me and Cousin Giselle are tired of waiting. We want that dawg. Today. This evening. My uncle wants him for a bait dawg."

The tent's door flap flew open. Winder strode in. "We're on the move again, Colonel. To reinforce General Pemberton at Vicksburg."

Marsden raised his fist. "Vicksburg! At last, a real fight. When are we to move out?"

"In a day or two. General Gardner got a ciphered dispatch from Pemberton."

"The dawg?" Zack's fingers drummed his chair's arms.

Marsden pulled off his gauntlets. "Park your wagon by the warehouses and wait till Sergeant Winder comes for you. No one loiters around the warehouses much in the evening. You'll get the mongrel tonight."

"Using my musket's sling and a bit of bait." Winder consulted his watch. "Time's getting short. Nabbing the mongrel might take a few hours."

"I'm as patient as a cat watching a mouse hole, Sergeant." Zack patted his crutch. "We'll stuff him in the hogshead I brought for the event."

His master's dress parade over, Squire pawed Jesse's leg. No response from his master. Too busy shouting at one of his men. What it was about, Squire had no notion. The soldier seemed to shrink when his master leaned nose-to-nose in the soldier's taut face.

Squire squeezed between them. Instead of this quelling his master's anger, it parted them wider.

Squire pawed his master's legs harder, more insistently. Why wouldn't his master calm down? Didn't they see he wanted their attention? He barked. *Stop fussing. Please stop fussing.*

"Quit, Squire," Jesse snapped before turning back to the soldier he was reprimanding.

Squire hung his head, his tail drooped, and he wandered off. No attention did he receive. He moped out of the regimental camp. Why was his master angry? What did he do to deserve his rebuke?

A familiar odor drew near him. Someone came at a steady pace. When he turned his head to see who it was, he recognized Winder. He didn't trust Winder. A low growl rose from deep within him.

"I ain't going to hurt you, you mangy cur doggie." Winder cracked his knuckles.

Unlike his previous angry tone, something Squire vividly recalled that day he stole Smythe's shoe, the man sounded strangely pleasant this time. Neither did he direct his gaze straight at Squire's eyes. Maybe he'd leave him in peace. Squire kept walking, the narrow path growing cooler beneath his paws. The lengthening day gradually grayed as it edged toward darkness. Shadows stretching across the earth pointed the way.

First stop, a wharf. Squire padded down the steep road to the river. He sniffed barrels of sour corn.

"Must've been here before the Yankees tried passing us." Winder picked up a rotten ear and hurled it into the Mississippi. "General Gardner's the blame for our food shortage."

Squire glanced up. The big man's hand swooped toward him. Off he bounded, back up the road to the bluff. Was that man trying to grab him or just pat his head?

"I ain't going to hurt you, cur doggie!" Winder's gruff voice lilted slightly.

Looking behind him, Squire noticed Winder following him, not at a run, but at a saunter like his master usually walked.

Squire's wanderings led him southward, downriver along the bluff, past river batteries. Soldiers spoke to him. His tail swept the air in happy reply. At the last river cannon, three soldiers built a fire. One produced a small square of cornbread from his haversack.

"Have one, Squire." The soldier tossed it on the ground.

Squire's teeth crunched it into crumbs as he swallowed it.

Winder approached. "I'd be careful about wasting food."

"What brings you this far down the line, Sergeant Major?" The soldier rummaged inside his haversack for more rations.

"I heard one of you men caught a load of catfish this morning before reveille. Thought I'd help y'all eat it."

"No one here caught a catfish."

"Reckon I was mistaken."

While they talked, Squire resumed wandering—through a deep ravine, in and out of ditches, past another earthwork near the river. Panting, he continued his southward journey, below the garrison's defenses. Darkness enveloped the woods and river. Squire sat on the bluff and thrust up his muzzle, enjoying the cool breeze and sampling a myriad of smells. Distant lights on the river commanded his attention, the lights of ships anchored off an island. His heart thumped fast. Though he didn't know the ships' deadly purpose, their lights fascinated him. Did men live on those boats? Could he swim to them and make another friend or get another treat?

"They'll be hitting us again soon, I imagine."

At the sound of the sergeant major's voice, Squire sprang to all fours and faced him. Casually, Winder closed in. The moon's glow danced off his square face, which appeared softer. Nothing in his body language hinted at danger. Should he trust this man who always yelled at him?

"What do you think, cur doggie? Can we stop the Yanks from landing a force on this spot? No. I reckon you don't understand nothing 'cept dog." The sergeant major pulled something from one of his trouser pockets. It was long and wrapped in paper.

Squire almost scooted closer to the sergeant major, till a warning inside him held him back.

"Hungry, you ugly looking animal?" Winder's voice was soft. He peeled back the paper.

Pork. The thing wrapped inside the paper was pork. Squire's tongue swiped his lips.

When Winder dangled the sliver of meat at his nose, he snatched at it but his teeth clamped air because Winder jerked it clear. The sergeant major continued downriver.

Something inside Squire screamed louder. "Don't follow! Don't go!" But the pork held a kind of magic over him, an allure that weakened his will to resist.

So Squire tagged after Winder. Down into a low, grassy area the sergeant major led him, to a spot almost directly opposite the Union ships. The remnants of a shattered building halted them. Mangled wood, smashed in halves and thirds and into splinters, littered the area. Barrel staves, blasted into bits. "The ships did it to us again." Winder cracked his knuckles. "Hope no skirmishers come here tonight."

Squire lifted his head toward Winder. His tail thumped earth. He licked his lips. *Food.*

"All right, you thieving cur dog. Time for your last meal." Smiling, Winder went to a willow tree. He drew more paper-wrapped pork from his pocket. "Better not make me waste this." He spread the slivers of meat on the ground.

Barking once, Squire dashed to it and gobbled it. This pork was good!

Winder jerked a thin rope he'd slid between Squire's collar and bandana while Squire ate. "Gotcha."

Squire turned to flee. Up flew his front feet; they slammed earth. Snarling, he whipped around to bite Winder, but the sergeant major shoved his head down hard and pressed it against the ground. Using the rope, he jerked Squire up again, so hard the back of his head smacked the tree. Winder whipped the rope around the tree twice and then back beneath Squire's collar.

Squire struggled and fought and snarled and snapped. Winder whipped the rope around the tree trunk a third time before tying it off. He did a similar thing with his musket's sling.

"Serves you right, you mangy cur dog." Winder whacked dust off his trousers.

The back of his head jammed against the tree trunk. Squire's collar pinched him. No slack remained in either sling or rope. He couldn't lie down; his forepaws could hardly move; his hind legs battled earth for freedom. Such battling yanked his collar tighter against his throat. He gagged.

Winder waggled his finger at him. "Don't you go nowhere now. I'll be back in a short spell."

The sergeant major headed off in the direction from which he'd come.

Squire's heart quivered. He was beyond terrified. He desperately wanted someone to hear him, someone to help. He barked and barked and barked, its pitch growing louder and louder. A long time seemed to pass. Still no one came to help him. Did he wander too far for anyone to hear?

Squire shut his eyes and eventually his barking died. Though a breeze washed over him, it didn't calm him, nor did it slow his pounding heart. Unable to move, he sat motionless for what seemed an eternity. Something pattered past him, maybe a rat, mocking his helplessness to give chase.

Clattering approached. He opened his eyes. A pair of horses halted a wagon close-by. Two men sat on its bench. Squire's ears popped to attention. What was this?

The big man, the wagon's driver, climbed down and went round the wagon where he helped down another man, who hit the ground on one crutch. A third man threw off a canvas cover and rose from the wagon bed. The man who tied him to this tree.

"I told you the dog wasn't going nowhere," Winder said.

"Good thing," Zack said. "I'd hate to have gone through all that waiting and jolting over rough terrain for nothing. No roads in these parts, 'cept that little trail we follered. Pretty near impracticable getting here."

"That's why this was such a good spot. Too far for anyone to hear this dog's carrying on trying to get help."

"Frank, the hogshead." Zack pointed at the barrel in the wagon bed. "We've found Brutus a training partner."

The dark man went behind the wagon. "Think this 'un's big enough, Mistuh Zack?" His large hands hefted up the barrel.

Zack narrowed his eyes at Squire. "It'll do. Roll it over to the cur. Easy, now."

Instead of rolling it, Frank heaved the barrel up onto his massive shoulder. When he reached Squire, the moon reflected his face's craggy features. He set it down.

Squire sensed this man's kindness, felt the gentleness pouring out of his mournful eyes.

"You and me in de same boat," he whispered to Squire. "You's a pris'ner and I'se a slave. Ain't no difference 'tween the two, 'cepting you's a dog and I'se a man."

"Hurry up," Zack said. "Sun'll be up soon."

In no great hurry, Frank worked off the hogshead's lid, pocked with breathing holes.

"Get the hammer and nails." Zack gestured angrily. "Fast, you lazy, good-for-nothing!"

"I'll stuff the cur in the barrel," Winder said.

Squire listened to this human chatter and correctly guessed from their tones that they were up to no good, except for Frank, who slipped nails inside his shirt pocket then turned his sympathetic gaze upon him. The barrel was meant for him. Squire sensed it.

Winder stepped forward.

Baring his teeth, Squire snapped for all he was worth.

Winder sprang back. "Better muzzle him first. Glad I brought a pillowcase. I thought something like this might happen."

Pillowcase in hand, Winder returned from the wagon a brief time later.

Squire snarled and snapped at the pillowcase blinding him. His teeth lashed into it. It swung over his muzzle twice, was jerked tight, and clamped his jaw shut. He struggled as it was knotted behind his ears.

"Zack, untie the rope and sling." Winder knelt beside Squire.

Squire felt Winder's arms clutch his midsection. The rope and sling around his neck fell limp. The earth swept out from under him. Up. They were lifting him up. His legs flailed. Twisting, writhing in Winder's death-grip, his hind feet shoved off the barrel's rim.

Winder screamed obscenities. As the sergeant major shoved his hindquarters downward, Squire shoved his hind legs off the hogshead in a last, desperate attempt to flee. His left foot missed the rim and he slipped inside it. His forepaws found the barrel's rim. Down smashed the lid, on his paws. Thanks to his pillowcase muzzle, Squire's yelp stuck in his throat. A painful shock sliced through his forelegs when he jerked them inside his coffin. Loud hammering overhead made his ears ring.

"Hurry up," Zack said. "Nail it shut before he gets out."

"I'se doin' it, Mistuh Zack."

Squire scrunched his legs against his body. Limited space afforded him scant room to move. His nose warred against the barrel's odor, and his forepaws bumped his coffin's staves as they came up to his muzzle. He batted the pillowcase squeezing his teeth.

Zack dropped Winder off at the nearest crossroad. Next, he told Frank to take them home. While they bumped along, the horizon's orange-red glow heralded the sun's ascent up the azure sky. Behind them, in the wagon bed, Squire banged and scratched the barrel staves. Zack wished that stupid dog would shut up. He was done for already. Frank's fate, however, remained undecided. He needed to consider Frank's punishment, what he deserved for his recent conduct.

Zack's fist pressured his knee. Bad conduct, for sure. For the past few months, Frank did the opposite of almost everything Zack told him, like when he carried the hogshead on his shoulder instead of rolling it over to the dog. He told him to hurry up getting the hammer and nails, yet he acted like he was on a Sunday stroll. Once they reached home he'd send him to the fields permanently, after a good taste of the rawhide ripping his dark back, slashing red stripes down his skin, a crisscross of torn flesh. This time, Frank would learn his lesson.

A loud clap sounded behind them. Turning, Zack saw the hogshead's lid pop up and down a crack. "Stop, Frank."

Frank stiffened his jaw.

"Did you hear me, stupid?"

Frank tugged the horses' reins.

"The dawg's trying to escape. Get out and nail that lid down tighter."

The hogshead thudded over. A golden mass scrambled out and vaulted over the wagon's end gate, his pillowcase muzzle flying off his head.

Zack cursed Winder. He should've tied a tighter knot behind his ears. The stupid…

"Run, dog!" Frank yelled. "Run! Run!"

Zack backhanded the slave's face.

Frank smacked Zack's rib cage so hard Zack tumbled off, onto the dew-soaked grass with a powerful ache.

Frank leapt down. Hands on his hips, his brown eyes flashed. "That dog's got as much a right to freedom as I do."

"You nailed it wrong on purpose." Zack glanced around him. Where was his crutch? If he could just stand.

"You got that right, Big Man Zack. I sho' 'nough did." He snatched Zack's crutch from off the wagon bench and flung it into the woods beyond Zack's reach. "Crippled man can't catch me, neither. I'se borrowin' de wagon and goin' to Baton Rouge to join de Yankee army. Maybe I'll find some of de other slaves who escaped yo' farm last time de Yankees was here."

Frank started to climb back onto the wagon bench.

Zack drew his knee up along the ground, bringing his foot close to his hand. He slipped his knife from his boot. Using his other hand, he managed to push himself up high enough to hurl it. It sailed past Frank and the horses drawing the wagon.

Frank gave a piercing whoop, cracked the whip, and drove the wagon back up the road. "Baton Rouge and de Yankee army! I'se on my way."

"You can't break that dog's legs, Cousin Zack." Giselle peered out her home's parlor window. Henry carried a canvas sack full of dog food.

"The cur can't run next time if I do it." Zack hobbled up to her on his crutch. "And I won't be careless like Winder, in such a blame hurry he didn't tie that dawg's muzzle tight enough."

Blevin mopped his forehead with his sweaty handkerchief. "I don't want his legs broken."

Giselle looked down at Zack's feet. "'Sides, he might bite off your other leg."

"You stay put and keep your eyes on the rest of our slaves from now on." Blevin crammed his handkerchief in his shirt pocket. "Losing Frank like you did, well, we'd better not lose any more of them."

"I ain't totally helpless," Zack said, "though I am grateful some of our horse soldiers happened by and got me back on my crutch. If you want him whole, how are we supposed to get him?"

Wicked mischief boiled inside Giselle. "Papa, I got me the most best plan. I know it'll work. I'll go get Ma's recipe book and get to work on it."

"How will a recipe help?" Zack said.

"It's all written down in Ma's special book, Cousin."

"Must be a good one, Cousin."

Giselle tapped Zack's shoulder on her way to the kitchen. "It is."

Seventeen

———◆———

"Did you know this train runs tri-weekly?" Rachel spoke to Matilda, who sat opposite her in the Clinton train's only passenger car.

"Really?" Matilda fingered a blond curl slipping out from beneath her bonnet.

Outside their window, cotton fields seemed to roll past as their train rocked and rumbled along its track.

"It'll go to Port Hudson one week and try weakly to get back to Clinton the next."

Matilda giggled. "Where'd you hear that one?"

"At the Clinton Depot. I heard someone telling it to a child."

"Mister Collins was a real dear, bringing us here. We're lucky he didn't live far from Newton." Matilda reached into her reticule for a small mirror. She studied her reflection.

"You look fine, honey."

Matilda put the mirror back. "We never could've made it without Mister Collins, not after what those awful Yankees did in Mississippi, burning those trains and tearing up the railroad."

"Humph! We might have been here sooner if it hadn't been for them." Rachel giggled. "Why, I do think it was kind of me and my flattering little ole mouth to persuade him."

During their brief stay at Newton, Mister Collins and his daughters were wonderful hosts. It took several days, though, before he finally agreed to bring them in his carriage. He'd been in Vicksburg visiting his son, an officer in General Pemberton's army. "Let's get rid of the Yanks first," he said. "I wouldn't want you ladies falling into some ruthless Bluebelly's hands."

Grateful for their uneventful trip, Rachel told herself there wasn't a Yankee alive who could handle her. Arriving here on the seventh of May wasn't so bad. Better than not arriving at Port Hudson at all.

She clutched her cameo hanging from her neck. It once belonged to her maternal grandmother. Though Rachel harbored rarely uttered doubts, her grandmother always assured her she was beautiful, even when her thoughts told her otherwise. Her older sister Margaret, a mayor's wife in a small north Alabama town, had a tinier waist and a prettier face. "You are pretty, child," her grandmother always told her. "And my dear, you have a wonderful personality that suits it like a tiara suits a princess."

Therefore, Rachel exercised her personality to her advantage.

Pine trees zipped past them. What was her Jesse doing at this hour? Marching? Playing with her Squire? Perhaps he'd grown thinner, perhaps even lost some hair. Soon she'd be secure in her adoring husband's strong arms. Jesse still adored her. He must still adore her, the way she'd always adored him way back to their childhoods, till Marsden's brief interruption when Jesse went off to the university. She deserved Marsden's betrayal. After all, she'd betrayed Jesse's trust during that period. But they weren't in love then, were they? Not real love, not till after he returned home to work in her father's furniture store. It wasn't really a betrayal on her part, was it?

Then again, the war might have changed Jesse. He might have become like certain other men who cheated on their wives, or on their fiancées like Hampton Lafayette Marsden did to her. No, not her Jesse. He'd never broken his word on anything save for his failure to return home quickly after he took Squire off to war, and that wasn't his fault.

The train rumbled on.

Rachel daydreamed about her husband and Squire.

"Squire! My honey melon!" Rachel cried.

Bent ears flapping, he sprinted to her full tilt as she stepped across Port Hudson's tracks. Barking and leaping, his molasses eyes aglow, he cavorted around her till she grabbed his collar and gently settled him down on his hindquarters. She knelt and wrapped his wriggling body in a huge hug; his wet kisses slobbered her face.

Pale hands propped on her willowy hips, Matilda smiled down at them. "Well, hello to you again, Mister Squire."

Rachel let go. Squire lifted his head to receive Matilda's petting.

"The bandana you made him's gotten sorta dirty." Matilda stroked Squire's back.

"I'll get it off him later. Maybe I can get it washed."

Squire ran a tight circle, stopped and looked at them, then started running it again.

Rachel waved "come on" at her friend. "He wants us to follow him. I'll betcha he'll lead us to my husband." She made a broad sweeping gesture. "Forward and away, Sir Squire."

"What about our trunks?"

"They'll still be at the depot when we get back. The trunk thief's up in Maine right now. Come on."

His gait jaunty and his curved tail held high, Squire led them down the long road leading into town.

By the time they reached Jesse's camp, his company's drill ended. Soldiers and a sprinkling of spectators loitered on the bluff. One freckle-faced girl's green eyes flashed at her as though in recognition.

Who is she? Rachel wondered.

The girl sashayed around several soldiers.

"Where's Captain Webb?" Matilda said.

"In Port Hudson." Stooping, Rachel leaned into Squire's ear. "Show us where he is, boy."

"Rachel. Matilda. Uh, uh…When did…uh…when did y'all get up here?" Mitchell broke away from a lady with whom he was chatting and hurried to them.

Rachel grinned, getting to her feet. "Surprised?"

"I, uh…"

"Where's my husband?" Rachel said.

Mitchell's eyes darted left and right. "I thought you two were still nursing down in Mobile."

"We were. Our new orders sent us up to Vicksburg, but when our train pulled into Newton Station, some Yankee cavalry raided it, set our trains on fire, and tore up the tracks." She clasped her hands. "Oh, quite frightening and exciting. A fine gentleman who lived near there happened to be on the train. My matron Mrs. Harris let him bring Matilda and me here. Isn't that grand?"

"Yes, well…have y'all reported to Doctor Barnett yet? He's our chief surgeon." Mitchell steered Rachel and Matilda away from the small crowd. "You're supposed to see him first."

"Oh, pshaw, Lieutenant Hayes. We'll see him later."

"No, Mrs. Webb. We'd better get on over there now."

"Why?"

"Because…" Mitchell turned his head and coughed. "Because uh, uh…" He coughed again.

"Good gracious, Lieutenant. You act like you're trying to hide a gold mine or something. Is anything wrong?"

"Me? Hide a gold mine?" He snatched a passing private by his shirt sleeve. "Perkins, escort these ladies to Doctor Barnett. Double-quick."

Perkins gave them a greeting.

"I'll tell Jesse, I mean Captain Webb, that you're…uh…that you're here. He'll meet y'all at the post hospital."

When Perkins started to lead Rachel and Matilda away, Rachel glanced back after Squire gave a bark. To her left, the freckle-faced girl closed on Jesse. *Oh!* Rachel's heart thrilled and she started toward him till the freckle-faced girl…What? Frowning, Rachel stopped in her tracks.

Miss Freckles stood close to him. Too close. Directly in front, face to face, noses practically touching. Her slender fingers marched up the buttons of Jesse's frock coat, her hand eased around his elbow and she…she kissed him. "Smack on the lips!"

Jesse shoved the girl clear when he heard Rachel's cry.

Rachel screamed, turned, and hurried back up the road as fast as her hooped skirt allowed her.

"Rachel," Jesse yelled through cupped hands. "I didn't see you."

"Obviously." Rachel quickened her pace, her limbs working hard beneath the gored skirt hindering her movement.

Jesse ran around in front of her and blocked her path. She swept around him. He jumped in front of her again. "Rachel. Darling. I have no idea what possessed Giselle to do that. We're just friends. She's never—"

"Very close friends, I take it." Her mind and heart tossed and tumbled and flew every direction as though smashed by a tornado.

"You don't understand."

"We've known each other too many years, Captain Webb. I guess now you're tired of me. Private Perkins, please escort my friend and me to the post hospital as quickly as you can."

Long face quizzical, Perkins looked at Jesse. "Sir?"

"Not yet." Jesse shot in front of her a third time. "I'm not done talking to my wife."

"You will not talk to me again, Husband."

"I will, too, Wife. Hear me out. Giselle isn't—"

Waving him off, Rachel swept around him. Though Jesse kept after her, shouting lame explanations, she shut her ears. Nothing could justify his behavior.

A bugle call turned Jesse back.

Rachel and Matilda kept walking. Perkins's unencumbered limbs kept pace. Squire, his tongue dangling and dripping saliva, trotted alongside them.

Rachel and Matilda entered the office of Chief Surgeon Doctor James Barnett, quartered in the hotel near the depot along with General Gardner and his staff. Seated at his pine desk, mumbling, the doctor scribbled his steel-tipped pen across a sheet of paper. He dipped his pen in an inkwell and slapped the paper atop a fat, leather-bound medical book near his left elbow. Rachel cleared her throat.

"Yes, miss?" he droned, slowly lifting his weary eyes toward them.

"Doctor Barnett." Rachel's voice cracked. "I am Rachel Webb, and this is Matilda Rutherford."

"How may I be of service to you ladies?"

"We're nurses. Our matron sent us here. From Newton Station."

Thick gray brows knitted, he studied her. "My dear, it is my observation that your eyes are red. Have you, by chance, been crying?"

Rachel sniffled. "I'm fine."

"Are you certain?"

"Please, Doctor. I said I am very fine. Thank you for asking."

"If you say so, my dear. Well, if you ladies have any questions or require anything, you may ask me, or Doctor Hereford, our post surgeon. We do have a matron on the premises, a Mrs. Garrison, but she's…Nah! Don't bother about her." The doctor grunted. "I'm afraid you will not see much of me, though." He gathered up a stack of papers. "All this fool paperwork prevents me from helping our boys. Case books, prescription books, diet books, two reports a day." He went to his open door and peeked out, turning his head left and right as though looking for someone. "There you are, Sergeant Leeds." He stepped back and allowed the sergeant entrance.

"Yes, sir, Doc?" Leeds eyed Rachel and Matilda curiously. He stood Rachel's height, five foot five. His head was round and his neck, thick.

"Sergeant Leeds is one of our stewards," Doctor Barnett said. "He'll show you ladies around the regimental hospitals and help you get settled in."

"Thank you, Doctor," Rachel said.

Outside the hotel, Leeds led them toward the depot. "We're hurting for food," he said, "and our medical supplies aren't what they used to be, though a smuggler did bring in some laudanum and quinine the other day, courtesy of our fine Bluebelly friends down Baton Rouge-way. We make do with what we have and improvise when we need to. I'll take y'all to the hospitals after we fetch your belongings. I'm sure we can find you a place to stay."

"What does Mrs. Garrison look like?" Rachel asked.

"Can't miss her when you see her," Leeds said. "She's got this awful stringy brown hair, and her nose takes up most of her face. Her husband's posted here."

Leeds's brisk stride challenged Rachel's and Matilda's efforts to keep alongside him.

Tail up, Squire tagged after them.

Warmth spread through Rachel like sweet melted butter. At least Squire still loved her. Dogs loved everybody.

From her right sounded hoofbeats. Colonel Marsden, galloping his stallion toward her. He reined in his mount directly in the trio's path. Rigid in his saddle, he doffed his cap. "Mrs. Webb."

"Colonel." Rachel stiffened. Though she may not be her most presentable at this moment, her former suitor's arrival didn't embarrass her regarding her appearance. Long ago he'd ceased being her turtledove.

Marsden swung down from his saddle. "Where's your husband?"

Rachel glared at him.

Hand on his sword's hilt, he swaggered to her. His dark falcon eyes and a jerk of his head signaled Matilda and Leeds to step out of earshot, which they did.

"I'm departing for Vicksburg tomorrow," he said. "Since you haven't seen your darling husband yet, I'd better inform you before you discover it. He's betrayed your love. Truth is, he never really loved you. I planned to write you a letter about it, but seeing as how you're here now, you can observe his treason for yourself rather than believe my words."

"We grew up together. In the same town."

"What does that matter, Mrs. Webb? You still married the wrong man. I would never have done to you what he's done. I'm not the cad he is."

"What about Stella?" Rachel said curtly.

Marsden cleared his throat as though stifling a retort, mounted his horse, and galloped away.

Rachel bit her lip. She'd never truly loved Colonel Marsden. That was a hard lesson she'd learned. Why did they ever start courting? He made arrogance look like humility. Lifting her chin, she moved ahead of Leeds and Matilda while Squire brushed against her broad skirt. She blinked rapidly; mist clouded her vision.

Eighteen

"Sergeant, I'd say I'm happy to see Marsden go." Jesse felt Squire's warm body rubbing against him, an earthy smell wafting from his fur.

"Me, too, sir," Hickam said.

Dust clouds kicking up from beneath his soldiers' feet, General Maxey's brigade tramped past them. Marsden, back erect and eyes flashing, sat astride his prancing stallion as he rode in the vanguard of his ragtag column. Miles's Legion would be the last to depart today and, of course, General Gardner and his staff. General Beall commanded Port Hudson now, assigned the duty of defending the place.

Hickam scratched his stubbly chin. "I wonder why Colonel Marsden's so popular with his men."

"Well, I'd say they're likely deluded."

Squire wove a figure-eight between Jesse and Hickam.

"They think he's not only a fighter," Jesse continued, "but a living, breathing, sure 'nough military genius." Jesse grinned. Maybe some Yankee would kill Marsden for him.

A bugle sounded skirmish drill. Jesse and Hickam, also Squire, hurried back to the river batteries. After this drill, Jesse determined to set things right with Rachel. He'd explain everything to her, tell her

Giselle drank some "crazy water." Giselle, he'd tell her, was to blame for the kiss. Not him. He'd make Rachel understand.

Inside a regimental hospital two days later, Rachel nursed a gaunt soldier, his left arm broken from a tumble down one of Port Hudson's ravines. Splinted, it was at rest in a sling brace. He sat on the edge of his cot. "I heard tell you're married to Captain Webb."

"I need to wash your face." Rachel scooped a rag from a bowl of water.

"He's a mighty good man. I ain't in his company, but I am in his regiment."

Rachel spread the rag across the soldier's forehead. After she patted it, she mopped off its dirt.

"A few days ago, he helped me write my fiancèe a letter."

"Sh-h-h. Don't talk. You need to build back your strength."

"He gave me some fine, fancy words to say to her."

She bathed the soldier's sweat-flecked beard and heavy sideburns. She swept the rag over his lips for a time longer than normal. It was the only way she could stop him, politely, from talking about her husband. "Your fiancèe must be a beautiful lady." She pulled the rag away.

"She sure is, ma'am."

After she washed all the dirt off the young man's face and hands, she admired his handsome features. No wonder his fiancèe loved him. His high cheekbones and heavy black eyebrows, why, his handsome looks pretty near matched her husband's. The soldier's hazel eyes held a glimmer. This man knew love. Had he ever experienced love's loss? Never in her wildest imagination would she believe Jesse would betray her and wouldn't believe it now even if Marsden had written her and told her. Maybe her fears had been fulfilled. Maybe the war *had* changed him. *No.* She shook her head. Not her husband. She pulled herself to the next patient.

"Mrs. Rachel Webb, darlin'!" Giselle's trill sounded from the tent door. In all her despicable glory she stood there, poised like a prima donna.

Squire poked his nose around Giselle's skirt.

Leeds strode to her. "Miss, unless you have business here, you'll have to leave."

"I got business here. I got business tellin' Mrs. Webb to get on back where she come from."

"I will not," Rachel said. "You go home and stay home, Miss Freckles."

"Your husband belongs to me, dearie. He's mine."

Rachel gulped so hard it was like swallowing a rock. The attendants gazed at them. Doctor Carter and Matilda shifted uneasily in the tent's eastern end. Now everyone knew about her humiliation. She started to fire a verbal shot at Giselle when a shriek pierced her ears. The blast that followed nearly knocked her off her feet.

"Mortars," Leeds said. "The mortar boats are at it again."

"Getting the range of our river batteries, I'll wager," an attendant said. "Certain there'll be a bigger bombardment tonight."

"Or the Yankee ships will have another go at passing us," Leeds said.

Another shell followed the first one, then another. The river batteries roared their response.

Screaming, Matilda cupped her hands over her ears.

Rachel's knees became mush. She'd never heard a mortar shell before.

Leeds's strong arm secured her waist. Her thumping heart calmed...up to a point.

"Back to work." Doctor Carter bent down to examine a patient. "All of you."

Another blast ripped the air a good distance away. Though a few mortar shells strayed from their path and struck outside the tent, they buried themselves in the earth without exploding. Forcing steadiness into her shaky hands, Rachel muttered, "Fireworks. They're just fireworks." She washed her patients' hands and faces, fighting to maintain a calm, confident demeanor.

Some hours later, the fireworks ceased.

"What a commotion." Matilda seized a roll of bandages off a table.

"Where'd Freckles go?" Rachel looked left and right. "Did anyone see her leave?"

Everyone shook their heads no.

The notion that Giselle must have run off more scared than they were amused Rachel. But her humor died when her husband, arms outstretched, rushed inside the tent, Squire trotting alongside him.

"Rachel. Rachel. Are you all right?" Jesse maneuvered a brisk path between the patients and started to hug her.

Rachel shoved him back.

"Rachel. Please. Listen to reason. Like I told you the day you arrived, Giselle and me, we're just friends." Drawing her tintype from his trouser pocket, he moved around to face her.

Rachel showed him her back a second time.

"It's not what you think."

"Isn't it?"

"How long have we known each other? Since we were children, that's how long. Do you honestly believe I'd betray your trust? Did I ever do that? Remember all those grand ole times we used to have before the war, eating your fine fare at parties and celebrations, and dancing till midnight? You were the only gal I ever wanted to dance with and marry. The only gal, Rachel." Jesse's hands crossed his heart. "I swear it."

"I don't know what to believe anymore, Captain Webb. Nor do I know what to think."

"Rach—"

The bugle sounded another drill.

Muttering, Jesse departed. Squire tagged after him.

Rachel got fresh bandages off a table. She needed to change them on a patient's blistered foot. Perhaps she'd misjudged Jesse. If so, well, she'd teach him a lesson, a hard lesson about getting too friendly with women of questionable morals such as Giselle. She'd take no pleasure doing it, but it must be done, at least for a spell. He could not let women like Freckles get the better of him, ever again. She was going to teach him this lesson because she loved him. That is why she was going to do it, wasn't it? Because she loved him?

"Let's all get back to work, ladies and gents," Doctor Carter said. "Back to work. Back to work."

"Sweet laudanum." Giselle set the drug's bottle on her square dining table before joining her father, his hands behind his back and looking out a window.

Outside, Henry trained Cato. The powerful dog sprang high and seized the huge knot at the end of a thick, heavy rope, swinging back and forth many feet above the ground.

"Them Yankee mortar boats done me a favor, Papa. While other folkses worryin' about 'em and talkin' about 'em, I stole me some of this here laudanum from a hospital tent."

"Nobody saw you do it?"

"Shucks, no. Mortars got all their attention. Not me."

"Suppose you give the cur too much laudanum?" Blevin didn't turn from the window. "Folks have died from taking too much of that medicine, and you ain't a doctor. Laudanum's for people, not dogs. I told you I wanted him here alive."

"I'll bring him back here alive. Ma wrote down a list of dosages in the back of one of her recipe books. She just didn't leave me no laudanum when she passed. Used it all up, I figger, what with all them aches and pains she was always complainin' about. That's why I stole it from the hospital."

"You're giving him just enough to make him sleep?"

"A sleep so deep I can lock him in a cage before his peepers pop open."

"When?"

"I need me four days."

"Half-rations for my gladiators. They need to be good and mean by the time the cur arrives."

Nineteen

———— ◆ ————

J esse crept through the dusky dawn, working his way through dense foliage till he arrived at a redoubt south of the river batteries, shoveled up the previous evening. He moved between the small fortification's two cannons and peered at the enemy vessels anchored in the river; mortar schooners hurled shells toward the river batteries at regular intervals, their explosions punctuating the otherwise quiet day.

Several hundred yards further down, two more cannons glowered from an old gun position. Soldiers from his regiment manned the oddest of this pair, a small brass rifle salvaged from an abandoned Yankee vessel on the Amite River this April past. Dubbed "The Baby," they'd mounted the little gun on a twenty-four pounder siege carriage.

Yesterday Lieutenant Colonel Paul De Gournay, commander of the river's southern batteries, transported these four cannons down here. From this spot, he'd bombard the enemy vessels. Although Jesse had no reason to come, nor did anyone order him to do it, he came anyway. Who cared that he might die? Certainly not Rachel, and, well…he fought a needlelike pain in his throat…if he did get killed, he deserved it.

Why Rachel didn't believe him when he tried explaining about Giselle, he didn't know. Suppose Rachel did still care about him.? If she did still love him, she'd sure as sand worry about him and pray for his safety. His coming here would test that love.

Jesse fixed his attention on the ships. Though distant, a screw sloop's silhouette stood in bold relief against the awakening day. Her black funnel not smoking, her sails furled upon her three towering masts, her rigging streaming from her masts to her hull, not a man one did he see moving aboard her. She seemed asleep.

But the ironclad gunboat—her twin stacks situated forward, her freeboard mere inches above the waterline and her sloping iron casemate spanning her from bow to stern—had opened her gun-ports.

Colonel De Gournay, who observed the ships from behind Jesse, lowered his field glasses. "That ironclad is the *Essex*, and the screw sloop anchored near her, she is the *Richmond*." A French marquis, De Gournay owned estates in Brittany, Louisiana, and Cuba. When the war broke out, he'd been a newspaper editor. "The mortar schooners appear to be moored under the bluff. I am uncertain regarding how many of them we will be able to hit."

"We can at least try to hit them, sir," Jesse said.

"*Oui*, Captain Webb. *Oui*."

Ever since their attack two days ago, the schooners had harassed Port Hudson's river batteries. Jesse reasoned this resumption of a daily pounding meant Banks was either preparing to attack, or else the navy would make another attempt to pass them. Too late for Banks to beat General Gardner back here, though, because the general had already returned, ordered back by President Davis to hold this spot at all costs. Such was the rumor making rounds through the garrison.

The Union men-of-war opened the fight, firing their guns louder than a warehouse full of fireworks exploding. The schooners quickened their bombardment. A shell arced toward them. Jesse smacked dirt. Rising to his knees, he peeked over the parapet. He breathed a sigh of relief. The wind carried the shell back toward the river batteries farther up.

De Gournay passed the order for his cannoneers to target *Essex*.

Gripping his flintlock musket, Jesse drew a cartridge from the leather cartridge box slung across his shoulder.

Cannoneers loaded their artillery, inserted primers to their cannons' vents, and stepped back while other members of the artillery crew kept their lanyards at the ready, awaiting De Gournay's order.

De Gournay's sword scraped out of its scabbard. "Fire!"

The cannoneers yanked their lanyards. The carriages recoiled as their artillery belched fiery roars. "The Baby's" shell detonated before it reached *Essex*. Other shells scored ineffective hits. The schooners, well out of De Gournay's range, responded with deafening fury.

Having no illusions about his own effectiveness against ships, Jesse nevertheless raced downriver through falling fragments. Mortar shells arced his direction. He tasted dirt when they slammed the soft earth and exploded. Maybe, if he could get close enough, maybe he could get off a few shots.

He crouched near "The Baby," barking at their foe, and bit off the paper-wrapped cartridge. *Essex's* forward battery thundered. *Richmond* weighed anchor, her cable heaving up through her hawse-hole. All around him, shells exploded and shrapnel showered them. Trees leaped off the ground, branches and trunks scathed, sundered. "I love you, Rachel." A shell burst at the cannon beside "The Baby." Jesse's musket flew out of his hands. Clutching his head, he tumbled forward.

Rachel gazed at her Jesse, asleep on a cot. Squire padded up beside her and licked her knuckles, his way of reassuring her everything would be all right, she guessed. Then he walked over to Jesse. His jaw clamped and expression serious, he sat beside him as though standing guard.

Because Squire knew how to behave in hospitals, Doctors Carter and Barnett allowed him inside the hospital tents. Rachel was glad, for Squire's presence comforted her, too.

She swatted at mosquitoes. "Thank you, God," she whispered. "Thank you the shell's explosion only knocked him out. Thank you that he's just sleeping."

Regarding Freckles, Rachel's thoughts smoldered. The ignorant little man-stealer. Why did he let her get the better of him? What did he see in that other girl, a girl so uneducated she butchered the English language? And who wasn't pretty, except for her eyes. Why didn't she own eyes as pretty as hers? Kissing her husband... the way she did it...but Jesse did shove her back.

"He'll live." Mitchell eased up alongside her.

"He's been sleeping a mighty long time."

"Because he suffered a concussion." Mitchell removed his kepi. "A mild concussion. I think that was Doctor Carter's diagnosis. Jesse couldn't focus his eyes when he was brought here, and he complained about a powerful headache. According to the doc, folks suffering concussions sometimes sleep longer than they normally do. No apparent injuries other than that, he said."

"He needs the rest."

"Jesse truly does love you, Rachel."

Rachel shrugged.

"As sure as my name's Mitchell Asheworth Hayes, he does."

Rachel studied him. Mitchell's face was sad, serious, unlike the excitable, animated Mitchell she'd known before the war. Something troubled him. "How come he and Freckles kissed each other?"

"Her name's Giselle, and he didn't cotton to her. Not at first."

"Obviously, he simply adores her now."

"Adore? Not by a cat's whisker."

"Humph. I find that hard to believe."

"She's been hankering after him for weeks, wanting to court him. He wasn't after her. You are much more educated than she is, Rachel. And prettier by far. Her grammar and her speech—"

"It's atrocious. I doubt she can read a lick."

"She gets by, barely."

"All right, then." Rachel's hands clapped her hips. "Why was she after my husband if he didn't like her?"

"Because he likes her now."

"Huh?"

"At the time." Mitchell flung down his kepi. "It came out the wrong way. I didn't mean to say…Argh! He likes her, but he doesn't like her, not in the way you think he does."

Rachel hiked up her skirt and flounced out the hospital tent. Mitchell followed.

"I tried warning Jesse about that woman," Mitchell called after her. "He didn't listen."

Rachel scurried up the path toward town. Liking and loving were two different things. Why was Jesse so blind when it came to women?

She glanced back. Did Squire follow her? No. *Faithful Squire, still protecting him.*

"I loathe coming back here same as you do, boys." Marsden's heavy eyes, burning from exhaustion, blinked while he addressed his fatigued troops. A little rest would recover his spirits.

His men stood, slouched, in two ranks behind their breastworks on Slaughter's Field. He searched their haggard faces and stifled a yawn. Where was that good-for-nothing Eakin? Since he'd discovered Stella's identity, the man held an ace in his pocket. If word ever got out about her, it might ruin him, especially if Webb found out and sent word to his father, who'd certainly disown him. He'd lose his inheritance and his family's wealth. When the right opportunity presented itself, when he could kill Eakin without getting caught, he'd do it. Until that opportunity arrived, he'd bide his time and hope Eakin didn't make known his and Stella's secret.

He stifled another yawn before he resumed his speech. "We had a chance at glory and renown in Vicksburg, but our superiors, well, General Gardner received orders to return here. There's nothing we can do about it, so we might as well make the most of it." Thumbs stuck between his gun belt and trousers, he started pacing. "The enemy will return here in short order. And we will destroy him, men. Not one enemy will penetrate our lines, except he's dead. We are the best, the finest regiment in this garrison. Let no man forget that."

Hoofbeats distracted him. Giselle was driving her wagon through the sally port. He dismissed his men.

They fell out of ranks.

Marsden seethed. Soon they'd engage the enemy. Perhaps command of this center wing would devolve upon him. General Gardner had ordered General Maxey's brigade, along with Generals Rust's and Gregg's, to continue their march to reinforce Pemberton while he and Colonel Miles's Legion had returned. Thus, Gardner brought back a mere two thousand men. Perhaps, by obtaining command of the center wing, he'd finally win greatness and prove his worth to his father.

He dragged himself toward his tent. A little sleep was all he needed now. He'd throw his weary self onto his cot for a nice, long nap.

Hunting Squire, Giselle made her way into Jesse's camp. Rumors that the Yankees were advancing again stirred fear in most of the region's civilians. Many were either leaving their homes or had long gone already. Those Bluebellies didn't scare her, though.

At the river batteries, soldiers went through the motions of loading and firing the cannon while Webb, his back to her, directed some men who aimed rifles at the river below. No one noticed her.

She passed blankets spread out around campfires' charred wood, peeked inside each of the three willow log cabins. Now where was that stupid dog? She hurried out of the camp. Further hunting finally led her to him, snoring beneath a pine tree, his muzzle at rest between his forepaws and his eyes closed. She perked up her voice. "Hello there, feller."

Squire lifted his head, his alert eyes open and ears pricked forward. Giselle crouched and stroked his fur's tangled mass.

Squire sat up. His tail thumped earth.

"Want to join me, Squire? Want to have some fun?" Standing, she snapped her fingers like Jesse snapped his, twice, Squire's signal to follow. She led him to a deserted street where she'd parked her wagon. Squire scurried behind a watering trough. Here he crouched, warily watching her, as though he recalled his previous experience in Zack's hogshead.

"There, there, feller. I ain't goin' to hurt you." Reaching inside the wagon, she produced a small canvas bag. "See what I got? A treat. I have you a treat."

Squire's head cocked left. He focused on her every move, every flick of her hand, every flutter of the bag, and the stringy beef she pulled from it. At the trough, she let him sniff it.

"Yum, yum," Giselle said. "Beef. It's good."

Squire snatched it and gobbled it.

"Want some more?"

This time, she opened a small box on the wagon bed and grabbed her bottle of laudanum. From out of her skirt pocket she produced a spoon. She showed Squire the drug. "This here's laudanum, feller. It's got opium in it. My ma couldn't go nary a day without takin' some. She loved it 'bout the same way I love my snuff."

She poured a drop of laudanum into her spoon. Next, she let it drop from the spoon onto the string of beef. Squire's teeth snatched the drugged food.

While she fed him more laudanum beef and waited for him to doze, she surveyed her surroundings. Shades blocked the windows of every shop on this street, their owners up and gone.

A familiar man sat in a rocker, arms folded over his chest and his head bobbing. *Eakin, getting hisself a little nap.* She never knew Yankees could be such lazy critters. Marsden must be some mad he wasn't at the breastworks on Mister Slaughter's field.

Squire stretched out on the ground, front legs extended and hind legs splayed. He lapsed into a drug-induced sleep.

Giselle lowered the wagon's end gate. Not even its squeaky hinges awakened snoring Squire.

She squatted beside him, wormed her hands beneath his belly, wedged them between him and the dirt, but when she tried lifting him, she grunted and groaned and cursed his odor. Every muscle in her slender body strained.

"Need some help?"

Eakin's question stopped her efforts. "I can do it."

"Of course, but if you'll let me help—"

"Get away. *I said I can do it.*" She worked her hands between Squire and the dirt.

"Here." Eakin shoved her aside. He hefted Squire onto the wagon and pushed him into an iron cage, hindquarters first.

Giselle slammed the cage shut, locked it, and tossed a blanket over it. She glowered at Eakin. "I told you I don't need no man helpin' me."

"Consider it a favor then."

"Are you goin' to tell folks what I done?"

"I helped you, didn't I? Your secret is mine. I'm not fond of that dumb dog either."

"If you do—"

"I won't. Now are you going to get out of here before a less friendly person catches you?"

"Goin' to get right now." After climbing back onto her wagon bench, she drove Squire out of the garrison.

Congregating around campfires, while the late afternoon sun lingered over the treetops and cool air settled in, soldiers ate their meager rations. Jesse had finished what passed for supper when Eakin ambled up to him. He'd learned a lot about him from the garrison gossips. If everything he'd heard about him was true, he didn't like him, not one bit.

"Captain Webb." Eakin saluted lazily. "May I have a word with you?"

"A word?" Jesse said.

"Yes, sir."

"About what?"

"A transfer to your company, sir."

"I want no deserters under my command."

"I'm no coward, sir."

"Uh-huh."

"The slaves, sir. General Banks has former slaves in his army now. They're called the Native Guards. From New Orleans. I won't fight with any black man. It violates my conscience."

"Uh-huh."

"Will you do it, sir? Will you get me a transfer?"

Jesse pivoted his foot back and forth along the ground as though clearing away pebbles. After a moment's consideration, he locked his eyes on Eakin. "I have no quarrels about black folks, and I don't much care for slavery."

Eakin blinked. "Sir?"

"Slavery's an awful thing, but as far as I'm concerned I'm defending my state, my Southland, my new country, not keeping the black man in bondage. Once we win this war and have our new country, those of us Southerners who hate it can then work harder to rid ourselves of it."

"Sir. Excuse me. That makes no sense."

"It does to me."

"If the Confederacy wins this war, Captain Webb, and I sure hope it does, your slaves will always be slaves." Eakin shrugged. "I'm no abolitionist, so keeping them slaves is fine with me. A lot of us Northerners don't care about the issue one way or other, but they do care about keeping the country intact. You didn't work to end slavery before this war started. I doubt anyone will end it after the war, in which case, sir, your fighting on the Confederacy's side means you've helped your people keep them for yourselves and your future generations." Eakin shrugged again. "Makes no matter to me, sir."

"You listen to me, Eakin. If we win, I'll have helped my country win its freedom from your people's tyranny."

Eakin flashed a grin so broad Jesse swore he saw all his teeth.

"What's so funny?"

"Don't mean to sound disrespectful, but if the South does win, ending slavery is no sure thing. Your government has made it legally acceptable, what I read in the papers early in this war."

Jesse flushed. "Legal now, illegal in the future. Laws can and do often change."

"I'd like a transfer to your company. I like your command style, sir. You are a fair man."

"Well, I'd say your real reason is you hate Colonel Marsden, same as me."

Eakin spat on the ground. "Mainly, sir, I do confess."

"It's out of my hands."

"You can make a request, sir."

"I reckon I sure can, except for one wee little thing."

"Sir?"

"I won't."

Eakin spat in the dirt again. "I have some information that could ruin the dear colonel for good, about a certain lady who goes by the name of—"

"Stella. What sort of information?"

"Get me a transfer, sir. To your company, sir."

"I already know about her."

"Do you know who she really is, Captain? And your dog, sir. You'll never see him again, either."

"What're you talking about?"

"Promise me a transfer, and I'll—"

"Eakin!"

"Promise?"

"I can make no promises. Even if I did try, your transfer request may not be approved."

When Eakin turned to leave, Jesse seized his arm and wrenched it behind his back, eliciting his piggish squeal. "Tell me what happened to Squire."

"G-Giselle...Ugh...St-Stole him."

Jesse twisted his arm harder, making him wince. "When?"

"This afternoon. A...a few hours ago. At the...ugh...on a deserted street. North end of town. I saw her do it."

Jesse shoved Eakin down and ran to find Colonel Stonebridge so he could borrow his horse. He hoped the colonel didn't ask why he needed it because he'd have to tell him the truth since he couldn't bring himself to lie. And telling the truth, with the Yanks closing in...

"My apologies, Captain Webb, but you've got to go back." The lean-faced, hollow-cheeked trooper sat astride his horse. Behind him, two other troopers sat their mounts. Moonbeams played upon their rugged features.

"I must get through," Jesse said. "Somebody stole Squire."

"I'm sorry about your dog, sir. Plumb sorry. But unless you have a pass, we can't let you through. Yankees about these parts again, and sure as I'm sitting my horse, more are on the way." The trooper laid his carbine across his saddle. "Sir, you will have to return to the garrison."

"Did any of you see a gal go down this road?"

The cavalrymen shook their heads no.

"All right. I'd say I'm going." Jesse reined Colonel Stonebridge's horse around and nudged him into a slow walk. Squire, gone. Rachel, still not talking to him or letting him explain about crazy Giselle. Why did he deserve this? His heart tightened so hard it felt like he was squeezing the blood out of it. Where'd he go wrong? Should he try a different direction, evade the cavalry? Suppose he encountered a division of Yanks? He'd be either captured or killed, that's a fact. He wished he possessed a nose as keen as Squire's. Then he could smell his way to him and rescue him.

Ten minutes later, he guided his horse up a narrow path stretching north. Maybe it'd reach a major road. Perhaps, if he kept his ears open, perhaps he'd hear Squire barking.

"Turn back, sir." A muscular cavalry sergeant dismounted as Jesse approached a crossroads.

"Someone's stolen Squire," Jesse said. "I must find him."

"Sorry, Captain. Our pickets guard every crossroad. We can't let you through right now."

"But—"

"I'm sorry, sir. As much as I'd like to allow you, we can't."

"Not even for Squire?"

The sergeant wagged his head.

"Yankees?"

"They ain't that far away, sir."

Jesse swore under his breath. He turned his mount past the sergeant and the ten troopers under his command. "So long, my big furry friend. Please forgive me. I want to help you, but I can't. You're on your own, boy." *On…your…own.*

During his ride back to the garrison, Jesse's insides heated like water rising to a boil. When he first met Giselle, he didn't like her. Her flatteries and her lies, they lured him into her trap. Marsden, speaking to her that Sunday when Squire stole the tintype of Rachel, he'd wondered about them then.

Like a mortar shell bursting at night, the truth burst within his brain. Marsden was after him to wreck his marriage by using Giselle, probably so he could write Rachel and tell her about their alleged affair, which was no real affair. Giselle wanted Squire for her father. The two struck some sort of deal in this regard.

Jesse galloped his horse through the sally port, dust clouds rising round him. He reined his mount to a stop.

"Let's have it out, Colonel Marsden. Sir! You and me." Jesse swung down from the saddle and stormed up to Marsden, smoking a cigar.

"What's your problem, eh?" Marsden blew cigar smoke in Jesse's face.

Jesse coughed. He hated cigars.

Winder, standing behind Marsden, cracked his knuckles. "Need me to get him out of here, Colonel?"

"I think not, Sergeant Major. What's this all about, Webb, you and me having it out?"

"You ruined my marriage. You got my dog killed."

"Imagining things again?"

Jesse pulled off his frock coat. "Colonel, sir. Your coat. Take it off."

"Don't give me orders." Marsden dropped his cigar and crushed it beneath his boot.

"Sir, I'm giving you one now."

Marsden calmly shed his coat and spread it across his camp table. "I could have you arrested for addressing me in that manner."

Jesse flung down his kepi. "Arrest me then. I don't give a care."

Murmuring excitedly, soldiers circled the combatants.

Marsden spread his legs apart and planted his large fists on his hips.

Jesse swung at him. Marsden ducked, dodged, charged, knocking Jesse onto the ground. On his back, Jesse grunted and kicked beneath Marsden's weight. Marsden pinned his shoulders to the ground

"Captain Webb!" The voice boomed from behind the spectators. "You're under arrest. Assaulting a superior officer."

General Beall! He gained his feet once Marsden got off him. "Colonel Marsden—"

"I saw you threatening him," General Beall said, "and swinging at him. The colonel was merely defending himself. Guards!"

Two provost guards flanked Jesse's elbows.

"Take him to the guard house." Beall aimed a finger in its general direction.

Sullen and seething, Jesse accompanied them.

Twenty

———◆———

Giselle exchanged the dim firelight of her smoky house for the Rebel gray of dawn and followed her father to Squire, inside a pen.

Squire loosed two barks, hesitated…A louder bark followed.

She scratched her head. Her knuckles rubbed her sleepless eyes. All night Squire barked, ever since he'd woken from his laudanum-induced sleep. Chained flush against their T-post, he sat rigid. His fetters prevented him from standing. Scared? Calling for help? She waved his bandana at him. "Holler all you want, stupid dog. Ain't nobody comin'."

"He'll shut up quick enough." Blevin rested his arms on the pen's top rail, sighing as though now, since he had Squire, he was totally at ease.

"When will we sic the others on him?"

"After breakfast. Is Zack up?"

"Henry's helpin' him dress."

Blevin's critical eyes studied her. "Do you figure on walking around in your nightclothes all day?"

"I'll get to changin', Papa. I just didn't want to miss out seein' that cur get his just reward after what he done to Nero."

"You ain't gonna miss nothing, sweetie." Blevin moved down the line of pens to the first one, Cato's. Cato, Caesar, Brutus, all lowered their battle-scarred heads in filthy padlocked cages. All wore long chains secured to a thick post. Their rank odors hung heavy enough to choke a skunk. Dust floated in Cato's water bowl, whereas Caesar's and Brutus's water bowls were dry. All of the dogs' food dishes were dirty…and empty.

By starving his dogs, her papa was making them angrier and more aggressive, readying them to attack Squire.

Blevin raised his fists, his expression triumphant. "Good. They all look like they're in a fighting mood now. Squire's minutes are numbered."

The pop-pop of gunfire echoed in the distance.

"Sounds like it's drawing closer," Blevin said.

Zack and Henry emerged from the house.

"Probably a skirmish." Hunched on his crutch, Zack leaned forward slightly. "If the Yankees get on our land, we'll more'n likely lose the rest of our slaves to 'em."

"All three of our cotton-pickers, Zack?" Giselle said. "Lots of money we'll lose, losing them. Tee hee."

"We won't be able to work the farm anymore, Cousin."

"We can still fight our dogs and make us some money that-a-way…Cousin."

"Henry, my shotgun." Blevin jogged to the narrow path leading to his house.

"I'll hide in the stables," Zack yelled behind him. "We'll ambush 'em if they come here. Catch 'em in a cross fire."

Minié balls whizzed past Sergeant Buck Dooley, galloping ahead of his platoon. He fired his carbine at the retiring Rebel troopers. More shots from the two Bluecoat cavalry regiments scattered them off the ribbon-thin road into a small cotton field. From various points, the gray-backed horsemen wheeled their mounts around. They leveled their guns at Buck's men. A final volley crackled between regiments and Rebel pickets before the pickets galloped off.

"Halt!" The command reverberated down the blue column.

Colonel Grierson, riding in the column's van, ordered forward Dooley's company commander, Captain Pierce. Upon Pierce's return, he announced their new orders. "The Clinton Railroad's about a half mile from here. We're to tear up as much of it as we can. Let's get moving, men."

Buck's company cantered toward the railroad till his ears caught the sound—ear-piercing whines. It came from a white farmhouse up ahead.

For most of his life Buck had observed dogs. He understood them, and he loved them, and he often thanked God for creating them. Buck spurred his chestnut to overtake his captain. "Sir, that poor dog down there." He pointed at the house. "It sounds like he may be in some sort of trouble."

"You believe that's what his whining means?" Pierce said.

"It may be the case, sir, but I won't know for sure till I check on him."

Pierce's brows lifted. "So, you speak dog too, huh?"

"Please, sir, may I have your permission?"

Pierce studied the house. "You ought to have been born a dog, Sergeant."

"May I go check on the poor fellow, sir?"

"No. We've been ordered to tear up the railroad."

Buck firmed his resolve. He had to help that poor animal. "Sir, that dog."

"Sergeant? You heard what I said."

"Yes, sir. But that dog, maybe he's whining because some Rebels are there. We ought to at least check on that, sir. Permission, sir? To investigate possible Rebel activity there, sir?"

Pierced sighed heavily. "Oh, all right. Take three men with you in case you need them."

"Thank you, sir." Buck saluted. Turning in his saddle, he yelled at Privates Reynolds and Tucker, and Corporal Ingram, to accompany him. They steered their mounts away from the column and galloped toward the barks.

By the time they reached the house, a rotund old man cradling a shotgun blocked their path. Behind him, several dog cages inside pens. Snarling, the caged dogs bared their sharp teeth, but the golden-furred dog, chained to the T-post, barked loud enough to rend earth and sky.

"This is my land," the old man said. "Get out."

"What's your name?"

"Get off my land."

"Sir," Buck said, "let me see your dogs."

"They ain't hurtin' nobody."

"Not if I can help it." Buck laid his carbine across his saddle and drew his revolver from his holster. "Will you kindly lay down your weapon?"

The old man's jaw stiffened.

Buck gestured to Reynolds and Ingram.

Reynolds and Ingram walked their horses to the man and flanked him on both sides.

The old man thrust his shotgun's muzzle at Buck's face. "I'll blast you to pieces, Bluebelly. Tell 'em to back off."

Reynolds and Ingram swung down off their mounts. Tucker lifted his carbine to his shoulder but didn't aim it yet. Buck fixed his eyes on the man's gun. He'd check on those poor dogs if it took him all day or die trying. He hoped he didn't have to hurt this evil man in the process.

The old man's finger caressed his shotgun's trigger.

Buck caught Reynolds's and Ingram's glances. He nodded, and at the precise moment the man squeezed the trigger Reynolds and Tucker knocked him off his feet. The gun didn't discharge.

Buck scoffed at the man, now on his buttocks. "Load that thing next time." He strode to the dog pens.

When Buck neared the dogs, their powerful jaws clamped shut and their fierce stares locked on him. Wrath fired his brain. Their ears were torn up. The brindle one had lost an eye. All three bore ugly scars on their broad skulls. The black one suddenly lunged at his cage door, but his chain jerked him back, so he snarled.

"Fighting dogs." Buck fumed at Blevin.

"They're mine. I can treat 'em any way I want," the man said.

"Sergeant. Someone else is coming." Tucker spoke from behind him.

A girl clad in calico emerged from the house, followed by a lanky slave.

"I didn't load the gun, Marse Aaron." The slave beamed, his expression full of self-congratulation.

"You'll pay for this, Henry," Blevin snapped.

Buck gestured the slave toward their horses.

"Henry's our property," the girl said. "Everything here's our property."

"No one has the right to own another man," Buck said. "It's a sinful thing."

"We ain't believin' in sin."

"Obviously. According to the Good Book, 'A righteous man regardeth the life of his beast.'"

"We ain't righteous, either."

"So you own and abuse men, and you brutalize dogs."

"We can do anything we want," Blevin said. "Giselle and me ain't answering to nobody for nothing."

Buck raised his fist to slug Blevin. Having second thoughts, he lowered it. Blevin was way up in years. He couldn't hit him, no matter how tempted he was to do it. "Dogs are a kind and noble animal. No truer friend could a man ever have. All you have to do is give them the chance."

From the T-post, Squire let loose a piercing howl.

Buck strode to him. The stable doors banged open. He swung toward the sound and fired his revolver the same instant Zack fired at him. Zack's bullet flew wild. Buck's hit Zack in the stomach. Zack let go his crutch and tumbled forward, dead.

Screaming, sobbing, cursing the Yankees, Giselle dashed to her fallen cousin.

"Ole Buck's here, boy." Smiling genially, Buck approached Squire in a leisurely manner and offered Squire his knuckles. Squire sniffed them, licked them, then started barking again.

Buck scratched Squire's chin. "Calm down, boy. It'll be all right."

Squire's barking somewhat subsided, but he was obviously still stressed because his constant licking continued.

"You're not going to be anybody's bait dog, boy. I'll take good care of you. You're safe now." With an ache in his gut, Buck observed the bulldogs leering at his men. They also could've been good dogs if only Blevin had treated them right. "Ingram, Tucker, I'm taking this one."

On her feet, Giselle raised her fist. "You can't do that."

"No!" Blevin shouted. "No. You can't."

"Shut up. Like you two said, I can do anything I want." Buck went to his horse and took its reins from the slave. "Tucker, you and, uh…?"

"Henry, suh," Henry said.

"Henry, saddle yourself a horse and join me and Reynolds."

Henry hurried to the stables.

A sigh, deep and painful, rose inside him. Beyond him, gray clouds scudded across the sky. He squeezed shut his eyes. *God, please forgive me for what I'm about to do.* Blevin gave him no choice. At least it'd be more merciful than their present suffering. If only there wasn't this war, he could've perhaps turned them back into gentle creatures. "Corporal Ingram, you and Tucker kill these other dogs after we're gone then rejoin me at the railroad."

"We'll take care of it, Sergeant."

Buck blinked, stifling a sob. His men couldn't see him cry. It wasn't manly, but these poor dogs…tears exploded through his manly dam. Like a waterfall, they streamed down his cheeks.

Giselle watched. Giselle wept. Her father's legs fettered to Squire's former T-post, his flushed cheeks puffed. He fought the rope binding his wrists—twisting them, jerking them, and cursing up a tornado. Unarmed, she was helpless. Why, oh why couldn't she stop Ingram and Tucker from chaining him there?

Ingram's thick lips curled. "Say, Tucker, seeing as how Dog Dooley's gone, I got me a idea."

"What kind of idea?" Tucker said.

"Got food in your smokehouse, Rebel woman?"

"Ain't we supposed to be killing these hounds?" Revolver in hand, Tucker spoke from the animals' cages.

"I'm talking to the little Reb here. I asked her a question."

Hatred steeled Giselle's heart. Her eyes burned. Silently, she swore. Of course, there was food in the smokehouse.

"Keep a eagle eye on her, Tucker. I'll be back directly." Ingram crossed the small yard to a long brick building, the smokehouse.

Once he entered it, she addressed Tucker. "Ain't you men tired of war?" Gathering up her skirt, she stepped toward him.

Tucker cocked his pistol.

Giselle halted at arm's length. "You ain't goin' to kill a lady. Don't it go against your morals?"

Tucker aimed his pistol at her chest. "We're birds of a feather, you and me, woman. I got no morals. Besides, you're one of them fancy women. I'd lay money down on it."

She started forward again.

"Get away, Rebel woman," Ingram shouted from the smokehouse entrance.

She retreated and sat on her top porch step.

While her father's curses bombarded him, Ingram stuffed chunks of meat inside his shirt, boots, and trousers.

Shouldn't she tear Ingram away from him? But if she did, Tucker would kill them both. Her attention wandered to Zack, sprawled face down in blood pooling round his lifeless form. His pistol, not far away. The distance from the porch to his pistol…maybe about… thirty or so yards thereabouts. Her hands on her knees, she made a move to stand.

"Don't try it, woman." Ingram and Tucker went around behind the dogs' padlocked cages.

Giselle raged, angry unmentionable words roaring through her mind, mingling with her stifled tears of grief.

Ingram held up the keys to the shackles he'd locked onto her father's ankles. "Where are the keys to the dogs' chains and the cages' padlocks?"

"Don't tell him," Blevin screamed.

"I ain't," Giselle shouted.

"My oh my, you sure are a fistful of feisty, aren't you?" Ingram flashed an amused grin. "Keep your gun on her, Tucker. Kill her if she moves. I'm going inside their house and hunt for those keys." Minutes later Ingram returned outside, keys in hand.

"Now what're you doing, Ingram?" Tucker said.

Ingram waved his revolver at Giselle. "These dogs know you. Take off their chains and collars."

"I will not."

Ingram thrust his pistol's muzzle against her breasts. "I'll kill you."

She steadied herself. Her words came out strong. "I ain't unchainin' our dogs."

His demeanor dark and dangerous, Ingram cocked his gun's hammer.

"Aw, don't go killing no female," Tucker said. "We don't want that on our conscience, least I don't."

Ingram shoved her hard. "Sit down. I'll do it. Tucker, if she or those dogs make any sort of false move, kill 'em."

"My dogs'll kill both of you, all right," Belvin shouted. "You two are fools. Fools!"

Talking softly to the animals, Ingram entered Caesar's pen. At that dog's cage, he stretched forth his hand in a friendly gesture and beckoned him to come. Crouching low, Caesar growled.

"Let me see your collar here, fellow."

As though he understood Ingram's intentions, Caesar ceased growling and wagged his tail. Ingram reached between the bars and unlocked his leather collar. His chain thudded on the crate floor. Next Caesar whirled on him and snapped. Ingram jerked his hand clear of the dog's teeth. "Whew. Not getting a piece of me today, dumb varmint."

At Brutus's cage, the dog banged against it barking and snapping. Ingram reached between his cage's bars, partway before he jerked back.

"I told you he was going to kill you," Belvin shouted.

"Shut up, old man." Ingram tossed Tucker the keys. "Unlock 'em from their posts while I distract 'em."

"I don't know, Ingram. Maybe we'd better—"

"Do what I say. You hear?"

Reluctantly, cautiously, and trembling a little, Tucker knelt behind the cages. When he tried taking Brutus's chain off his post, Brutus whirled toward him and charged. Tucker shot away; horror filled his eyes.

"All right, Tucker. Here. You feed 'em with this sack of pork while I do it." He took the keys and freed the remaining dogs, Cato and Brutus, from their chains while Tucker distracted them by tossing food between their cages' bars.

After this, Ingram tossed morsels of pork left and right on his way to her father.

Giselle's eyes went wide. *No!* He can't do what he's doing. She stormed to him, her hot blood racing, and snatched at the keys, but Ingram, who was much taller, held them high and out of her reach.

"Gimme those keys," Giselle said. "You ain't unlockin' our dogs' cages."

"I ain't?" Smirking, Ingram went to Caesar's cage. "Why don't you want me to do it? I thought they'd kill me if I did." He chuckled.

Giselle met him at the cage and swiped his hand aside.

Ingram plowed his fist into her stomach. "Don't do that again, little Reb."

Doubling over and collapsing from the pain, the wind whooshed out of her. Weeping, aching, all her efforts to stop him failed.

Ingram unlocked each cage's padlock but left the locks on their hooks. Before she'd recovered from Ingram's brutal punch, he and Tucker, guffawing, mounted their horses and galloped off.

Giselle dashed to Caesar's cage to lock it back, but Caesar hurled himself against the gate, popped out the lock, and sprinted past her to freedom. He snatched a morsel off the ground before glowering up at her, chewing and gobbling down his meat. Fear surged through her and jerked her out of his path.

"Over here," her father yelled. "Hurry."

Cato and Brutus banged out of their cages.

Giselle made for Zack's revolver.

"Brutus," her father screamed. "No! Heel! Heel!"

She wheeled toward the dogs and fired at them as they sprang atop her father. Her shaky hand made the first shot missed Cato. The second shot missed Caesar. Brutus sprinted for the woods. Another shot cracked at him and missed.

Her father's bones crunched beneath his powerful attackers' jaws.

She steadied her tremble. Three bullets left. *Stay calm.* She must make them count.

Cato and Caesar lunged at each other, Cato atop Caesar, Caesar on his back, Caesar's legs flailing. At point blank range, she cocked her revolver and triggered a round, an action she repeated three times. *Pop! Pop! Pop!* Cato dropped limp, over her father's body. Caesar, too. Both dead. Like her father. Blood covered his face and neck. Brutus, though, cheated its cold grip.

Outside the guardhouse, Jesse saluted Colonel Stonebridge. "Thank you for getting me released, sir."

"Be aware, Captain, that General Gardner merely suspended your arrest. Considering the circumstances and what Marsden did to you,

I might be able to get you off completely." Stonebridge punched his shoulder in a friendly manner. "Maybe if I succeed in that, your father-in-law will give me a discount on a desk next time I visit his store."

"If he doesn't, sir, I will. My solemn guarantee."

"The day of battle is near. We'll need every available man to fight the Yanks. From now on, you will steer clear of Marsden. After all this is over, perhaps we can prove he was behind Squire's getting stolen."

"If he keeps on pestering me, sir?"

Stonebridge looked Jesse in the eye. "In that case, Captain Webb, I hereby officially order you to make him eat his teeth."

Parting ways, Stonebridge headed for General Gardner's headquarters at the hotel. Jesse shuddered beneath a blanket of cold misery. He shambled toward the post hospital. Rachel's accusations against him were false. Why, then, should he be a disgrace in her eyes? He wasn't a disgrace. He felt like a disgrace. Giselle. Yes, Giselle was the disgrace. He knew better than to trust that ignorant gal, yet he'd done it, and his foolishness may have cost poor Squire his life.

Squire's whimpers blared in his mind, also his barks and his howling pleas.

"Jesse Webb," he muttered. "You are an idiot. You are the disgrace." He paused just shy of the hospital tent. "Please, Squire. Please come back to me alive."

Rachel nearly bumped into him as she hurried out the tent door. Halting suddenly, her eyes hardened. Her face was red as fire; she trembled like a bomb about to explode. "You!" she screamed.

Jesse backed against a tree.

"You are to blame!"

"Rachel, Giselle and I—"

"I don't mean that ignorant girl, Husband." She poked his chest hard. "I'd forgiven you for that. I was trying to teach you a lesson. But now you've done it. You've really done it. I am supremely mad. It's your fault Squire's gone. Your fault... Husband." She jabbed his chest harder. "You... you should've never let him go to war with you. I warned you, you stubborn man. All you men...stubborn as mules." She jabbed him a third time. "Mule-headed, all of you."

Jesse seized her hand and glanced around them. "Shush."

Three nearby women who'd been watching them turned their heads and continued washing pans and hanging clothes. Jesse knew they'd heard Rachel's every word, though. Thankfully, they were Creoles who'd accompanied a Louisiana regiment. They didn't understand much English, only French.

"How did I know the war would last this long?" His question flew out of his mouth louder than he intended it.

"I also asked you not to hurt Colonel Marsden." Rachel lowered her volume.

"I kept my promise there, gal. I didn't kill him. Colonel Stonebridge made me promise to stay away from him."

"You'll keep that promise the same way you kept *my* Squire safe, I suppose?"

"Listen to me, will you? I love Squire as much as you do, and I'm just as devastated about it as you are. I don't need you heaping more guilt on me." Jesse stumbled over his explanation—how he'd fallen into Marsden's trap when he used Giselle as the bait. "I was stupid to fall into it, Rachel. It was total, absolute stupidity. I'm an idiot. Satisfied?"

"Humph. At least we agree on that. Don't blame others for your own misdeeds."

"I'm not blaming others."

"If Squire turns up dead, I'll never speak to you again."

"What about me? What if I get killed? Don't you still love me?"

Her countenance softened for a half-minute. She hurried back inside the tent.

Through cupped hands, he shouted, "I love you." He turned on his heel and left.

Buck dropped another hardtack cracker on the grass. Bivouacked on a plantation near the Bayou Sara Road, he'd roped Squire to a tree and allowed him plenty of slack so he could move around and stretch his legs.

Yawning and sitting on the ground cross-legged, the sergeant leaned his head against the tree. "Boy, we have had us one dickens of a day, haven't we? Tearing up the Rebs' railroad and telegraph wires and confiscating their beef cattle."

Squire quickly crunched the cracker Buck had moistened from his canteen's water, and then, lifting his head, swallowed it.

Buck scratched the dog's side. Squire licked his face appreciatively. Now what would he name him? Buck pondered. No, he wouldn't give him a name. He'd let Molly, his four-year-old daughter, name him. He hoped she and her mother weren't too sad about his long absence. He knew they prayed for him every day. This comforted him. "You'll make my little Molly a fine companion." His fingers vanished through Squire's soft, rich fur.

Cows mooed.

Squire stood and stretched, his forelegs extended and his back arching. Then he sat and offered Buck his right paw.

"Look at you, boy. We know a few tricks, do we?' Buck shook Squire's paw.

Squire lowered it and offered his left paw, which Buck also gently shook. Then he padded closer, stretched out on the grass, and rested his head on Buck's lap.

Some folks considered him crazy, the way he talked to dogs. "Dog Dooley," his men called him behind his back, unaware that he knew it. Well, he liked that name. People could learn a lot from dogs if they paid attention to them—observed and studied them—gratitude, love, respect if well trained. Dogs were good listeners, the best listeners, and unlike most humans, they never gossiped.

"She can't walk, you know. You see, she has this, uh, this problem in her limbs. She gets around in a wheelchair tolerably good. She doesn't have many friends, boy. Most children don't understand her condition too well. Some even tease her. Her best friend died a few days before the war started. Know who her best friend was? He was a little white dog. I promised her I'd get her another one. Once this campaign is over and I can manage a furlough, I'm taking you to her. You are a gentle soul. You will make her a very fine friend."

"I'm sorry, Mistuh Buck. I couldn't help but listen." Henry emerged from a thicket of pines.

"Well, get your body over here and join us."

"I heard you talking about your Molly. That dog does have an owner, suh."

"Do you know him?"

Henry shook his head. "Some soldier feller in Port Hudson. The dog's name is Squire. He kilt one of Marse Blevin's dogs in a fight, and that's why my marse—"

"You have no more marses," Buck said. "You're free now. Many thousands of men in my army's ranks are fighting for your people's freedom. It is an unfortunate thing, however, that many other thousands of my people still look down on yours. Not me, though. I'm glad you are your own man now. That's why I'm in this war—to liberate your race from bondage. Skin color doesn't matter. Every man has a right to have his freedom."

"And I'm mighty grateful to you for that, suh, but as I was saying, Squire kilt one of Blevin's dogs in a fight and that's why Blevin wanted to have him kilt."

"You mean you're telling me this dog killed a fighting bulldog?"

"I reckon he was smarter than ole Nero, the dog Squire kilt."

"Smarter, indeed. Do you know Squire's owner's name?"

"Jesse Webb. A cap'n he is, I think, suh."

"Thank you, Henry." Buck massaged Squire's neck. Funny, how dogs loved everyone no matter their skin color or where they came from. Dogs had more sense than humans in that regard.

Buck considered Squire's owner. Although they fought on opposing sides, and though they didn't know each other, they held a sort of kinship, a kinship bound by this dog called Squire. He'd once heard a story about how General Washington's soldiers captured a British general's dog. Under a flag of truce, Washington returned his enemy's dog to him. If he ever got close enough to the Rebel lines, maybe he'd do Squire's owner a similar favor, his superiors permitting, of course. Maybe, before this war ended, he'd find another kind dog to take to his Molly during a furlough.

Evening cloaked Buck's bivouac. He'd gone off on a raid against a nearby Rebel cavalry camp. Squire stretched out on his stomach and rested his head between his forepaws. He gazed at the vast acreage, at the flickering campfires, and the thousands of tents. Beside one of these fires, Henry slept. The earth cooled Squire's belly. He liked Buck, even enjoyed his company and his soothing speech, but this wasn't home. Down this road, there was home. How far down? Squire didn't know.

Squire got to his paws and moved forward till something jerked him to an abrupt halt. That thing stopping him—the rope. Frustrated, he collapsed on the grass and puffed air out his nostrils. Home. He wanted to go home. Turning where he could seize the thin rope between his teeth, he clenched it with single-minded purpose. Strand by strand, the restraint yielded to his determined jaws.

A short time passed. Squire quit gnawing when some nearby bushes rustled. An evil presence lurked there. Squire sensed it, smelled it. His hackles rose. He growled.

Evil emerged from the bushes. Brutus.

Squire's heart lurched. Brutus charged. Squire leaped sideways, his gnawed rope snapping apart like a whip and draping his body. With Brutus breathing behind him, Squire dashed for some horses grazing in a pasture. Brutus stayed on Squire's tail.

"Stop, Brutus!" Suddenly awake, Henry sprang to his feet and frantically waved his floppy straw hat.

Squire stoked his engine, drove himself harder, faster, to escape his foe. He veered toward some slave cabins just ahead. A look behind him…Brutus had dropped back though his pursuit continued.

Squire passed a flock of sleeping geese, wedged his muzzle between a cabin's door jamb and its door. No one inside the small cabin. He eased back the door and darted inside.

Scooting beneath a wooden bed, his heart galloped. While he awaited Brutus, hoping he'd go on past, time crept on. Soon the door opened wider. In its entrance, Brutus loomed. Frightened down to his paws, Squire's muscles refused to budge.

Outside Squire's cabin, hisses sounded the attack. Wide-spreading wings charged Brutus from all sides— the geese Squire saw earlier.

Brutus lunged at the goose on his right, but rolled over twice in a flurry of feathers. From his left, another goose attacked, his bill pecking him hard. Brutus scrambled to his feet, sprang for that bird's neck. Three ganders walloped his hindquarters.

Down went Brutus, rolling against another goose. The others attacked. Yelping, and after a brief struggle, he regained all fours and rabidly snapped at every bird as they, hissing and honking and huge wings flapping, tightened their circle. A frenzy of feathers followed, feathers and dog everywhere, like a storm. Had Brutus not been outnumbered, he might have waxed victorious. Instead, he killed one goose before barreling through the feathered mass and retreating down the road.

For a long time, Squire cowered beneath the bed opposite the cabin's opened door. His nose twitched. He didn't smell Brutus. What about the geese? Would they attack him, too? Finally deciding he'd make a run for it, Squire crawled out from beneath his hiding place. He went to the doorway. First his long muzzle, next his wedge-shaped head poked out into the fresh evening breeze. No Brutus. Heads tucked into their bodies, the geese appeared to be sleeping again.

Squire sprinted down the road. Since neither hisses nor flapping noises pursued, he dropped to a walk. His internal compass urged him eastward, away from the scene of near-death.

For the rest of the week, Squire wandered from crossroad to crossroad. Union soldiers occupied some of these spots. They fed him hardtack and salt pork. At a couple of camps, he spent the night, lingering for a day or two while he fattened on the spoils. One soldier liberated him from his rope. He sensed something big brewing. The Yankees' excited voices told him this, as did the occasional, distant musketry.

One morning during sunrise, distant booms awakened him. Squire rolled to his feet and squished the soft earth as he strolled to a road, where he happened upon a large body of Union soldiers chattering quietly. They marched in disciplined order and mashed the dirt road into powder, their muskets at shoulder arms.

Squire trotted past these soldiers, past their horse-drawn cannons rolling on creaking wheels, and down the long column of soldiers on horseback.

Instantly, Buck spotted him. "I thought you were a-goner, boy." The wiry sergeant's bright eyes held joy.

Squire barked happily and trotted alongside Buck's clopping horse.

"Henry told me about the bulldog chasing you. I arrested those men who didn't kill him like I ordered them to. Go on, now. Go find yourself a good hiding place. There's a big fight in the making."

Buck's pleasant tone soothed Squire. Understanding "go," he ranged ahead. A short time later, how many minutes Squire did not know, he rounded a crossroad. Quite a ways ahead, a two-story building attracted his attention. He'd passed it two days ago. What was inside it? What was about to happen?

He wandered around the building, peered in its windows, and sniffed it. No outside stairs. He went around to the front. Shouts caught his curiosity. Infantrymen stacked their guns. A treat! Did any of them have a treat? He ran toward them, past horses drawing cannon farther down the road.

A large man eyed him mildly. "Take a look at this, Sergeant."

"I remember seeing that dog the other day, Lieutenant. I wished he'd gone back home. I'd hate to see him get hisself hurt or killed when our fighting starts."

The lieutenant tugged his mustache thoughtfully. "See if that store up the road is unlocked, Jones. If it is, put him in there till after the battle. We can't go any further till General Banks arrives."

"Yes, sir." Jones tapped his thigh. "C'mon, good boy. Follow me now."

Squire sat and held up his right paw.

Jones knelt almost eye-level with him and shook it. Squire held up his left paw next, which Jones also shook. As Jones stood, Squire put a huge, wet lick on his cheek.

"That's enough, good dog." Jones wiped his cheek with the back of his hand. "Let's get now. C'mon."

Tail batting air, Squire followed Jones back down the road to the two-story building. Jones gave its door a shove. "Good. It's open." He tapped his thigh. "C'mon. Let's get inside."

Squire followed him through the doorway. To their right, flush against a wall, stood a dusty upright piano. A big chandelier hung from the ceiling, and a counter stretched out along most of the store's left side. Behind the counter stood two tall shelves. One of them held bottles of all sizes and shapes. Pigeonholes lined the other one.

Jones picked up a bowl and some kind of fat stick from off the counter. "Mortar and pestle. Must be a drugstore. Post office, too, by the look of those pigeonholes."

Squire wagged his tail fast when Jones stooped beside him.

"Listen, good boy. I want you to stay here for now. All right? I'm going to close this store's door so you can't get out. I don't want you outside in case any shooting starts."

Squire's quick licks bathed Jones's cheeks.

Again, Jones wiped off Squire's saliva with the back of his hand before he returned to the door. Though Squire followed, he didn't get far. Jones slipped out too quickly and closed the door behind him.

Squire pawed the door hard and barked as loud as he could. No one responded. He padded over to a window. Nose pressed against a pane, he watched the soldiers make battle preparations. Unable to see Jones among them, boredom settled in. He found a spot behind the counter. Here he stretched out completely, his hind legs splayed and his muzzle rested on his forepaws. He hated this place.

Sometime later shooting roused Squire. He ran to a window. Deafening explosions everywhere. He scurried back behind the counter. One shell smashed through the window he'd been peering through.

He poked his muzzle past the counter. A shell banged the store's piano, exploding and scattering its ivory keys and pedals all over the floor, its housing and lid practically smashed into firewood amidst its keys' hammers and strings. It also smashed enough panes out of a window for him to escape, so he scrambled out the window and ran from the store amidst shells and flying Minié balls, through the smoke of gunpowder and away from Port Hudson and away from the fighting. Again, home would have to wait.

Twenty One

———◆———

While General Banks's army slowly strangled Port Hudson, Jesse and his comrades worked themselves into a sweat defending it. General Gardner reassigned his commanders. To Colonel Miles went the right wing, General Beall the center, and Colonel Stonebridge the left clear down to the Mississippi River. Lieutenant Colonel Cox commanded Jesse's regiment.

Stonebridge posted himself on a hill they called Commissary Hill, from where he could conduct the pending battle in the works about a mile beyond him. Behind it were the garrison's commissary depot, arsenal, and grist mill. "Observe the enemy, oppose his advance, but don't get into a serious engagement," Stonebridge told Jesse and his other subordinates. "General Gardner's orders."

The harder Jesse drove himself into military duties, the swifter his worries swirled inside his mind. Squire's death, Rachel's stubbornness, and, despite all his efforts to convince himself that he wasn't defending slavery, that he was fighting for his state, his Southland, driving the Yankees out of it, his private struggles mounted. Though admitting it irritated him, maybe that sorry excuse of humanity, Eakin, was right, maybe if the South won this war, slavery would never be abolished and he…he berated himself. Before the war, he'd rarely voiced his opinion against it. He'd fretted too much about what others would think and how it would affect his father-in-law's business. So, what made him think he'd voice his opinion after the war, after they won it, if, indeed, they did win it? Alabama had a right to secede. The Yankees started all this bloodletting. They were the invaders.

"For a man who has a college education, Webb," he muttered, "your thinking sure gets twisted out of sorts at times. Once we win this war and have our new country, I'll do everything in my power to bring an end to human bondage. Then everyone will know where I stand."

Though he'd come to despise war, Jesse's blood was up. He'd lost his dog and his wife's affections. Fight and get it over with fast. He wanted to go home. Go home? Without Rachel? Without Squire? He berated himself.

By midnight, four Yankee divisions surrounded Port Hudson, and more kept closing in. Rebel cavalry fought to hold them back. Stonebridge threw out skirmishers, four companies, including Jesse's, under Cox's command.

Firefights erupted between Cox's skirmishers and Federal troops beyond Big Sandy Creek. Repeatedly, Jesse and his men repulsed the enemy until finally, on the eve of May 25, he and his men fell back through the swamp to some high ground not far from their main defenses. Here, they stacked arms and rested. From somewhere below, enemy soldiers took shots at them, their ammunition wasted since no one was hit.

Bone-weary from the fight, Jesse lay on his back, his hands behind his head. Mitchell and Utley stacked wood for a small fire. Staring up at the sky, he imagined its stars mocking him. Never again would he and his dear Rachel dance beneath the moonlight at socials back home. Never again would he and Squire enjoy hunting and fishing trips. Sleep forsook him. He imagined himself rising, rising, rising up into the blackness overhead.

The Yankees had sealed them tighter than a corked jug. Cut off by land and by the enemy's river fleet, they'd suffocate like a rat trapped in that jug unless they dealt the enemy such decisive blows they'd be forced back from whence they'd come. At least they'd bought another day to strengthen their weak line.

Hoofbeats neared. Jesse lifted his head to see Colonel Stonebridge astride his mount. He sat up, followed by Mitchell and Utley.

The colonel continued on to meet Cox, coming up from behind them. Stonebridge spoke his order loud and clear enough for the entire Alabama regiment to hear him. "Colonel Cox, General Gardner has ordered me to advance and feel for the enemy. Take your regiment and go forward until you have found him. When you do, hit him hard."

Cox snapped a salute. Turning to his men, he shouted, "On your feet, my good lads. On your feet. There's more work to do."

Groaning, Jesse loaded his pistol. His men scrambled for their muskets. Back down the bluff they moved, into the swamp, the full moon's light guiding their path.

The lunar light fanned through the swamp's heavy foliage and skimmed its brackish water. His nose revolted against its stench as his legs bumped logs, stirring the fetid water. Natural obstacles broke up their formation. Where were the Yankees? He'd not heard any gunfire since they'd entered this place.

Once through the swamp, the Rebels came upon a clearing. Dead trees, shrubbery, briars…

Pop-pop! Up ahead, Yankees, shooting from behind the timbers and other brush.

Unable to manage a clear shot, Jesse cocked his revolver and fired wildly. From the underbrush, gunfire clattered and musket barrels fumed black powder. Minié balls whistled past. He dropped to one knee; the mud sucked at his leg. Clutching his thigh, a nearby soldier fell. A second man dropped, a big crimson hole knocked through his chest.

Someone jerked his arm from behind. "Let's go, Jesse. We're retiring." Mitchell jerked him harder, Minié balls zipping. "Colonel Cox ordered us to fall back."

"Fall back? Where to?"

"Back to where we came from, stupid!"

Aware that Mitchell's excitable nature provoked his outburst, Jesse withheld a reprimand. Truthfully, he probably didn't realize he'd called him a name. Jesse followed Mitchell and the others through dense battle smoke and a hailstorm of bullets, back to their breastworks.

The Yankees' failure to launch a major assault on the twenty-fifth and twenty-sixth was a gift to the garrison, allowing the Rebels more time to build up their position.

Along Jesse's line, engineers supervised slaves erecting its fortifications and breastworks. Rifle pits were dug, trees felled in ravines, and four cannons were brought to Commissary Hill to defend the commissary depot. Every vulnerable spot Stonebridge could think of, he ordered strengthened. Before dawn on the twenty-seventh, the work was done and Stonebridge told Cox he was confident he could repulse any Yankee attack.

This was said before he ordered Cox to take four companies to a forward position north of the granary. Jesse's company was one of them Cox selected for this duty. As Jesse led his men to their new position, he pondered Marsden, posted along the center wing. Jesse mumbled a "thank you" to no one in particular. A "thank you" to General Gardner, perhaps, for not sending Marsden's regiment to this sector, because he'd probably kill him. That way, he could tell his dear, trusting Rachel that an enemy bullet felled him in battle, which would not have been a lie.

Meanwhile, shells from the enemy's mortar boats rained down on the garrison, making for an uneasy night.

Starlight seeped through the trees, illuminating a dim path for Henry as he and his regiment, the Third Louisiana Native Guards, marched toward their battle position. Frank, Blevin's former slave who'd helped Squire escape from the hogshead, marched behind him. Frank had gone to Baton Rouge where he'd enlisted in this regiment. Ahead of them marched the First Louisiana Native Guards. They moved swiftly, in a long column, till their officers halted them for a rest.

Henry settled down against a tree. Frank stood beside him and peered at the distant Rebel position. They'd been deployed on the farthest end of Stonebridge's left flank. Here, on the other side of a creek, the Rebels' defensive line turned southward toward the Mississippi River.

Before the war, New Orleans's free black population was the largest in the South. Now many of its free black men served in the First Louisiana Native Guards. French-speaking, some were educated and wealthy. Black line officers, lieutenants and captains, commanded many of these men.

For the former slaves who comprised the Third, however, all their officers were white.

Henry looked up at Frank. "Do you think we'll get us a chance tomorrow? At them Rebels?"

"Now how in tarnation do I supposed to know dat?" Frank said. "Ain't neither one of us got much soldier training. I got more'n you, but not by much. If we do attack dem, dey may not let me and you do it."

"We may not be ready yet, Frank, but I'd sure like to do it." Henry stood up. A week earlier, he'd been handed a musket and joined Frank and the Third. He wore no uniform yet, and it was only by constant begging that he'd been allowed to join this regiment in time for the battle. No training, no army discipline... "You'll be doing garrison duty behind the lines, anyway," a lieutenant told him. "But I'm still supposed to teach you how to use this thing. General Dwight's orders." Dwight was their division commander.

"Frank." A soldier offered Frank his canteen. He winked at them. "Got some fine whiskey in this one. You men wanna share?"

"Where'd you get dat?"

"One of them white officers sneaked it to me. Promised me all of us men would get us some come morning."

Frank seized it and took a swig. "Thank you, Pete. You is a good man."

Pete offered some to Henry.

Henry shook his head.

"He don't drink," Frank said.

Henry's eyes followed Frank as his friend accompanied Pete to a more private spot. Well, they weren't behind the lines anymore. Question is, would he and his fellow soldiers be given a chance to prove themselves tomorrow? And more importantly, if they were allowed to fight, would he run from the first bullet fired at him, or would he be brave?

Twenty Two

─────◆─────

Jesse stayed the night in a wooded region north of the granary. While the enemy's mortar schooners harassed them, Jesse pondered Rachel. Except when necessary, she no longer spoke to him. He still loved her. He wanted to visit her. Why couldn't she forgive him about Squire? Then again, why should he expect her to? If only he could embrace her one last time, experience that spark that once resided within her, and hear her merry laugh.

An enemy cannonade announced the dawn; the mortar boats' bombardment died. Flying iron blackened the skies; shot and shell blasted the Confederate right and center. In Colonel Stonebridge's sector, however, artillery and muskets remained mute. Five hundred men defended this wooded position, keeping the enemy at bay long enough for Colonel Stonebridge to finish his defenses, or so they all hoped.

"Wonder what they're up to." Mitchell unholstered his revolver. "I don't like it. Too quiet where we are."

"Those blame mortar boats kept me awake all night." Utley yawned and stretched his arms skyward. "Since I couldn't sleep, I'm exhausted."

"Don't you worry," Jesse said. "We'll all forget our weariness once our little fight starts here."

"You think this is where they're going to attack?" Mitchell said.

Jesse nodded. "You know something, Mitch? I wish we'd all managed to settle our affairs peaceably, the Yankees and us. You and I both hate slavery. We both know it's wrong, but the Yanks—"

"The Yanks tried bullying us and invaded our land." Mitchell turned on his heel and started walking off. Over his shoulder, he said, "That's also wrong. My conscience is clear about this war."

"Have you suddenly turned abolitionist on us, sir?" Utley said.

"I'm just sick and tired of this war," Jesse said. "I wish those Yanks had just minded their own affairs, then none of this killing would've ever happened."

"Bluebellies a-coming!" Hickam screamed.

From out of the opposite woods the soldiers in blue advanced, a great human wave threatening to engulf Jesse and his comrades.

Grudgingly, the Rebels surrendered ground. Foot by foot, inch by inch, they popped off rounds as they retreated through the pines. From behind trees and felled timbers, they turned and cut down Yankees stepping and stumbling over their dead while tightening their lines.

Chest heaving, knuckles whitening round his revolver's butt, Jesse jumped behind a magnolia tree. Catching a whiff of gunpowder, he glanced up through the tree's limbs, drew a deep breath, then stepped out from behind it to face his foe.

The enemy halted, leveled rifled muskets at them, and fired. Two men beside Jesse fell, one shot in the chest and the other man in the forehead. Jesse triggered a bullet.

"Fall back!" Cox waved his sword. "Fall back! Back, my lads! Back!"

Stubbornly, the Rebels continued their retreat, pausing to duck behind trees, shrubs, and logs to answer the enemy's rifles. But five hundred Rebels against thousands of Yankees? Jesse doubted they'd stop the Bluecoats for very long.

Moving south, they fought the advancing foe, scattered by ravines as they struggled down them.

Rebel musketry crackled, picking off dozens like slaughtering chickens in a coop.

More than an hour later, the Federals closed around them. The blue tide surged toward their ranks.

"The redoubt!" Cox screamed. "Move it! Move it!"

Jesse snatched a shotgun from a dead soldier. Hoping it was loaded, he whirled and squeezed its trigger. Three Yankees closing on him suffered its blast. He and his comrades continued southward, soon making their way through the rugged valley of Little Sandy Creek, past rifle pits and over breastworks. Jesse stumbled, regained his footing. Utley and Mitchell ran behind him, following their men.

Artillery fire punctuated their retreat— the 15th Arkansas occupying a lunette and the batteries on Commissary Hill dueling with recently arrived Union batteries, which had gained the crest of the ridge.

At the crest overlooking the valley of Little Sandy, some two hundred yards from Jesse's fortification, the Yankee advance stalled. Far beneath them stretched the ravine-pocked valley full of felled timbers. Jesse guessed they might be debating whether or not to continue their attack through the intimidating terrain.

For the moment, though, the artillery duel captured Jesse's attention. White crosses nailed to trees on the enemy's ridge gave the Rebel cannoneers their range. One hit after the other they scored, exploding Yankee cannon off their carriages, dealing death to men and horses.

"I reckon we didn't get spared after all," Mitchell said.

"I reckon I told you right," Jesse said, "and they didn't even leave us a calling card."

Mitchell chuckled bitterly.

The enemy didn't hesitate long. Down into the ravines they came, not in any disciplined order due to the obstructions, natural and manmade, which fragmented their lines. Like big blue ants, they moved over hillocks and around fallen tree limbs.

"Hold your fire." Cox paced behind them. "Wait till they're within range."

One of Stonebridge's aides hurried up to Cox, saluted, and said, "Colonel Stonebridge's compliments, sir. He wants you to take command of Major Bennett's redoubt."

Cox returned the aide's salute. "I'm on my way. Major Knox, you're in command here."

"Yes, sir," the major said.

Yankee shells exploded near Commissary Hill's battery, spewing iron fragments, smashing the granary. Shooting from fallen trees below the battery, snipers picked off its gunners. Colonel Stonebridge, observing the battle through his telescope, dropped behind the parapet, followed by survivors of the sniping. One by one, their battery's guns suffered destruction from Union artillery, till the enemy's cannon blasted them out of commission.

Cox ran toward the lunette, which guarded the garrison's bull pen, its cannons blazing away at enemy artillery.

Disorganized as it was, the blue-clad infantry advanced ever closer. Behind their parapet, Jesse's men stood five feet apart. Two provost guard companies manned the works on their right.

"Buckshot and ball," Major Knox said as he went down the line of men from captain to captain. "Wait till the enemy gets within forty yards of our rifle pits before opening fire."

Jesse repeated these orders to Sergeant Hickam. Hickam passed them on to Mitchell and Utley, who relayed them to their platoons. Armed with flintlock muskets, their guns' effective range stopped at forty yards.

"Here, sir. I got this off Lane during our skirmish." Hickam handed Jesse a powder flask and a shot pouch.

"He got killed?" Jesse slung the flask across his shoulder.

"'Fraid so, sir. We lost about ten men so far."

"We're all gonna have to answer to God one day for all this killing." Jesse started loading his shotgun. Suppose he did get killed today? Would Rachel mourn his passing? Despite her fierce stubbornness, he'd loved her so much he was willing to overlook that. She was, after all, beautiful. Maybe they should get a divorce when this war ended. If he did survive this war, he'd ask her for a divorce. But wouldn't that disgrace her? Yes? No? Wouldn't…?

Onward the Yankees came, struggling over rocks and logs, past underbrush and through trees, the ravine's obstructions breaking them into squads.

"Forty yards they are, boys." Knox raised his saber. "Fire!"

Rifle pits and parapets cut loose, a barrage of flame and white smoke. The blasts sliced holes in enemy lines. The Yankees wavered, fell back.

Rallying for a second charge, they came on the Alabamans at a run, yelling, shooting. The Alabamans' muskets clattered like a string of fireworks. Clutching their heads and faces, hundreds of enemy soldiers toppled over brush and felled timber.

Jesse reloaded his shotgun, his pistol next.

Mitchell dashed past him. "On fire!"

Flames danced off the provost guards' breastworks. Jesse and Utley raced to the pending disaster. With Mitchell, they ripped out its revetments—the burning fence rails—threw them in the dirt and stomped out the fire. Mitchell gripped his chest and tumbled forward.

"Mitch!" Jesse dropped beside his friend.

Groaning, Mitchell barely moved.

Blinded by fury, Jesse leaped atop the parapet. A blue mass spread out before him. Swearing, he blasted it with his shotgun and emptied his pistol at them.

"Cap'n!" Hickam yanked him off the parapet.

Jesse landed on his buttocks as a bullet whistled over his head.

"They're retiring back to their ridge, sir. They're out of range."

During the fracas along Jesse's line, the First and Third Native Guards waited their chance in the woods.

Henry clutched his musket. Nervous sweat dampened his palms. Though his gun weighed a mere ten pounds, today it felt heavier. His mouth tasted like sawdust; his heart pummeled his ribcage. *Don't run. Whatever you do, don't run.* "I heard someone say last night General Dwight don't believe we can fight." Henry assumed his position beside Frank.

"De man got de stupids, same as dem Southern whites," Frank said.

Henry eyed him curiously. "You drank too much of that whiskey them white officers give you. I smell it on your breath."

Frank peered down at him.

For all his gruffness, Frank really was a decent fellow. Henry understood this because of their long time together on Blevin's farm. When Frank told him how he'd helped Squire escape the hogshead, that good deed didn't surprise him.

The shouts and musketry and artillery booms in Jesse's sector subsided. Their conversation ended when their colonel, astride his white horse, rode a narrow path through the timbers. He pointed his sword at the rubber pontoon bridge engineers inflated and set in place over the creek just ahead.

"Men," he cried, "we have our orders. The Rebs have halted our assault across the Little Sandy. It is up to us to turn this flank, to penetrate the enemy's lines here." He rose higher in his McClellan saddle. "We are attacking the Rebs' strongest position. We'll be attacking a very high bluff, and we'll be charging it on low ground. Since they occupy the high ground, they have a clear advantage. Do your people proud and never run from the enemy. Take it, my brave men! We will take it and hold it."

Hurrahs rose from the Native Guards.

Raising high his musket, Henry's shouts mocked the memory of his old, dead master, Aaron Blevin. The cheering quieted when artillerymen drew two cannons up a road toward the engineers' bridge.

The First's column, six companies strong, advanced behind the cannon and Henry's regiment, nine companies strong, followed, reinforced by some white cavalrymen on foot.

From childhood, Henry had endured Blevin's ridicule and been told he was less than a man. Blevin's words were daggers hurled into his soul. His back bore the scars of many a whipping, the sharp rawhide lashes digging into his flesh. Though he once resigned himself to this fate, this war lifted his hopes for freedom. Sergeant Dooley told him they were fighting for his people's freedom. He was right. Now he was free to be his own person. He would not run. He would be a man. A brave man.

"Is you scared?" Frank said while they approached the bridge.

Gulping, Henry swallowed his response.

"Me too."

This was their first battle. Anybody claiming any sense ought to be scared. Henry shifted his musket from his right shoulder to his left to ease his right shoulder's burden. Running and being scared were two different things. Men with yellow in their blood ran, but he'd seen men full of scared who behaved bravely. These men kept going on like scared was nothing, even though every bone in their body rattled like a skeleton dangling in a storm. He hoped he was this kind of scared. Nothing wrong with being scared, everything wrong with running.

The terrain's lethal layout revealed itself after they crossed the bridge. To their west, the swollen Mississippi River spilled over its banks and swamped most of that area almost to the road on which they marched. Overlooking them was a high ridge stretching alongside the road till it met the bluff about a quarter of a mile dead ahead. Another, lower outcropping stuck out from this bluff, almost inaccessible as well.

As they crossed the creek's pontoon bridge, their cannoneers ahead unlimbered their two cannons. Rebel artillery roared from the bluff. One Union gun flew off its carriage. The second cannon fired once before its cannoneers hastily limbered up and withdrew.

The First and Third hurried into the willow trees. While each regiment struggled to form battle lines two ranks deep, the river batteries rained mortal lead on them. Shells crashed through the trees, smacking the dry riverbed where they stood, spraying dirt and limbs and shrapnel.

Cold fright clawed Henry's mind. Lacking artillery support, this fight was entirely theirs. No, he couldn't skedaddle. He couldn't, he wouldn't do it.

Sabers raised, the officers shouted, "Fo-o-or-ward!"

Led by the First Louisiana Native Guards, two ranks deep, the thousand men marched out of the woods. Using the same military formation, Henry's regiment followed.

Musketry stormed from the ridge paralleling their route. A hail of Minié balls felled soldiers. Nevertheless, they continued their advance against the enemy-held bluff. They moved at quick time, then at double-quick. Screaming themselves hoarse, they surged toward the bluff. Henry's screams drove off his fear.

Canister cut through the First's ranks—from the bluff, from the river batteries—bursting and severing arms and legs and heads. Blood pooled the ground.

Henry's regiment moved at the double-quick. Minié balls hissed and canister spewed. Henry and a retreating soldier collided.

Wide-eyed, Henry glanced around him. Other men collided into the retreating soldiers. Confusion. Men thrashing and hollering. Cries of pain. Frank and others made for a large brick sugarhouse. Should he go there?

A bullet smashed Henry's leg, another his shoulder. Determined to prove his mettle, Henry continued his charge amidst canister and bullets. Weaving through the disorganized First, he made for the Rebel-held bluff. A third bullet, in his thigh, felled him.

The smell of chloroform permeated the post hospital tent. It sickened Rachel the first time she whiffed it in Mobile's Marine Hospital the previous year, but since then she'd learned to ignore it. She sat on a stool and clasped a wounded soldier's hand. Moans rose and fell from its every corner, melding into the rumbling cannon all along the garrison's lines.

The soldier coughed. "D-Don't leave me, miss."

The youth's haggard face stirred Rachel's pity. Her fingers traced the powder burns splotching his hollow cheeks. These poor men didn't deserve this. North or South, none of them did. Slavery was an abomination, a stain on their culture, so maybe this was…No. Not every Southerner approved of it. She certainly loathed it and thousands of men in their army, like her husband, didn't own slaves. Many were just poor farmers defending their families and their homes. *Why, oh why, must they all suffer this way?*

"The doc's taking my leg from me, ain't he?" the youth said.

A doctor's bone-saw sent a shudder through her. She'd never get used to hearing that dreadful thing. She peeled the soldier's fingers off her hand, lifted the big shears from a camp table beside her, and cut his bloody trousers up to the gaping wound above his knee. Its stench…she turned her head and made a face. *Get hold of yourself.*

Across the tent, Matilda gave a mangled man water from a canteen.

Behind Matilda stood an amputating table. An unconscious soldier lay on it, knocked out by chloroform. Doctor Hereford swept an amputation knife around his putrid arm, down through its fat and skin. A bloody tub on the ground stood ready to receive it when it dropped off.

Another surgeon, a stethoscope dangling from his neck, strode past Rachel.

Rachel forced merriment into her voice. "Oh, Corporal. You're going to be all right."

The corporal's fearful gaze rested upon amputated arms and legs, stacked like cordwood on the long wall tent's south side. "Promise?"

"I promise." All she could do was give these poor men hope. She knew not the truth of her encouragement.

Wide-eyed and trembling, the man stared up at the tent roof.

Rachel scanned the crowded scene of wounded, dirty men. Any one of them could be Jesse. Was she behaving selfishly? Childishly? *Oh!* Her heart screamed louder than the loudest screaming man. Her cries caught her throat. Her Jesse mustn't die. She did love him, after all. She loved Squire, too, but she loved Jesse even more. How could she bear her guilt, for the way she'd treated him, if he got killed? Matilda once reprimanded her for refusing to make amends. She shook her head as though ridding it of cobwebs. She didn't know, nor did she have time to think about it.

She seized a rag and patted dry the wound's blood. More blood spurted onto her skirt.

A sergeant burst inside the tent and strode to Leeds, the hospital steward who'd first shown Rachel and Matilda around the camp many weeks ago. "Colonel Miles sent me to get these men's guns, Sergeant. We need them fast. Hurry."

Marsden's regiment waited behind their breastworks alongside other regiments. More Confederate troops poured in from other sectors. All morning long they'd endured a heavy cannonade, but the enemy had not yet advanced against their position.

Marsden plucked his watch from out of his frock coat's pocket. It ticked toward two o'clock. Things were about to change. Marsden was confident of that. A disparity in numbers, no doubt, since four-and five-foot gaps separated his men. During this lull, he knew the enemy was preparing to attack his line in close order and vastly superior numbers. Miles's men, reinforcing them from their right wing, carried three rifles apiece, thanks to the guns he procured from the hospitals' sick and wounded and the garrison's arsenal.

Despite the enemy's superior numbers, they'd give him a time of it. Except for the ravine running alongside the road passing Mister

Slaughter's rubble, his residence which the Yankees set afire the previous day, the enemy lacked places to hide and take cover. Four parallel fences separated Mister Slaughter's cornfields. An abatis of sharpened timbers and limbs massed across the level field and rifle pits behind them, which dotted the level terrain like moles' holes, would prove a challenge to any enemy assault. Right in front of their breastworks ran a gully, a final obstacle.

For what seemed an eternity, the thin Confederate line awaited the attack. Though numerous faces were tight with seriousness and worry, others sang songs like "Dixie's Land" and "O Susanna." A few men cracked jokes about "killing them Yankee pigs." Some even danced, as though such things would throw off the tension gripping them all.

Through binoculars, Marsden followed trotting horses wheeling enemy cannon into position, out of the woods and nearer their lines. About six hundred yards away, Marsden estimated. *Ah. This was war. A glorious conflict in all its glorious gore.* Skirmishers fired on the enemy artillerymen unlimbering their guns. Though the Rebels picked off a few enemy soldiers, their artillery belched shot and shell, skedaddling the skirmishers back behind their earthen fortifications.

"Pass the order, Winder," Marsden said. "Have the men place their cartridges on their works so they can fire faster."

Winder delivered the order to the company commanders, every man of them holding either a musket or a shotgun.

From out of the woods several hundred unarmed black soldiers, shouldering long thick poles, advanced.

"What do you think they're up to?" Lieutenant Ransom said. "Bridge the gully?"

"Of course. What else would they be trying to do?" Marsden said.

Ransom raised his musket and aimed it at them. Some hundred white soldiers carrying planks followed the black soldiers, skirmishers advanced behind them, and behind the skirmishers came the Bluecoat infantry marching shoulder-to-shoulder. Their officers galloped back and forth, waving sabers and urging their ranks forward.

Rebel cannon smoked and thundered. Yankee horses stumbled, buckled and fell, struck by cannon balls, their officer riders knocked off their saddles.

Still the Bluecoats came on. Slaughter's rubble disrupted their formation as they stepped over piles of bricks and maneuvered around scorched wood. At the fences, they halted amidst exploding shells and deadly shrapnel.

Marsden grinned when the Confederate batteries found their enemy's range. After ripping out the fences, the Yankees forged ahead amidst the iron missiles. The soldiers carrying the poles dropped them and struck out for the rear while others hugged the earth.

Likewise, the white soldiers carrying planks dropped their burdens. Whipping out revolvers, they fired at the Rebel cannoneers before skedaddling to the ravine.

Marsden thinned his lips. *Ah!* Once they'd reached the abatis, the enemy was done for.

Yelling, the Yankees rushed the abatis. Grape shot and canister shattered their ranks. Broken chains and rusty nails spewed from Rebel cannon.

Shotguns and rifled muskets decimated the Bluecoats when they attempted to climb over or go around the obstructions. Like animals snared in a trap, the abatis entangled them. Field pieces smashed them straight on from the road, raked their flanks, and chewed them to pieces. Men in the forward rifle pits fired with astounding accuracy. Bluecoat after Bluecoat stumbled and dropped, victim to their bullets. Finally, untangling themselves from the obstacles, they turned and ran.

Marsden raised a cheer and fired his revolver. "That'll show those cowards!"

Enemy officers waved their swords, screamed, and pointed them at Marsden's position. The Bluecoats stopped running. They reformed their lines. Again, they advanced. Musketry crackled from the breastworks. Yankee casualties mounted. Hundreds of dead men in blue littered the field.

During a third enemy attack, the Rebels in the rifle pits maintained their accurate fire. The Bluecoats made for the ravine. Their sharpshooters peered over the ravine's ridge and popped off rounds at the men in the rifle pits with equal accuracy, so accurate, in fact, they forced the Rebels back behind the breastworks. Marsden swore up a storm when they joined his men.

He paced hard, his strides long and angry. All around him, bullets clipped air. When he spotted Eakin sitting against the earthwork, his musket in his lap, blood rushed to Marsden's head. "Get up there and fight."

"Stella don't want me to!" Eakin screamed back at him.

"You'll never hold her name over me again, you yellow-livered…" Marsden seized Eakin by the collar, jerked him to his feet, and rammed his back against the works. A knife blade slashed the back of his hand when he landed a punch on Eakin's jaw. The knife dropped from Eakin's hand; he crumpled to the dirt. Marsden aimed his revolver at Eakin's chest.

"You will get up there and fight."

Eakin spat and moved to rise, collapsed when Marsden shot him clean through his heart.

By five o'clock, quiet settled along the lines, save for the moans of the wounded and haunting pleas for water from sunbaked, thirsty men. They'd stopped every Union assault. On the Plains Store Road, Confederate casualties numbered fewer than thirty. Among the Yankees, more than a thousand dead and wounded lay strewn across this same field.

Gloriously bloody. Marsden scratched the bandage wrapped around his hand's knife wound. *Glorious war.*

Twenty Three

O n May's last scorching day Giselle dragged her shovel through the small picket gate and into the family cemetery where her parents and cousin Zack were buried. Sweat pasted her disheveled hair against her face and neck. Her unwashed calico dress carried an odor, or was it her body? She hadn't bathed since the Yankees killed her father and Zack. Not like her not to have a bath most days. She just didn't feel like doing much of anything anymore. Not even dip snuff.

She trudged to a clump of crabgrass in the cemetery's farthest corner. Shoving her shovel's blade beneath it, she worked it under the crabgrass roots. After momentary effort, she lifted it out and tossed it over the picket fence. She'd not let weeds crowd this cemetery. No weeds among her family's gravestones, either, not today, not ever.

She searched the ground for more crabgrass. The Yankees ruined her life. Her father and cousin dead, the handful of slaves they'd owned gotten up and joined them. Nearby farms, large and small, all abandoned. Mister Slaughter's house, burned to kindling. Even Henrietta and her father had left. Just like her unwashed body, she'd not cleaned her house. Loneliness was no friend.

She plodded to a large rock, her father's gravestone till she could acquire a proper one, and Squire emerged from some nearby trees. She swore at him.

Tongue dangling out his mouth and his countenance friendly, Squire padded toward her.

"Scat!" she yelled.

Squire stopped for a second, and then he came on.

"You heard me, dog! Get out of here! Scat!" She waved her shovel at him.

After another moment's hesitation Squire, wagging his tail, trotted through the cemetery's opened picket gate and up to her. She raised her shovel to strike, its blade poised to smash him.

Squire cocked his head.

"I'm goin' to smack you so hard with the back end of my shovel, dog, this'll kill you deader'n..."

Panting, Squire sat in front of her, his tail thumping the earth. He pawed her dress.

"What're you doin'? Tryin' to make amends or somethin'?"

Squire kept pawing.

"It ain't gonna work, dog." She lifted her shovel blade higher, but before she could swing it down buzzing launched a chill straight up her spine.

Her eyes slid toward the tall grass at her father's gravestone. Coiled against his stone and shaking its black tail, a big canebrake rattlesnake, identified by the reddish stripe coursing the middle of its back, over its dark brown cross bands. Her heart almost stood still.

Canebrakes, the deadliest snakes in these parts. One of them killed her grandfather when she was barely out of diapers, or so she'd heard. He'd accidentally stepped on it while walking through the woods.

This canebrake's triangular head rose swiftly. It lunged at her and missed... on purpose she knew...its warning shot, as though telling her to leave it alone.

Mouth dry, she inched back farther. If she gave it space and didn't bother it, it'd slither off...she hoped. Canebrakes were known to do that when they didn't feel trapped or threatened. But terror refused to lower her shovel blade.

Higher the snake lifted its head, its mouth open and its baleful black eyes riveted on her. It reared back farther...

Squire leapt between them when the snake lunged. Quicker than lightning, its fangs flashed and sank into Squire's left foreleg. Yelping,

Squire whirled like a top out of control. Round and round he slung the snake till its grip on him loosened.

Down went Squire's jaws. His teeth seized the snake behind its head. Back and forth, like snapping an old rag, Squire shook his hapless foe till he dropped its mangled body into a lifeless heap.

Giselle lowered her shovel when Squire returned to her. Breathing a sigh of relief, she stooped to examine his bitten leg. Squire licked her face then turned away. He limped down the path leading into the woods.

"Squire!" Giselle cried. Tears welled her eyes. "Come back, Squire! I'm sorry!"

Sobbing, she put her face in her hands. The snake's venom was in him, and as big as the snake was, Squire faced certain death. She'd been mean to him, yet he'd answered her meanness with kindness. All she'd known were dogs that tore each other apart. She'd never known a dog to be as kind as him and…she sniffled…and he'd sacrificed his life to save hers.

June 1863
Port Hudson, Louisiana

Twenty Four

—◆—

"Get back where you came from, woman." The burly Yankee sergeant thumbed at the road.

"I ain't botherin' nobody." Giselle peered beyond him, at the plantation's white-pillared mansion. Not far from her, a soldier pulled a bottle from a medicine wagon's chest. Several miles away, sporadic gunfire echoed.

The sergeant's narrowed eyes assessed her. "You're no nurse. I'll wager you're either a spy or a smuggler. Go home."

"Don't your peepers see I'm wearin' mournin' clothes? How could you say sech a thing?" Giselle put her face in her hands, sniffled and boo-hooed. Somehow, she must get to that wagon and steal some quinine for the garrison. This was her third attempt in three days.

"Put a cork in it, woman. I know every female trick ever tried. Your bawling doesn't move me. This is the last time I'm telling you. Get."

Riding crop in hand, Giselle mounted her horse sidesaddle and nudged him into a trot. She guided her mount down a narrow trail into a stand of pine. Through these trees, she studied the plantation's outbuildings some two hundred yards distant. The Yanks were using them for operating rooms. Where did Squire wander off to, to die? Her heartbeat hitched.

Her long-dormant conscience awakened, she decided that somehow, whatever it took, she'd have to get into Port Hudson. She

191

must make amends for her evil deeds, both with Mrs. Webb and her husband, if he was still alive. Maybe, if she could only get her hands on some quinine, maybe she could make amends for her misdeeds and help the Southern boys enduring this awful Yankee siege.

Concealed by the timbers, she stayed in her spot. She started devising a plan she'd carry out at dark.

Jesse nodded at Mitchell. "That's got it."

On his knees, Mitchell finished adjusting the blanket on a ridge pole. After he and Jesse spread it atop two three-foot stakes planted in the ground, they fastened each of its corners with four other, shorter stakes planted ninety degrees from their taller cousins, a shelter from the sweltering day. "Not a bad looking shebang, Captain."

Jesse got up off his knees. He trudged to the works fronting the ridge. Sour-smelling sweat puddled his chest and shirt.

"Get down." Mitchell spoke in a loud whisper. "Snipers around here. You aiming to get yourself killed?"

"A bullet in my heart suits me fine." Jesse hesitated before he plopped behind the works and hunched low to the earth, Mitchell beside him. When Mitchell was shot he'd been hit by a spent bullet. He'd suffered nothing worse than an ugly bruise on his rib cage. On every front, they'd repulsed the Yanks. Now they'd settled into a siege, but the enemy's grip couldn't compare with the agony besieging him.

While a man slipped past the enemy fleet below the garrison bearing a dispatch for General Joe Johnston, Gardner devoted himself to strengthening their defenses. The soldiers did everything they could think of to make their position impregnable: sandbags arranged so as to make loopholes for sharpshooters, pits dug for their cannons' protection, land mines made from unexploded mortar shells, which they planted in front of their works.

Though they possessed an abundance of gunpowder, their limited supply of ammunition forced them to use whatever a cannon could shoot that inflicted damage—iron scraps, ramrods, broken bayonets. What shot and shell they did have, they husbanded in the event of another major assault.

One of Jesse's men crawled out from his shebang, an Enfield rifle in his hand, one of many Enfields gotten off dead Yanks after their fight last month. With these guns' longer range, the enemy faced an even sounder licking if he attacked again, Jesse told himself.

"Has Rachel started talking to you?" Mitchell asked.

Yankee cannon fire rumbled in another sector.

"When she's a mind to," Jesse said. "I'd say I'm done with her. She and I are going to get us a divorce after the war. I'll move to Mobile and find work there. I might even find employment at the bank where my brother-in-law works."

"Captain Jesse Carlton Webb, I forbid it."

"I can move to Mobile if I want to."

"Sure you can, but not without Rachel. You and Rachel cannot divorce. I forbid it."

"As do I."

Jesse looked at the speaker behind him—Colonel Cox.

"Giving up is not the way to go, Captain Webb." Cox wriggled down a hill to get closer.

Jesse heaved a painful sigh. "She doesn't trust me anymore, sir. I'm not bitter. Why, I can't say I even blame her. It is all my fault, after all."

"She'll learn to trust you again. Be patient."

"I want more than her trust, Colonel. I want her love, her respect. I can't have that? Well, I'd say we might as well part company. And I'll say it again. I'm not bitter about it. It was all my dang stupidity, trusting that Blevin gal. I've lost Rachel. I've lost Squire."

"Be patient, Jesse," Mitchell said. "Wait till we send the Yanks back to Baton Rouge, then try reasoning with her again."

Cox handed Jesse his testament. "Please keep your heads down till I say otherwise."

"Yes, sir." Jesse and Mitchell spoke this at the same time.

When Rachel entered the hospital tent, Yankee artillery slackened its fire. Marsden was lying on his back, atop a thick hay mattress. His eyes followed her as she maneuvered around a cot. He'd suffered a minor knife wound. A mere scratch. *Yet it caused him to end up here?* Rachel wondered. *Or was it something else?*

"H-Hello." His jaw moved with great difficulty when he spoke.

"I am sorry." Rachel sat on a stool beside him and touched his shoulder.

"Trouble… moving…jaw. Speak…not much."

Tears pooled Rachel's eyes.

"Mrs. Webb?" the doctor approaching her said.

Rachel got to her feet and brushed away a tear.

The doctor drew her out of Marsden's earshot.

"Is it lockjaw?" she asked

"It's possible. Today, spasms started affecting his face. His neck and jaw are also getting stiff."

Marsden's eyes studied them.

Rachel gasped and looked away. "Can you get word to my husband? He ought to know about this."

"I'll dispatch one of my stewards to him." Bowing his head, the doctor went to another patient.

She returned to Marsden and gazed upon him. Her thoughts traipsed back in time. Here lay a man, a tall, powerful, ambitious man, member of a prominent Mobile family, a man who longed to become a great man himself, her love for him long ago abandoned. In his dying, did he still love her? She'd lost her love for him when he killed her husband's brother. But now she pitied him and her pity, like a baptismal pool, washed away all the filth, all the hatred, from her heart. She hoped the same would happen to her husband once he received word of Colonel Marsden's fate. They both needed to forgive this man.

A spasm twitched his face. His jaw clenched and then opened a little. He spoke, but she couldn't understand him, so she leaned into his face and he repeated the words. "Pocket. Shirt."

A white piece of paper…folded…inside his shirt pocket. She eased it out. After unfolding it, she gasped at its salutation.

February 15, 1863

My dearest Brother,

> *I hope this letter finds you safe.*
> *We do so miss you. I think about you night and day. Little James is always asking about his favorite uncle, and he wonders when he'll come home. James turned six yesterday. I wish you were*

*able to visit him on his birthday. You are the only one I can count
on in our family to continue loving us, the only one who never
turned his back on me because I married a barkeep. And I shall
always love you, dearest brother, for always loving me....*

Rachel's eyes skimmed down to the letter's ending and read it
aloud. "Your affectionate sister. Stella." Stunned, she stared down at
Marsden. "Stella's your sister? Why didn't you tell me?"

His jaw muscles tightening, Marsden made an unintelligible sound.

"Hampton," she said. "What is it? I...I can't understand you."

More sounds. Two words she did catch when he spoke between
clenched teeth. "Disowned her."

Disowned her? Stella? Who? Why?

A loud bone-saw sent his face into spasms. He struggled to open
his mouth, but when two patients screamed another round of spasms
followed. "Letters. Tent." He spoke these words through his barely
opened mouth.

"In your tent." Rachel repeated this to be sure she understood.

Marsden made a sound, which she took for a "yes."

Tears streaming, Rachel hurried out. She'd find those letters, read
them, and perhaps learn more about Stella. Oh, she'd done him, and
Jesse, so wrong!

Afoot, holding her horse's reins and her riding crop, Giselle led her
mount through another pine thicket some fifty yards closer to the
field hospital. All was quiet, save for the persistent cannon banging
out rounds along the front and the occasional flashes of shells lighting
the midnight sky. Sizzling campfires had long since died. The men
who once sat beside them, now sleeping inside their pup tents.

Three men guarded the camp's perimeter, at least in her vicinity.
One stood to the south. Not a problem, that feller. The others, though,
did present a problem. Cradling their rifles, they stood close by. One,
smoking a cigarette, wandered toward the road.

A medicine wagon was parked behind the other soldier. In a
nearby pasture, mules grazed. Reaching inside her saddlebag, she
pulled out a cloth doll stuffed with sawdust.

"Get on." Her palm swatted the top of his hips. "Get!"

Her horse trotted out of the trees to the mules. The medicine wagon soldier headed toward him to investigate, quickly distancing himself from the wagon.

Giselle hiked up her skirt and made for the vehicle, her dark clothes blending into the blackness. Upon reaching the wagon, she peeked around it. Good. That soldier was stroking her horse's nose, and the cigarette soldier had returned from the road. They appeared to be talking to each other while examining her animal's saddle.

A guard she hadn't noticed ambled her direction. Crouching behind a wheel, she clutched its spokes and tried to muffle the thump thump of her heart. Once the guard passed her, he disappeared around a small brick building. Easing open the chest on the wagon's rear, she scanned its bottles. Too dark to read the labels. If not quinine, anything would do. She snatched up a small bottle, thrust it through a slit in her doll's back, and buttoned it back.

She glimpsed the two soldiers, who'd investigated her horse, heading her direction.

"I'll bet that pesky woman's around here somewhere," one of them said.

"We'll find her, Haywood," the other one said. "Go wake the sergeant."

Clutching her doll, Giselle ducked beneath the wagon. Before many minutes passed, guards swarmed the camp. At least eight of them, maybe more, peeking under ambulances and inside tents. Giselle gulped. How'd she get out of here? *They ain't goin' to shoot a lady...or...*

A guard neared her hiding place. She drew a quick breath, crawled out from beneath the wagon and, unencumbered by a hoop beneath her dress, she hiked it up and sprinted toward her horse.

"There she goes!" a guard shouted.

"After her!" the burly sergeant yelled.

Soon as she pulled herself up, into her saddle, the sergeant seized her horse's reins and aimed his pistol at her. "I suggest you don't go anywhere, miss."

"Takes a big ole man to shoot a lady, don't it?" Giselle popped his hands with her crop; he let go the reins. She next popped her horse, put her heels to her animal's barrel, and galloped him onto the road when two shots rang out. One clipped her dress's sleeve; the second one whizzed past her shoulder. Doll and medicine in hand, she was quickly out of range.

After riding almost a mile, she approached the Union army's front lines. She slowed her mount to a walk. Batteries discharged a brisk fire at the garrison. The earth rocked. A steady din of destruction rent the sky.

"Where do you think you're going?" The captain who spoke seized her horse's bridle. His voice boomed between cannon blasts.

"To Port Hudson," Giselle said sweetly, feigning innocence.

"You can't go there. There's a battle in progress."

"Is that what that ruckus is all about?"

Brilliant explosions cast a bright hue on the captain's commonplace face. "You have no business being out this late. You ought to be home."

"I must get through. My husband…"

"Not tonight. Too dangerous. You'd better go back."

Giselle steered her horse off to the left, a pretense of obeying the captain's orders, before she wheeled him back, nose to the garrison. The captain shouted at her to stop, but she galloped past him in clouds of dust and smoke. Guns blazed away. A shell exploded, knocking her off her mount at the Rebel sally port.

Twenty Five

When morning splashed the horizon orange-red, Giselle stirred awake on a straw mattress atop an oak bed. Before her stood a tiny lady staring at her, her face pale and blond curls hanging out of her bonnet. She fumbled with its big red bow.

"What're you gawkin' at?" Giselle almost growled her question.

"My name's Matilda, and I'm gawking at you." Her dark lashes blinking, Matilda dropped her hands to her side. "I can't believe you're still among the living after riding through all that awful shelling last night."

Giselle's bandaged shoulder throbbed. She sat up. "It was stupid of me."

"You'll live." Rachel entered their cabin. "The shrapnel hit a muscle. It didn't penetrate deep. Doctor Hereford cut it out of you last night."

"I ain't rememberin' that."

"Of course not, stupid. You were chloroformed, with what little we have left, the little we needed for our poor wounded men. Unfortunately, they stuck you in this cabin with Matilda and me."

"Where's my doll?" Giselle sensed Rachel's coldness, evidenced by her wooden face. She couldn't blame Rachel for feeling like she did.

Rachel grabbed the doll off a bunk bed and flung it at her.

Giselle jumped in time to catch it, wincing when a pang stabbed her. "Don't throw it. I got a bottle of medicine in her." She worked out a small, square bottle from the doll's back. The word "quinine" was written on the label. So, she did get it. Grinning, she held it up for Rachel and Matilda to see.

"Well, I'll be!" Rachel grabbed the bottle from Giselle and handed it to Matilda. "See this gets to Sergeant Leeds right away."

Matilda hurried out.

"It ain't much." Giselle fell back on the bed, her shoulder aching.

"Better than nothing." Rachel moved closer to Giselle. "Why did you risk your life to bring it?"

"Y'all needed it, didn't y'all?"

"We need lots of things."

Giselle reached beneath her thin sheet and grasped Rachel's hand. Rachel recoiled as though stung.

"I ain't the same girl I used to be, Mrs. Webb."

"And you expect me to believe you?"

"Sit down yonder in that wicker chair. I'll tell you everythin' you got to know."

Rachel sat in the chair beside the cabin entrance.

Then starting with the day Squire killed Nero, when she met Marsden at the sally port, Giselle confessed the whole story—how she and her father and Marsden conspired against Jesse, how she used Lady to catch him, and on and on. Not one aspect of their plan did she omit, including how she recognized Rachel from her picture on the tintype Jesse once showed her. That explained why she'd kissed and flirted with Jesse when Rachel and Matilda arrived on the train— she recognized her.

"I knew none of that business between you and my husband was serious," Rachel said. "But you had no right stealing my...my and my husband's dog."

"Your Squire's what's changed me."

"You've seen him? He's alive?"

Giselle next recounted Squire's rescue by a Yankee sergeant. Then how Squire came back a few days later and killed a canebrake rattler before it could strike her. "He saved my life, Mrs. Webb. Canebrakes are the most deadliest snakes in these here parts. After all Papa and me done to him, he still loved me and saved my life. If your dog can forgive me, can't you and your husband?"

"Where's Squire now?"

"The snake bit him. He wandered off."

"He's dead."

Giselle shook her head seriously. "Ain't no way a dog can survive that snake's venom. Ain't no way on this here earth. One of 'em killed my grandfather once."

Swallowing a sob, Rachel hurried out their cabin.

Giselle fumed at herself. Why did she go off and tell Mrs. Webb about what them snakes did? Why did she panic and not swat that ole canebrake with her shovel?

Lying shoulder-to-shoulder in their crude shelter, practically tasting foul-smelling dirt, Jesse and Mitchell turned their heads at the sound of heavy breathing.

"Long climb, Leeds?" Jesse said once the steward got close.

"I'd make a poor worm, sir." Leeds puffed then drew his thin lips into a grim line.

Cannon fire exploded behind them.

"What news?" Jesse's and Leeds's noses almost touched. Sweat popped along the sergeant's narrow forehead.

"Winder got brought to the hospital this morning, sir. Mortally wounded by a sharpshooter."

"Marsden?"

"Dying, I fear. Have you seen him yet?"

"Haven't the chance. Can he still talk?"

"Not very well, sir. His jaw's pretty much locked now. Talks through his teeth when he can."

"I'm sorry."

"I didn't come here to tell you that, though, sir."

Jesse and Mitchell swapped curious looks.

"Blevin's daughter brought in some quinine last night and dang near got herself killed doing it."

"She's all right?"

"Hit in the shoulder. Nothing too serious."

"That doesn't sound like her, Captain," Mitchell said.

Jesse shook his head. "Not at all."

"One other thing," Leeds said. "Your wife asked me to tell you that she loved you. She says if you're willing, she'd like you and her to make a fresh start."

"A fresh start?" Jesse paused for a moment. "Leeds, tell her we'll do it, soon as this little fracas we and the Yanks are having is over."

"One more thing, sir. One of our prisoners, a member of the Native Guards we captured after he was wounded…calls himself Henry. Anyway, sir, he says he was Blevin's slave and this Yankee sergeant rescued Squire from Blevin's pen, took him with him, but ole Squire gnawed his leash apart and skedaddled when one of Blevin's dogs chased him. The Blevin girl, she also said that later on Squire came back to her place and got bit by a snake. A canebrake rattler, I think she said. I'd best get on back before Doctor Hereford has my hide."

While Leeds crawled back out of sniper range, Jesse's throat caught. "Squire's dead."

"We don't know for sure," Mitchell said. "Remember that man I told you about when we went snake hunting? The Snake Man? Remember his dog I was telling you about, the one that got bit by a rattler and didn't die? Well, the Snake Man told me venomous snakes, like rattlers and copperheads, don't always have enough venom to kill things, and sometimes they don't even inject enough. Sometimes they just bite. Snake Man really knew his snakes. Those venomous varmints don't kill too many dogs, he told me once."

"But Blevin's dog, if he hasn't already, might find him and kill him." Jesse's fist pounded the soft earth so hard it made a shallow crater.

Twenty Six

—◆—

Squire arose from beneath a cool shade tree. Gone was the pain in his left hind leg. Though the snake's venom caused some swelling, he'd survived. While he lay here during this past week he dined on crackers and salt pork, fed to him by soldiers marching past.

He padded into the scorching sunlight. From deep inside him stretched a yearning to return to his master, his master's wife, and his pack. It was time to go. Go where? To his master, to home.

His nose tested the air. He smelled myriad things, but he also heard distant cannon fire right down this dirt road. The promise of seeing his master again set him in motion, renewed strength in his legs.

Tail swishing, he happened upon a large house. No sign of life in it. No one in the yard. He attempted another scent. From among the trees, he whiffed something sinister trailing him. Stepping out onto the road and striding into view… Brutus.

Squire sprinted toward the empty house. Brutus pursued. Madly pawing a door and finding it open, Squire bolted through the entrance and darted into a large room on his right. Ducking beneath a piano, he next awaited Brutus's attack. When Brutus lunged for his head, he scrambled out from beneath it, Brutus on his tail. Squire jumped out an opened window onto a portico. Brutus scrambled over its sill, and out.

Up the portico's stairway Squire dashed. His paw swatted the upper portico's door to get back inside the house, but the door was locked. He swerved around to face his foe, Brutus's cruel eyes promising death.

Squire scrambled behind a tall vase on his left and knocked it over. Down the steps it rolled and crashed toward his enemy. Though delayed but for a moment, Brutus plowed right through it when he mounted his charge.

Driven by terror—an impulse, actually—Squire shut his eyes and crashed through a window on his right. When his eyes popped open, he leapt onto a high bed and whirled on its mattress to confront Brutus. Brutus sprang for his nose. Squire danced aside. Down went Brutus, onto the floor. Squire snarled and snapped and flashed his teeth. He'd kill first, before Brutus killed him.

Scrambling to his feet, Brutus went to the bed steps against the bed frame. He charged up them, onto the mattress.

Anticipating Brutus's maneuver, Squire sprang off the bed and landed behind a large trunk angled in a corner. Not much room to move. Nowhere to run. Jaws open, Brutus vaulted off the bed toward him.

Wide-eyed, his heart in his throat, Squire sprang up from his tight spot and seized Brutus's throat between his jaws during his enemy's mid-flight. Brutus collapsed atop him. Backed against the two walls' corner, Squire squeezed and squeezed till Brutus's life failed him. Afterward, Squire collapsed on the floor.

His breaths came hard. His chest heaved. He needed to get out of here, but Brutus atop him trapped him in this corner between the trunk and the wide bed post. Whimpering, Squire pawed at Brutus and wriggled against the wall. His breaths shortened. Frustrated, he puffed air out of his nostrils. He tried rising, his paws pressing hard on the wooden floor. He collapsed back down, for Brutus was too heavy to shove aside.

How to get out of this plight? How to go home? Home. His master. Squire moved one of his forepaws, touched the trunk, pawed it hard. It budged…a little. He pawed it again, harder, and the trunk moved a little more. Maybe it wasn't too heavy, after all. Squire kept pawing it, harder and faster, till a narrow space opened between it and the wall. Squire rose as high as he could, which wasn't very high, and then crawled forward, struggling and wriggling out from beneath Brutus.

Strengthened by the hope of freedom, he crawled past the trunk. Fresh air poured through the window he'd crashed through when he'd fled his enemy. Freedom. Home. Giving lifeless Brutus a final glance, Squire climbed over the window, went back down the portico's stairs, and headed for home. Happy and triumphant, his tail wagged high.

Sporadic musketry crackled along the Confederate lines while Rachel and Matilda made their way to a hospital tent. Rotting flesh's nauseating stench permeated the garrison, the odor of decomposing enemy dead abandoned on the battlefield.

The Confederates' predicament deteriorated to desperation— their medicines almost depleted, hundreds of men suffering malaria's torture. Yankee prisoners, in addition to their own sick and wounded, crowded their tents. The day after their engagement a week ago, the Northern soldiers delivered drugs through the lines for their men.

"I can't believe the Yanks can be so cruel," Rachel said. "You know Lieutenant Mitchell Hayes and my husband went out just beyond their works to give water to their wounded and got shot at?"

"Compassion isn't in their vocabulary," Matilda said. "Those poor men, their corpses just lying out there baking in the sun. I heard a rumor that General Gardner sent General Banks a message, a request asking him to bury his dead. The stupid general said he didn't have any dead on the battlefield."

"Lieutenants Hayes and Utley, and some other soldiers, dragged a couple hundred dead Yankees inside their works a few days ago and buried them. General Banks didn't permit it. Another Yankee general did. That's what I heard tell."

A provost guard met them as they ducked inside a tent. "Mrs. Webb, Miss Blevin wants you to meet one of those black soldiers we captured. He's in one of our hospitals but on the mend. I believe he has some information about Squire."

Rachel's heart skipped a beat. "Is Squire alive?"

"Don't know, ma'am. You'll have to ask him."

"Oh, let it be so!"

Twenty Seven

---◆---

"**T**hings have slowed down a bit, H. L." Hands dangling between his knees, Jesse sat on a stool and faced his former enemy, lying on his back, on a cot.

His teeth clenched and his lips pulled back by his facial muscles, Marsden held a malevolent grin, one characteristic of tetanus victims, Doctor Carter told him.

"You'd have been proud of your men last week. They fought like tigers." Could Marsden hear him? Was he wasting his time talking to him? Jesse continued his monologue. "We have little truces every now and then. It's sort of peculiar, I'd say. There's not a lot of hate between us. Not between some of us, anyway. I never really hated the Yanks, just didn't like them trying to tell us how to run our lives. I just figured on the war being sort of an adventure. You know. Fun. Well, I was sure enough wrong. Real war's no game. Sharpshooters do most of the fighting these days. We raid each others' ditches, bombard each other. I suppose you can hear our cannon blasting away. The Yanks dig most of the ditches now. Did I tell you? Their black soldiers do it, and a few former slaves. A lot of the black soldiers got wiped out...the Native Guards they were called...from New Orleans...back during their attack in May. The Yanks are advancing on us at several points, but we'll stop 'em. The gristmill at Commissary Hill's gone. Our Yankee friends blasted it to pieces."

"Too bad." Marsden's words came between his clenched teeth.

Jesse started. So, he could hear him, couldn't he? And he could talk a little between his teeth.

"They're not stopping us, though. Know what we did? We rigged us up an old locomotive, and we used us a belt from the mill. We put it around one of the locomotive's wheels. It does a tolerably good job grinding meal for us."

Jesse considered telling him about other food woes but refrained. Why torture Marsden by painting verbal images of food? Not many days from now, he expected they'd be living off rats and horseflesh.

"Hampton," Jesse said, the first time in years he'd addressed him by his first name. "I know you think I put Elliott up to tracking you down in Pensacola, but I didn't. Never in this whole entire world did I know you'd gone there. I'd have stood up for my Emma, too, if she'd been in Stella's place. If Elliott had known she was your sister and you were taking care of her behind your parents' backs, he wouldn't have challenged you. And he would not have told your parents. I wouldn't have told them, either. It was all one great big unfortunate misunderstanding. I hate all this tragedy happened. I'm sick and tired of hating and sick and tired of killing."

"Me too."

Marsden's odd grin shuddered Jesse. Hate him because he killed Elliott? Because he helped the Blevins steal Squire? Seeing his former foe in this pitiful state…what good had hating done? It accomplished nothing. To continue harboring it against his dying foe…Jesse leaned close to his ear and whispered, "All is forgiven, Hampton. I'm sorry this happened to you."

"I…I forgive you…t-too."

Minutes later, Jesse practically bounced out the tent. A peace passed through him. At last, he and Marsden were reconciled. When Jesse turned onto the road to return to the front lines, joyful barks rang out. Jesse whirled right. Squire sprinted toward him, bent ears flapping and molasses eyes beaming.

Jesse burst into laughter. "You ole rascal!"

Squire bounded into his arms and knocked him to the ground. They playfully rolled and tussled while Squire's rough, wet tongue lathered Jesse's face and neck. His dog's dusty odor delighted him. Finally, Jesse managed to crawl out from beneath Squire.

"Come on, boy." Jesse snapped his fingers. "Let's go see Rachel."

Jesse headed for the next hospital tent, Squire trotting alongside.

Twenty Eight

———◆———

The humid days dragged on. The Yankee siege dragged on as the soldiers in blue slowly advanced, digging zigzagging ditches toward Jesse's line.

The Confederates threw themselves into delaying the enemy's advance. Raids, skirmishes. Nothing they did discouraged the Yankees' persistence.

Every time Jesse's men charged the enemy's trenches Squire, instead of running away like he did in the past, would scramble over their earthen parapet and race ahead raising a string of barks. Bullets clipped air, almost always whistling over his head. Then he'd leap into a trench, seize a Union soldier's trouser leg, or pounce atop him snarling and snapping. Once the fracas ended, he'd bound out of the trench and follow Jesse and the others back to their lines, tail high and batting air as though this siege were a game.

During one such sortie, Jesse and a Yank struggled hand-to-hand. The Yankee slugged Jesse's jaw, plowing him backward against a pile of fascines. Jesse's pistol dropped from his hand. The Yankee whipped out his revolver and fired, while at the same time tumbling beneath Squire's weight when Squire launched against his chest. Yelling clamored around them, and shooting, yet Squire stayed atop this man long enough for Jesse to snatch up his and his enemy's pistols before rejoining the fight.

That evening, Jesse sat beside a campfire and stroked Squire's back. "Our boy saved my life today, Mitch."

Squire rested his head on Jesse's lap and closed his eyes as though welcoming Jesse's affection.

Mitch patted his head. "He's one fine animal, Jesse. Good thing he came back, else you'd likely have been killed today."

"A sure enough fact." Gratitude spread throughout Jesse's soul. His fingers threaded up and down Squire's furry spine. "The good Lord brought him back to us just in time. I reckon our boy would like to get on back home now, same as we all do."

"Yessir, I reckon he does."

On June 26, Jesse's men laid down a diversionary fire while thirty Arkansans raided a Yankee ditch some two hundred yards distant. At the cost of one wounded, they brought in seven prisoners, fourteen rifles, and lots of sandbags.

"That dog looks familiar." A prisoner, passing through their lines, indicated Squire.

"He's our mascot," Jesse said. "He wandered off for a few weeks. Maybe you saw him then."

"Likely. He may have been the one wandering the roads we were marching on."

Suddenly, Squire lunged at him and knocked him onto the ground. Snarling, he seized the prisoner's shirt between his teeth. He jerked it and ripped it and....

"Squire." Jesse almost reprimanded him, till he saw the reason for Squire's behavior. A pocket knife lay on the ground. Jesse scooped up the weapon. "Enough, boy. Stop it." He snapped his fingers. Squire returned to Jesse's side.

The Yankee regained his feet.

"Our mascot also happens to be my dog. I brought him to war with me when all this craziness started."

"Captain, I didn't intend hurting you. I was going to give the knife to you. I'm tired of fighting."

"Well, I'd say my dog didn't know that."

The Yankee lifted his palm. "May I pet him?"

"Of course."

Bending low, the man patted Squire's head. "There, there, good feller. Are we friends now?"

Squire licked his knuckles as though answering "yes."

The Yankee captive hurried to catch up with his six captured comrades.

Another week passed.

Their ammunition expended, Jesse detailed some men to help gather Minié balls the Yankees fired into their garrison, which their ordnance department used to produce several thousand Enfield cartridges a day. Regarding the Yankee shells that didn't detonate, those that fit the Rebels' cannon the ordnance department made usable again. Fuses inserted into the smaller shells turned them into hand grenades.

Along other sectors similar things were being done, Jesse heard.

So close did the enemy get to the Rebels, Yankee snipers picked off those going for supplies. It didn't take long for the besieged to do what Jesse suspected they'd be forced to do—eat horseflesh and rats.

Squire became quite adept at catching rats, bringing them to Jesse and his men. He comforted the sick and dying, too, those under Doctor Carter's care since he was the one doctor who allowed him inside his hospital tent. Every day he visited that doctor's hospital, he let the patients pet him, licked their hands and faces, and lent them all the strength he could give.

On June's final day, Marsden died.

After pickets brought an official dispatch to General Gardner regarding Pemberton's surrender to Grant at Vicksburg on July 4, the general convened a council with his senior commanders. When Colonel Stonebridge, who'd attended this council, returned to Jesse's line he announced the news: "You all fought well, boys. Whipped the Yanks at every turn, y'all did But the rumors are true. Vicksburg has surrendered. Continued resistance here is futile, therefore we your commanders have decided the wiser course is to surrender."

When Jesse, exhausted and sitting on the ground, heard these words, he breathed a sigh of relief. At last, his war was over.

Utley and numerous other angry men cursed up a storm. Some vowed to escape the garrison during the cease fire they knew would come.

On July 8, Generals Gardner and Banks signed surrender terms.

On July 9, Confederate defenders lined up in military formation to surrender. Though some of Jesse's regiment did escape through Union lines the previous night, Jesse made no effort to do it. Like the Yankee prisoner who'd given him his pocketknife he, too, had lost all desire to fight.

Banks's chief of staff led an occupation column through the sally port on the Jackson road. During the ceremony, Gardner offered the chief of staff his sword. "Having thoroughly defended this position as long as I deemed it necessary, I now surrender to you my sword, and with it this post and this garrison."

"I return your sword," the chief of staff said, "as a proper compliment to the gallant commander of such gallant troops—conduct that would be heroic in another cause." He kissed the sword's hilt, and then handed it to Gardner whose military bearing remained erect, even in defeat.

Though the garrison surrendered, its defenders didn't. In every stand-up battle, they'd whipped the Yanks. And could whip them again anytime and anywhere, they boasted, swaggering and holding their heads high. It was only because of Vicksburg's surrender they'd also surrendered.

Banks paroled the enlisted men. As an officer, Jesse faced a different fate.

"I think they'll be sending me on down to New Orleans," he told Rachel the day before his departure. "They say I'll be imprisoned in either the Custom House or in one of the warehouses down there."

"At least you'll be close to Mobile and to Emma." Rachel clasped his hand.

"I love my sister, darling." Jesse enveloped her in his arms. "But you're the one I'm really going to miss. You are, and always will be, the love of my life. You are very beautiful. Always remember that." He tilted up her chin and kissed her lips. "Will you remember that for me?"

Her eyes misting, Rachel said, "Yes."

A cough interrupted them. When they turned at the sound, Giselle stood smiling at them, not at all embarrassed by interrupting their private time. A small, wiry cavalry sergeant stood beside her.

"This here's the man who rescued Squire from my father's fightin' dogs," she said.

"Buck Dooley, Captain." Buck stretched forth his hand.

Jesse seized it. Gratitude swelled his heart. "I owe you a debt, Sergeant."

Rachel tugged Jesse's sleeve.

"Sergeant," Jesse said, "if you will please excuse us a minute." He followed Rachel to a relatively quiet spot off to the side of the other prisoners. "What's he all about?"

Rachel explained how she met Henry, Blevin's former slave who'd been wounded and captured during the First and Third Native Guards' charge back in May, after she heard he'd wanted to talk to her. She'd gone to the hospital where his wounds were being tended to during the siege. Henry told her about the Blevins' cruelty, Buck's rescuing Squire, and about his wheelchair-bound, friendless daughter Molly. He'd wanted her to have Squire for a friend. "Henry assured me the sergeant's a good Christian man," she said, "so he's probably not the sort to bring up the subject. After how he helped Squire, don't you think it'd be a nice gesture on our part?"

They studied the sergeant. Squire brushed against his legs and licked his knuckles.

"Do you really want to part with our boy?"

Sniffling, fighting tears, Rachel started to speak but her lips merely quivered. She glanced back at Squire, now sitting in front of Buck and thumping his tail while Buck scratched him behind his ears.

"Well, I'd say he can't go to prison with me. Can't you take him back home?"

Rachel shook her head. "Oh, I don't know. Maybe I could, but I'm not sure I'll be going straight home. Another hospital may need me. I still might be needed here for who knows how long to help the wounded and sick on both sides. Squire perhaps could stay with me, I reckon."

Jesse shifted his feet. "We both love Squire, dear. He's our dog. He needs to get sent where it's safer for him. Back home."

"Darling, I'd like him to go back home, too. But...why not...I mean...why not send him where he can help someone else? A little girl named Molly who has no friends. That's what Squire, and all dogs, are best at, Husband. They're the best of all God's beasts at making friends and showing love. And we would be showing Squire love by sending him to a safer place."

Jesse swallowed hard. Rachel was right. He had been selfish bringing Squire to war, and it almost cost Squire his life. Maybe it was in Squire's best interests to let Sergeant Dooley have him. He would be way up North, away from the fighting and the killing, and he'd be happy by making a little girl happy. Through cupped hands, he called for Squire.

Squire raced to him and threw his big forepaws up onto his chest.

Jesse gripped his paws. "What say you, boy? Would you like to go with the nice Sergeant Dooley? Go up North?" He rubbed Squire's soft fur and scratched his broad chest. He glanced at Rachel then back at Squire.

Lowering himself and sitting on his haunches, Squire let his tongue dangle out of his mouth.

Squire barked a "hello" when Buck approached.

Jesse's eyes misted. No, they couldn't be selfish. More than likely, the sergeant would be able to get a furlough now that Union forces controlled the whole entire river. Jesse smiled at Squire's gleaming eyes. "Good-bye, my good ole boy. Make little Miss Molly happy now, you hear?"

June 1866
Coughlin, Alabama

Epilogue

———◆———

Rachel waved at the elderly couple climbing into their buggy, parked on the main street in front of Montgomery and Webb's Furniture Store. "Come back and see us again, Mister and Mrs. Milton."

"I'm sorry we couldn't afford anything," Mrs. Milton said.

"I quite understand. These are hard times."

"Indeed, dear Rachel." Mister Milton grasped the buggy horses' reins. "The Yankees have all of us by the economic throat." He popped his whip, and the two black horses drawing his vehicle started down the street.

Hands on her hips, Rachel watched them turn the corner. The day couldn't have been more beautiful. Not a cloud in the sky, the avian choir rejoicing in nearby trees, yet her heart carried dark pain. No Yankees in Coughlin. The town was too small. At least, that's what she figured. They were all down in Mobile and other larger cities.

Yankees in Coughlin wouldn't bother her, though. Despite the recent war and her Southland's defeat, she harbored no ill-feelings toward them personally. Neither did Jesse. After all, a Yankee had saved Squire from certain death.

What pained her was her inability to conceive. She wondered if it was God's punishment, leaving her childless. At least she could still have a dog, if somehow another stray wandered into their store like Squire did that winter day before the war. They couldn't afford a dog. Not when their store was struggling, but she prayed every day that if God did not bless her and Jesse with a child, that He would at least give them another dog, a loving animal like Squire.

Sighing, she moved back into the store and into her office. She picked up a brown ledger from off her desk, frowned at the sales figures, the debits and credits. Disgusted, she shook her head.

"Mrs. Webb."

Rachel faced the familiar, somber voice. James Henley. He'd worked for her father since she was a child. Before the war, he'd been a free man of color. Thank goodness, all the slaves shared his freedom now.

Deep lines creased James's narrow face.

She handed him the ledger. "James, take this to Father."

James studied Rachel's figures. "Mrs. Webb, it's been a year since the war ended, and we're barely keeping this business above water."

"Go on, please. Show those numbers to Father. He won't like them, but he needs to see them."

James turned to leave her office. Pausing in the doorway, he said, "I don't like them either." He moved on, his feet slowly clicking down the hall.

Rachel went to a file cabinet. She opened a file drawer, then slammed it shut. Taking a long, deep breath, she muttered.

The war had devastated the South, its economy a shambles and most of its wealth gone. When would Jesse return from Mobile? He'd gone there to visit his sister, Emma. Since the railroad wasn't in the best condition, and Mobile wasn't far, he'd driven there in his wagon.

Her father's bills were barely getting paid. Like the Miltons, few customers purchased furniture because few could afford it. She imagined Squire was having himself a dandy time making a little girl happy.

"Rachel." Her father's firm hand clasped her shoulder.

"James showed you, sir?"

"Things will turn around, dear," Mister Montgomery said. "I'm not selling my store yet. We're going to survive. And as your Jesse would say, 'My guarantee.'"

Rachel forced a smile. "I wish he'd hurry back."

That afternoon, two customers visited the store. Neither made a purchase.

Before sunup next day, Rachel sprang out of her bed at the sound of shouting.

"Halloo, Rachel! Halloo, Mister Montgomery! Halloo—!"

Jesse's back.

Barking.

Barking? Rachel threw open her window. On the street below, her husband guided his wagon's two horses toward the street lights in front of the store. Someone sat on the wagon beside him…a little girl it looked like, wearing a pretty blue bonnet…and in the wagon bed…was that Mister Dooley and the lady, his wife? Tail wagging fast and eyes gleaming, a dog propped his forepaws up on the bed's edge. *Squire?* "Father! Father! Look who's come! Squire's back!"

She yanked open her armoire, pulled out the first skirt and blouse she touched, and dressed as fast as she could. It was a race between herself and her father to see who'd reach the store's entrance first. Her father won.

Unlocking the door, Mister Montgomery stepped out onto the boardwalk.

Rachel hurried to the wagon, nearly stumbling off the raised boardwalk's steps. "Oh, Squire! You're home! Home!"

"Mrs. Webb." Buck pushed down the wagon's end gate. Squire bounded onto the ground and rushed upon Rachel. His eyes gleamed.

She gave his head a happy rub, which he returned by licking her hands.

She laughed.

Glancing up, she noticed Buck had helped his wife down from the wagon. "This is my lovely Mary," he said.

"I am delighted to meet you, Mrs. Webb," Mary said.

"Likewise," Rachel said.

The ladies shook hands.

"I'll help you, Buck." Jesse ran to the wagon bed and hopped inside. He seized a wheelchair and rolled it toward his Northern friend.

Buck lifted it out and wheeled it to the little girl cradling a golden-furred puppy while she sat on the wagon bench. "This is my daughter Molly," Buck said. "She was sure happy to get Squire when I took him to her during my furlough after Port Hudson's surrender."

Rachel brightened. "Oh, I am delighted Molly! Your father wrote us a while back about how much you liked him."

"Yes, ma'am," Molly said.

Jesse took Molly's puppy.

Buck reached behind Molly and, gently, he heaved her off the bench and settled her into the chair. Jesse gave her back her dog.

By now the sun was on the rise, and Rachel could see everyone's features better.

"I got a letter from Buck a few weeks ago, dear," Jesse said. "He told me he was bringing back our boy. I wrote him back and gave him Emma's address so he could meet me there. I wanted to surprise you."

"Well, you most certainly succeeded in that."

Molly lifted the puppy toward her. "I want you to have him."

"For me?" Rachel reached for the pup. "Are you sure, dear?"

Mrs. Dooley laughed. "It's for all the happiness your dog gave her during the war. He and his furry little missus gave birth to some puppies about six months ago. We have plenty of dogs now to keep our Molly happy."

"Where is Squire's missus?"

"Oh, back home. A friend is caring for her."

The puppy's curved, bushy tail looked exactly like Squire's. Rachel hugged him close.

"Mister Montgomery." Buck eyed him. "If you could use another honest business partner, I have the funds to invest. I think I can help you make this store survive. You can have Squire back now, too, if you'd like."

Mister Montgomery and Buck shook hands. "No argument there." He gestured at his store's sign. "Montgomery, Webb, and Dooley. My good sir, it's a deal!"

The End

Author Notes

Many years ago, during a visit to the Port Hudson State Commemorative Area just north of Baton Rouge, an image of a dog flashed through my mind. The dog of my imagination resembled a beloved dog I once owned, except this imaginary dog sat beside a battery on the Mississippi River sniffing the coal that burned from the funnels of Union warships as they bore down on the Confederate garrison. Thus was born the story *Squire, A Mascot's Tale*, a revised edition of my previously published book, *Rebel Dog*.

Mascots were not uncommon during the American Civil War. Many went into battle with their regiments while others, such as Squire, served as morale boosters and pets. Most mascots were either dogs or horses. So, into my story trots Squire, mascot of a fictional Alabama regiment. Though I have striven hard for historical accuracy, I in no way pretend that this is pure history. It is not intended to be.

I have loosely based my fictional regiment on the First Alabama Volunteer Infantry. Three primary sources assisted me in my research: Edward W. McMorries's *History of the First Regiment Alabama Volunteer Infantry* (The Brown Printing Company, Montgomery, Alabama, 1904), Daniel P. Smith's *Company K, First Alabama Regiment, Three Years in Confederate Service* (Published by the Survivors, Prattville, Alabama, 1885), and *The War of the Rebellion: A Compilation of the Official Records in the Union and Confederate Armies* (1880-1901).

My secondary sources include Lawrence Lee Hewitt's *Port Hudson: Confederate Bastion on the Mississippi* (Louisiana State University Press, Baton Rouge and London, 1987), John D. Winters's *The Civil War in Louisiana* (Louisiana State University Press, Baton Rouge and London, 1963), and Edward Cunningham's *The Port Hudson Campaign, 1862–1863* (Louisiana State University Press, Baton Rouge, 1991). Mister Cunningham and I are not related.

Historically, Colonel I. G. W. Steedman commanded the First Alabama. I replaced him with my fictional commander, Colonel Edward Stonebridge.

Lieutenant Colonel M.B. Locke served as Steedman's second-in-command. In this book, Lieutenant Colonel Thaddeus Cox serves this role.

Major Knox, who appears toward the end of the book, is a historical figure.

Colonel William R. Miles, commander of Miles's Legion, receives more coverage in this book than any other historical figure mentioned. While he pursued Grierson, Miles encountered high water on the Amite River. According to the *Official Records*, he built a bridge across this river and crossed it within five hours "with my artillery and trains." I have based the details of its construction on the remembrances of Private Warren Lee Goss, a Union soldier in the Army of the Potomac. In his article "Campaigning to No Purpose," *Battles and Leaders of the Civil War*, Volume II, he described how they built such bridges.

No additional regiment accompanied Miles's Legion in its pursuit, though Gardner did dispatch other units to stop Grierson. In my book, a fictional regiment does accompany Miles, led by its colonel, Hampton Lafayette Marsden.

I also left out the action at the Priest Cap, which happened on June 14, because it didn't contribute to my plot and also because Jesse's Alabama regiment did not participate in this action.

About the Author

John "Jack" M. Cunningham, Jr. is a graduate of the University of Alabama. He holds a B.A. in history and taught school in the New Orleans area.

He's been writing professionally for over thirty years. His work has appeared in numerous devotional and Sunday school publications as well as Christian and secular magazines. His fiction has appeared in literary magazines. His two historical novels are a series titled Southern Sons-Dixie Daughters. Book 1 is titled *Vengeance & Betrayal,* and Book 2 is titled *River Ruckus, Bloody Bay.* They are available in e-book format at amazon.com. Paperback versions are in the planning stages.

He's also a speaker at writers' groups, a freelance editor, and a writing instructor. Visit his website at theauthorscove.com.